THe fisherMAN

Larry Huntsperger

Fleming H. Revell
A Division of Baker Book House Co
Grand Rapids, Michigan 49516

© 2003 by Larry Huntsperger

Published by Fleming H. Revell
a division of Baker Book House Company
P.O. Box 6287, Grand Rapids, MI 49516-6287
www.bakerbooks.com

Printed in the United States of America

Library of Congress Cataloging-in-Publication Data
Huntsperger, Larry, 1947-
    The fisherman/Larry Huntsperger.
        p.   cm.
    ISBN 0-8007-5844-7 (pbk.)
    1. Peter, the Apostle, Saint—Fiction. 2. Bible. N.T.—History of
Biblical events—Fiction. 3. Christian saints—Fiction. 4. Jesus Christ—
Fiction. 5. Apostles—Fiction. I. Title.
PS3608.U75 F47 2003
813'.6—dc21   2002014975

THe
fishermAN

For my Joni Sue, with Papa love forever.
You sifted through my fumbling efforts
to be your father,
chose to embrace only those things
that drew you closer to your Lord,
and then, with grace and kindness,
set all the rest aside.

Thank you.

Author's Note

The book you are about to read is fiction. It is not the fifth Gospel. It is not the Third Epistle of Peter. Apart from a few quotations from Scripture woven into the text, every word from the first to the last is the product of my imagination.

Having said that, however, I need to say more, for although *The Fisherman* is fiction, it is fiction unlike any you have ever read before. During the writing process, when asked what I was working on, I described the manuscript as historical fiction. I now believe this does not accurately describe the book. Authors of historical fiction weave their own imagined plot against their chosen historical backdrop, allowing the history to provide a frame through which readers can see the plot. I have done exactly the opposite. I have not placed a story into a historical frame; I have created a frame through which I hope you will be able to see history with a new clarity.

The entire plot of this book and the central events of each of the twenty-seven chapters are taken directly from the historical records. I have been careful not to alter nor amplify any of these events for the sake of the story. If I have done my work well, my words will simply enable you to personally enter into these events and the lives of those involved in them.

To the best of my ability, I have followed a chronology that is consistent with the Gospel records. I realize, of course, that scholars differ in their approaches to this chronology. It is my sincere hope that if my understanding of the sequence of events differs at some points from your own, it will not interfere with your enjoyment of the book.

And then just a final word about who the book is written to. Imagine being granted a private audience with the apostle Peter near the end of his life. He has given you permission to ask him anything you want to ask. In response to his offer, you say, "Peter, I want you to tell me what it was really like during those few years you spent with the Master. What was it like to be there? What was it like to be you?" If you can imagine yourself in such a conversation, this book is written to you.

Larry Huntsperger
Soldotna, Alaska

Prologue

I have brooded long over what I am about to do. In the end I have chosen to write because so few seem to understand. I am not a writer. Words on paper come hard for me. Even now my mind is filled with a thousand other things I would rather be doing. But if I do not speak, who will? Who knew the Master better then? Who knows him better now?

You see, it was not the way you think it was. There! I have said it. And unless you understand how it was, my friend, you will never be able to understand how it should be now.

I was born Simon Barjona. You know me by a different name—Peter. I am one of the twelve disciples chosen by the Master during his time among us. Several excellent accounts of those remarkable months have been written and widely circulated by others more skilled in such things than I. Those accounts accurately record many of the events we witnessed and shared together. I have nothing to alter or add to those accounts. I write now because so few seem to understand those accounts correctly. So few seem to understand *him* correctly—the way he was when he was with us and why it changed our lives forever.

Perhaps it would help if I allowed you to see those days through my eyes. I want you to know not just what happened but what it felt like to be there. I want you to know it was real, more real than the hot dust under our feet, more real than the flies buzzing around our sweat-soaked clothing. Somehow I want to help you to see the things I saw and feel the things I felt. I have seen what the enemy has done with the record of those days. I have seen what he has done with people's perceptions of me. I have seen the way reality has been twisted into ritual and religion. I have seen the way it sucks the life and vitality out of the people of God. When I wrote my second open letter to the family of God, I addressed it "to those who have received a faith of the same kind as ours." But unless you understand what my faith is like and where it came from, the letter's assurance will be of little value to you.

And so I write with the hope that I can help you to see the Master as a man. For, if we cannot see him correctly as a man, we have no hope of understanding him correctly as our God.

1

I was a fisherman before I met him. My brother, Andrew, and I fished together. I loved fishing. I loved everything about it. I loved the smell of the sea. I loved the look of the nets neatly folded on the deck of our boat. I loved that incredible sense of freedom I always experienced the instant we pushed away from the land and the world began to roll under my feet. I loved the creak of the wood and the feel of the sun on my back. I loved knowing I answered to no man, that I held my future firmly in my own hands. I loved those days when the catch was good and my wife, Ruth, and I could put a little extra income toward our dreams. I even loved those days when the catch was poor. Even if I brought home only a handful of fish, I knew at least I could always provide food for my family.

Andrew and I did most of our fishing with Zebedee's two boys, James and John. We grew up together—Andrew, James, John, and myself. John could run circles around me in a battle of wits, but the size of both my mouth and my muscles left little dispute about my position as unofficial head of our tiny fishing fleet.

I wish you could have known me back then, before he entered my world. I wish you could have known how . . . well, how common, how normal, how like everyone else I was. I wish you could have heard me blast poor Andrew when a fish or two slipped out of the net. I wish you could have seen me stomp out of the house in a huff when Ruth and I disagreed about something and I knew she was right. I wish you could have sat with the four of us after our nets were put away for the evening and listened to me babble on. I wish you could have known the smallness of my dreams.

"Someday I'm going to have two boats all my own. And I'm going to build a bigger house up there on that little hill overlooking the bay. Someday I'm going to be the most successful fisherman this town has ever seen."

You see, if my words to you now are to be of any value, this one thing you must understand—there was nothing in me or about me that made me any different from yourself. Before he entered my world, my life was an unbroken stream of work and family and eating and sleeping and selfish little hopes and dreams and plans for the future. I was a fisherman. That is all I was. That is all I knew how to be.

I attended meetings on the Sabbath in our synagogue as often as most men. But, to be honest, much of what happened there bored me to death. I knew the history of our people. I followed the feast days and the celebrations. But my mind was more often on the festival food than on the great historical significance of the events we were celebrating. I knew some of the young men who held aspirations for leadership in our Jewish community. Sometimes I listened to their endless debates over intricate and obscure passages in the law and the writings of the prophets. I saw their glow of satisfaction when they contributed some comment or insight the others considered significant. I sensed the urgency with which they approached their world of ideas. But it seemed like a waste of time to me. In the end it changed nothing, and it certainly didn't feed my family.

Does it surprise you to hear me speak this way? You call me the apostle Peter. My two letters written to my fellow Christians are read as words inspired by God himself. My presence in the church commands immediate respect and attention. This is as it should be, because it served God's purposes to place me in this role. But do not misunderstand—I do not hold this position because I now know things, because I have accumulated a great wealth of knowledge and insight that qualifies me for such authority. I am no more skilled in the ways of books and learning now than I was as a youth. Even now, when I read some of the letters written by my brother Paul, I find things difficult to understand. No, I do not hold my position of leadership because I know things. I hold it because I know *him,* and because he has chosen to use that knowledge of him in this way. But I'm getting ahead of myself.

How is it possible for two brothers to be so different? Andrew's restless spirit and hunger for truth never ceased to amaze me. He would spend hours, even days, churning over questions I never even thought to ask. I can remember the two of us, straining at our nets, soaked with sweat and sea spray, hauling our catch into the boat. My mind would be counting fish, calculating their value, dividing the profit. Then suddenly I would hear Andrew's voice saying,

"Hey, Simon! Do you realize it has been more than four hundred years since the last true prophet spoke? Four hundred years! How could that be? I wonder why we don't have prophets today. Why do you think that is, huh?"

How in the world should I know? And what difference did it make anyway?

Then the Prophet John entered our world and I lost Andrew altogether. Oh, his body was still with me, but his mind was absent on a permanent basis. The first time Andrew heard John preach, he was hooked. From then on all Andrew talked about was the Prophet John! The Prophet John said this and the Prophet John said that. "Oh, Simon!" he'd say. "The Prophet John speaks with a power and authority that makes you shake inside. And, Simon, nearly every time he speaks he talks about someone who's coming after him. I heard him say he wasn't even fit to untie the sandal of the one who's coming. Can you believe that? You have to come hear him, Simon. You just have to!"

But somehow I just never found the time. Besides, Andrew provided me with a word-by-word account of every syllable the prophet uttered. One disciple of John in the family was enough. We had a business to run, and there was no way it would run itself with both of us chasing around the country after traveling preachers.

Then came that morning when Andrew failed to meet me at the boat. The previous afternoon he and his friend Philip had taken off in search of the Prophet John and hadn't come back. I hung around the boat waiting, a little worried, a lot angry. How could he do this to me? I didn't really mind all this Prophet John stuff as long as it didn't interfere with our work. But now he was going too far. We were losing a full day of fishing, and there was nothing for me to do but sit and wait and plan my lecture for the slacker.

It was nearly noon before Andrew returned. As soon as I saw him walking up the beach, I sprang to my feet, ready for my attack. But before I could utter a word, Andrew broke into a grin and held up both hands as if to ward off the blast he knew was coming. He looked different somehow.

For a few seconds he said nothing. He offered no apology for being late, no immediate explanation for his absence, and no new flood of quotations from the great Prophet John. He just stood there staring at me through shining eyes, looking as if he were about to explode.

Then he spoke. "Simon, we have found the Messiah!" He wasn't trying to convince me. He wasn't attempting to bait me into yet another theological discussion. He wasn't soliciting my agreement. He wasn't looking for my approval. It was a simple statement of fact, spoken with absolute assurance.

I didn't say anything. I didn't know what to say. I just stood there in silence. My face must have mirrored my confusion and concern, because Andrew suddenly burst out laughing as he slapped me on the shoulder and said, "Relax, big brother! I haven't gone mad. When you hear what's happened, you'll understand."

The account poured out of him like a flood. He and Philip had found the Prophet John without difficulty, but he wasn't preaching and answering questions the way he usually did. He was engaged in an intense conversation with a man about his own age. Neither Philip nor Andrew recognized the stranger, but John seemed to know him well. They edged closer to the pair, trying to catch a little of their conversation.

The man's name was Jesus, and Andrew found this newcomer fascinating. The things he said, the way he laughed, the look in his eyes, even the way he carried himself communicated a confidence, an authority, a kind of contagious love for life. I asked Andrew if he was another prophet like John. Andrew struggled with the question for a few seconds, then said no, he was different somehow. When I pressed him for an explanation, he said the Prophet John drew you to his message, but this Jesus drew you to himself. At the time, that made no sense to me whatsoever, but I let it pass and Andrew continued his account.

He and Philip had kept edging closer, but just as they were within range to hear most of what was being said, John and Jesus ended their conversation and Jesus walked away. For a few seconds they just stood there next to John, watching Jesus go. Then John turned to them, pointed at Jesus, and said, "Behold, the Lamb of God." They had no idea what those words meant, but they were determined to find out. Andrew and Philip followed after him.

For a few paces the little procession moved down the path in silence, Jesus in the lead, his two shadows a few feet behind him. Then, without warning, Jesus stopped, turned around, looked straight into Andrew's eyes, and asked, "What do you seek?" Andrew said it was just as if he knew Andrew was following him. He wasn't angry. He wasn't irritated. Andrew said that as he stood there looking into Jesus' eyes, he suddenly felt as if this man was asking him a question to which he already knew the answer. Andrew, however, had no idea what to say. What *did* he seek? What he really sought was *him*. He wanted to know so much more about him. Who was he? What was he doing? Where was he going? Andrew wanted to be near him, to talk with him. He wanted to get to know him. But there was no way Andrew dared put that into words. Jesus would think he was crazy. Andrew said he stood there in terrified silence for a few seconds and then blurted out, "Rabbi, where are you staying?"

As soon as those words came out of his mouth, Andrew knew how stupid they must have sounded. "Oh, Teacher, we're just sneaking along behind you here because we were wondering what kind of house you live in." Dumb! Dumb! Dumb! Andrew said he could feel his face turning red.

Then, just as he dropped his eyes to the ground and began to turn away in embarrassment, Jesus spoke what for the rest of his life Andrew described as the five words that changed everything forever. Jesus said simply, "Come, and you will see."

When Andrew looked up, Jesus was smiling, his eyes filled with kindness, compassion, and an acceptance that made Andrew feel as if this man knew everything. He knew what Andrew had been thinking and feeling. He knew what Andrew was searching for, not just today but for years. He knew, and he welcomed it. In fact, Andrew told me, he seemed to be expecting it.

Andrew never said much more about that first night he spent with the Master. Whatever passed between them touched Andrew more deeply than anything else had ever touched him before. It touched and it healed. He didn't want to share it, and I didn't want to pump him. But he did share one thing more that sent a shock through me. "Simon . . . there's something else too. I don't know how, but . . . well . . . he knows about you. And, Simon, he wants to meet with you."

2

"Me? He knows about *me?* What do you mean he knows about me? What did you tell him? What did he say?"

Little brothers can be so irritating sometimes. That day Andrew proved to be at his irritating best. He was obviously enjoying this.

"I didn't tell him anything, Simon. I never even mentioned your name. But I'm telling you, somehow he knows about you. The last thing he said before we parted was that I should see if I could get that big brother of mine to come back with me next time. I was so shocked I just turned around and stared at him. I didn't say a word. Then he smiled and waved good-bye. I know I should have asked him how he knew about you, and where he'd met you, and why he wanted you to come back with me.

"But, Simon, it doesn't work that way with him. I mean, he is the most approachable person I've ever met in my life, but at the same time when you talk with him, you realize there are things he just knows, and at the time it seems natural that he knows, and it isn't until later on that you find yourself looking back and wondering how he knew what he knew. Oh, Simon, I can't explain it. You just have to come meet him and see for yourself."

Do you see what I mean about little brothers? I kept quizzing Andrew about who said what when, and how he thought Jesus gained all this knowledge about me, but the little runt kept saying he didn't know and I would just have to go ask Jesus myself. He knew exactly how to bait me. In the end there was nothing to do but to go with him.

We walked in silence on the way back to where Andrew last saw Jesus. Andrew was silent by temperament, and my own mind was busy creating a mental image of the man I was about to meet. I know what you're thinking. You have read the accounts of my history with the Master. You know about our first conversation together. You know about the events that would follow. You know about his teaching, his miraculous works, about his death and what happened afterwards. It's natural for you to assume that I must've been filled with excitement in anticipation of meeting this man who would change the history of the human race forever.

But you are wrong. Andrew and I walked along that day with no premonition of what was to be. Apart from the testimonial from my little brother and the rather strange words of endorsement from the Prophet John, I knew nothing about this Jesus. He had not yet begun his public teaching. He had not performed a public miracle; there was nothing to convince me he was anything other than just the latest in an endless stream of self-appointed messiahs who inflict

19

themselves upon our nation. To be honest, my first meeting with the Master was motivated by nothing more than a mild curiosity and a fervent desire to free my earnest, obviously misguided little brother from his messianic obsessions and get him back to work.

In my mind I pictured the man I was about to meet. I was certain I knew his type. There would be lots of charisma, lots of smiles and heartiness, great eye contact, and very likely a warm embrace for each and every one of his devoted followers. I was grudgingly forced to admit to the positive impact of his first contact with my little brother, but this claim to supernatural knowledge about me sounded more like some sort of trick than divine revelation.

The greatest events in my life have always taken me by surprise. They have been thrust upon me, unannounced and unanticipated. That initial meeting with the Master was such an event.

My first sight of him shattered my preconceived concept of the man I came to meet. There were no throngs of people around him, no thousands kneeling in adoration, no urgent multitudes seeking his wisdom and guidance. There was certainly no halo hovering over his head, no Shekinah glory, no radiant glow about him. Nor was there even a hint of that hideous charismatic facade I detest in so many of the self-styled messiahs parading about the country in recent years.

He was alone when we arrived, sitting on a rock, apparently enjoying the warmth of the sun on his face. I remember having the distinct impression he knew we were coming and had been waiting for us. He greeted Andrew and told him it was good to see him again. Then he looked at me. At first he didn't say a word. He just smiled. To my credit, I had one thing right—his eye contact was remarkable. But even that was not as I had anticipated. When he looked at me, I suddenly felt as if I had known this man my whole life. No, that's not it. What I really felt was that he had known *me* my whole life. He knew me, and he liked me, and he placed a high value on my friendship. The first words I heard him speak seemed to confirm what I was feeling. "You are Simon the son of John; you shall be called Peter."

I suddenly understood what Andrew had been trying to tell me. I don't know how he knew my name or the name of our father. He just knew. And it seemed right that he knew. And here is the amazing thing: His supernatural knowledge didn't make him seem supernatural! I have thought much about this since those days when he was here.

I know words will fail me in my attempt to share this, but I must try. You see, it was impossible to meet Jesus without being confronted with his tremendous spiritual power and knowledge. He possessed an authority that was rooted not in any position he held but simply in who he was. But the amazing thing is that those qualities were all contained within his obvious humanity in such a way that, though you could never deny his power and authority, those qualities never caused you to draw away from him in fear or awe. He was truly the most approachable man a person could ever meet.

It wasn't as though a supernatural being had squeezed himself into human skin, like you might expect if you met an angel. At the end of the day, you never anticipated catching a glimpse of him heaving a sigh of relief as he yanked off his cloak and finally stretched out a massive pair of wings crammed under his clothing. He was obviously a man. But he was a man who somehow possessed incredible insight, and power, and authority, and you kept asking yourself how someone who was just a man could possess such qualities.

I think his approachability must have had something to do with the way in which he never used his supernatural abilities for personal gain. He never had an angle or an ulterior motive. He never used another human being. It was something none of us had ever seen before. We all knew men and women who held positions of authority, and we knew, too, the way that authority corrupted those who possessed it. But to be in the presence of a person who possessed absolute authority, yet who exercised that authority with the absolute absence of corruption, did not fit with anything we had ever experienced. It changed all the rules.

Those first twelve words the Master spoke to me were perhaps the most important words I ever heard him speak. I came with my mind filled with questions, with suspicions, with a determination to get some explanations. I came to do battle. Then, in a single sentence, before I even opened my mouth, Jesus told me everything I needed to know. He told me he knew me. He told me he knew my past. And, most amazing of all, he knew my future! "You shall be called Peter"—the Rock!

Now where did that come from? I didn't know, but I liked it. I liked the name, of course. Who wouldn't? *The Rock!* It had a great ring to it. I was surprised I hadn't thought of it myself. But there was something I liked even better—I liked the thought that my future was somehow tied up with this man.

I drew all the wrong conclusions, of course. I assumed he recognized my obvious natural leadership skills, my exceptional physical strength, and my determination of will, and he knew he needed a man like me beside him. If he would have told me the whole truth that day, there is no way I could have handled it. If he would have filled in the blanks between who I was then and who I would one day become, I would have bolted in terror. Clearly he appeared to be selecting me and calling me to himself but not for the reasons or the role I assumed. How could I have understood that day the Master's plan to use me as the greatest illustration the world would ever have of the inability of any human being to live the life of the Spirit through the power of the flesh?

3

"So what do you think, Simon?"

Andrew broke the silence on the walk home. What did I think? I thought I was more confused and more excited and more terrified than ever before in my life.

I wonder if you know what it's like. The most perplexing, frightening, exhilarating *hope* had suddenly thrust itself into my life and sliced me in half. It felt horrible and wonderful all at the same time.

My rational mind was telling me this man, this Jesus, was dangerous. I wasn't sure how, but I felt as if he threatened all my plans for the future. I knew where I wanted to go with my life and how I was going to get there. A little luck, a lot of hard work and determination, and those plans would become a reality.

But now, suddenly, there was this man. And it wasn't just that he was an irritating distraction to my little brother. This was no longer about Andrew. It was about me. I knew that his prediction that I would one day be called Peter had nothing to do with fishing. It had everything to do with *him*. If I wanted the name and all that went with it, whatever that was, I had to go through him to get it. No, I didn't have to go through him, I had to go *to* him, *with* him. If, on the other hand, I was determined to cling to my own plans for the future, Peter would never exist. And why was I suddenly thinking about "clinging" to my plans, as if I were clutching at a chunk of debris in the middle of the ocean after a violent shipwreck? If I was determined to "follow" my own plans for the future . . . yes, that sounded better.

So what did I think? I thought the sooner we got home and put "Jesus" behind us, the better. In response to Andrew's question I just mumbled something about Jesus being a very interesting man. Andrew knew me too well to try to get me to talk when I was brooding. We walked the rest of the way home in silence.

I didn't sleep much that night. Ruth and I talked for several hours after I got home. She could always get me to talk when no one else could. I told her about the name discussion and tried to explain why it was so unsettling to me, but it must have sounded foolish when I put it into words. Mostly she just listened. It helped me to try to talk through it, but when we went to bed, I just kept churning things over and over again. I felt as though I was being asked to make some huge decision, yet I had no idea what the decision was. Should I just trot along after this man, listening to him talk for the rest of my life? I had a family, a career, a future. He was asking me to make no decisions. He was asking nothing from me. And yet . . .

Early the next morning Andrew, James, John, and I met at our boats. James and John were full of questions about our absence the day before. We gave them a brief account of our interview with Jesus, but I chose not to go into detail with all my confused introspection. Besides, having already missed one day of fishing, there was no way I wanted to miss another. The fishing went well, but Andrew and I didn't talk much. For once in my life I didn't know what to say.

Have you ever longed for something and not known you were longing for it until after it happened? Have you ever had a hope sitting in your mind just out of sight, a hope you didn't dare put into words for fear it would sound ridiculous once you brought it out in the open?

Two days after my first meeting with the Master, the four of us were once again at our boats early in the morning, preparing to push out from the shore. I was standing on the beach, ready to put my shoulder to the front of the boat, when I glanced down the shoreline and saw three men walking our way. The sight of the man in the middle suddenly brought my hidden hope to consciousness. It was Jesus. I did not realize until that moment how much I wanted to see him again.

He was walking with two of Andrew's friends, Philip and a man named Nathanael, another fervent follower of the Prophet John. When they reached us, Jesus greeted Andrew and myself with a nod and a smile, then turned to James and John. I immediately began to babble some sort of introduction, but as soon as the words were out of my mouth, I realized they were unnecessary. He knew them, just as he had known me.

"I know you're just heading out to fish, but the three of us are on our way to a wedding in Cana, and I'd love to have the four of you join us if you'd like to."

It was the first of many invitations extended to me by the Master during the next few years. And every one of them affected me the same way. On the surface it appeared to be simply a polite, casual, generic invitation to join the group. But inside I felt as if a great honor was being bestowed upon me. It wasn't the wedding, of course. It was him. He wanted me to go with him. No, it was more than that. He was *choosing* me to go with him. My response to his invitation was immediate. "Hey! That sounds better than fishing. We'd love to go!"

Three heads instantly pivoted in my direction. Andrew, James, and John all stood there staring at me in amazement. It wasn't that they didn't want to go. They simply couldn't believe Mr. Make-More-Money would so quickly walk away from another day of work. They knew enough not to say anything, but the expressions they exchanged with one another communicated their amused curiosity better than words ever could have done.

That was the first full day I spent with the Master. Cana was more than a four-hour walk away. I ran home to let Ruth know about our plans, then rejoined the group and we started off.

During the few years the Master was physically with us, he allowed me to share many incredible events and experiences with him. I heard nearly every one of his public teachings. I witnessed miraculous healings, masses of food created from morsels, direct confrontations between the Master and the violence of nature, raging debates with the established political and religious authorities. Once I even heard the voice of God himself speaking from heaven. But if I could relive just one piece of all that I experienced during those years, I would choose the times we spent traveling together. Those were the times when he wasn't on display, the times when we were free from the crowds clawing to get closer. Those were the times when we talked, when we joked, when we laughed, and listened, and learned more about the mind and the heart of the Master than all the other times put together.

If only you could have joined us on one of those walks, you would understand why I began this narrative by telling you it was not the way you think it was. That first trip together was typical. All of us were a little nervous, a little excited, and a lot unsure about what the rules were in our relationship with this man. Andrew and Philip, both earnest disciples of the Prophet John, certainly assumed their times with Jesus would follow a similar pattern. The Prophet John was all business and teaching. He valued each of his disciples, but he seemed to value them most of all as faithful tools through whom he could more effectively disseminate his call for repentance to our nation. It was the *message* that mattered most with John. In fact, he seemed to prefer being addressed as "the messenger" even more than "the prophet," calling himself "a voice of one crying in the wilderness." It was not surprising that Andrew and Philip and, to be honest, the rest of us too, kept waiting for Jesus to blast through with his message as well.

But we soon learned it didn't work that way with him. To put it in a single statement, whereas John was most concerned with how his followers related to his message, Jesus was most concerned with how we related to *him*. But please don't misunderstand me here. I am not suggesting he wanted us to trot along at his side, hanging on his every word, with expressions of reverent awe and adoration on our faces. Far from it! It was clear from our first day together that what he valued most of all was our friendship. He obviously deeply enjoyed each of us. He really liked us.

I cannot overstate the importance of those early days we spent with the Master. All too soon the eyes of the entire nation would be turned on him, and our lives would take on a public intensity that would strip us of the casual privacy we shared during those first few weeks. But those weeks were enough for him to establish the ground rules that would shape our relationship with him forever. In a thousand different ways he made it clear no phony religious facade was needed, and none was wanted. The multitudes would always bring their expectations and their assumptions about Jesus and how they should relate to him. Rarely did he try to correct those misconceptions. But with those of us who were close to him, it was different. To us he would give the responsibility of modeling for all the world what it meant for a created being to live in friendship with his Creator. We didn't understand that at the time, of course. We just knew this man loved us and valued our friendship as no one else had ever done before. The time would come when, just a few hours prior to his death, we would hear him say, "I have called you friends," and we would understand what he meant. Any form of ritualistic, religious adoration from us would have seemed absurd. Most of all this man became our friend, a friend who knew us fully and loved us completely just the way we were. Certainly his friendship produced profound changes in each of our lives. But they were not changes we attempted to paste on in order to be "good disciples of the great Teacher." They were changes that gradually infiltrated our lives the more we relaxed in his unconditional love and acceptance.

I sometimes think the greatest gift the Master ever gave me was his permission to be myself. It was a gift he gave me most of all through all the things I never heard him say. I look back over an endless stream of stupid things I said and did during the months I spent with him. Yet not once did I ever hear him say, "Peter, you're such a fool!" or "Peter, you blew it again!" or "Peter, just once would you try thinking before you speak!" or "Peter, I've had it with your endless egotistical stupidity—get out of here!" Amazingly, he seemed well content to have me forever blundering along at his side, knowing the only thing that would transform my life was the discovery that even my worst failures would never separate me from my Master's love.

4

Once again I had it all wrong. I began that day believing our journey was a thinly veiled test designed by the Master to find out which of us were really discipleship material and which were not. That belief generated within me an urgent desire to impress this man. After all, impressing people was one of the things I did best. I just knew by the end of the day I could have Jesus thinking to himself, "My, that Simon would certainly make a fine disciple. I need a man like that! I'll have to see if I can coax him into teaming up with me."

It was obvious he liked me. Now I just needed to round out his perspective on me—to introduce him to the greatness of my achievements and my aspirations for the future.

I talked about everything. I talked about our boat. I talked about our business venture with James and John. I talked about my grand plans for the future. I talked about anything and everything I thought might impress him. And he listened. He listened as if what I was saying mattered as much to him as it did to me. By the time we arrived in Cana, I was sure he was close to offering me a key position in his plans for the future—a position I might even consider accepting if the terms were right.

The wedding celebration we attended was for one of Jesus' cousins, the daughter of his aunt on his mother's side. His mother, Mary, was obviously pleased with Jesus' arrival. She had been deeply involved in the planning and preparation for the celebration and, though we all received a quick introduction as soon as we arrived, during the next several hours Mary was little more than a flying blur in and out of the kitchen. There appeared to be a far greater turnout for the event than the family had expected, with people standing, talking, eating, laughing, and sitting in every available corner. Though I didn't know the couple, it was evident everyone felt very good about this union. I heard snatches of a dozen different conversations; people took credit for getting the couple together or for helping their relationship along at critical points during the engagement. Cana was Nathanael's hometown, and he seemed to know at least half the people there. He introduced us to a number of his friends, and we spent several hours enjoying the food, the wine, and the celebration.

Then late that afternoon something happened that altered our perception of Jesus forever.

The seven of us were all in a group talking and joking when Mary came up to Jesus, obviously deeply concerned about something. She nearly had to scream to be understood above the noise of the party, and all six of us heard the one sentence she spoke to her son.

"They have no wine!"

The family had underestimated the size and length of the celebration, and the wine was all gone. Unless something could be done quickly, it meant embarrassment to the newlyweds and a premature end to the festivities, though I couldn't imagine what she expected Jesus to do about it.

I remember at the time puzzling over his response to Mary's words. His tone was not harsh, but his mother's statement seemed to face him with a difficult choice. He told her this was not his concern because it was not yet his time.

Then he glanced up at the six of us standing there, eavesdropping on their conversation, and made his decision. When he turned back to Mary, a tiny smile crept across his lips, and he gave her just the slightest nod. She immediately called several servants and instructed them to do whatever Jesus told them to do.

Just behind us, lined up against the wall, were six empty thirty-gallon water containers. Jesus told the servants to fill them to the top with water. The servants were not pleased with this added responsibility right in the middle of their other duties at the feast. Filling those pots involved more than forty trips between the well and the house. They were able to recruit several other servants to help, but even then it took more than half an hour to finish the job.

When the pots were finally filled, Jesus told one of the servants to draw some of the liquid from the pots they had just filled and take it to the headwaiter. I could see the servant from where I was standing, and as he drew out the liquid, the strangest expression crossed his face. He looked up at Jesus but said nothing, then went straight to the headwaiter. We all followed behind him to see what was going on. When the waiter tasted what had been brought to him, his face reflected first amazement and then irritation. He grabbed the pitcher from the servant, then charged over to the groom and began scolding him for saving the really good wine until so late in the feast.

The waiter's words brought two immediate responses. The groom whirled around and stared at the waiter with a look of helpless confusion on his face. At the same time six friends of Jesus grabbed goblets and bolted back to those pots. We must have looked ridiculous, pushing and squirming our way through that crowd, like a footrace mistakenly routed through the center of a public market.

One taste of that wine was all I needed. It was good—as good as any I had ever tasted in my life. But it wasn't the wine I was excited about; it was the future. I didn't know how he had done it; I just knew he had. And the implications were staggering. If he could do it again, we could sell this stuff and be rich overnight. If ever Jesus needed a partner, it was now, and I was clearly the man for the job. I could handle the whole business wing of the thing, and he could devote his time to the production side.

It was Andrew who finally jolted me back to reality. I glanced over at the pots and saw him sitting next to one of them in a sort of stunned silence. I went charging over, cup in hand, and blurted out, "Wow, little brother, did you see what he just *did?!*"

Andrew looked up at me and said, "No, Simon, did you see what *he* just did? This man just accomplished the impossible. Listen, Simon! This man isn't just a prophet. This man just performed a miracle. Prophets preach. Prophets exhort. Prophets don't change 180 gallons of well water into wine. And Simon . . . Simon, he didn't do this for them, for all those people out there laughing and having a good time. They don't even know about it. Simon, he did this for *us*, for you and me and James and John and Philip and

Nathanael. He wanted the six of us to see his power. Use your head, Simon. Even the great King David never did anything like this. And when our God performed miraculous works through Moses and Elijah, he did it to meet some critical need affecting our entire nation. But not like this! Not at their cousin's wedding! And certainly not simply because someone forgot to order enough wine.

"Listen, big brother—what just happened here isn't about wine. It's about him and about us. This man doesn't need us. This man turns well water into wine without even speaking a word. What in the world could we offer him? And yet, for some reason he wants us with him; he wants us to see the supernatural power God has given him. Something just happened here today that hasn't happened before in the history of our nation. And, Simon, I've never felt so honored in my life."

After hearing Andrew's words I decided to put my wine-selling scheme on hold for a little while. Somehow it just didn't seem like the right time to bring it up. I knew Andrew was right about one thing—Jesus planned this miracle for our eyes only. What a day! It began with a neat little bundle of expectations and assumptions about what it meant to be a disciple of this fascinating new prophet. Those expectations now lay in a shattered heap. In their place I was left with a man I couldn't even begin to understand.

The feast continued until well into the night. When things finally quieted down, we all found a corner in which to sleep for a few hours. We regrouped in the morning to discover that our little band was now considerably larger. The miraculous appearance of all that wine the night before demanded some explanation. Though Jesus said nothing himself, the servants were more than willing to fill in the blanks. Rumors flew throughout the crowd, and Jesus became an instant object of fascination.

Our trip back to Capernaum took on the look and feel of a caravan. Along with a number of fascinated followers,

Jesus' mother and several younger brothers and cousins also joined the pack. Though Mary's permanent home was still in Nazareth, she was determined to stay as close to the Master as possible. Her husband, Joseph, had died several years earlier, leaving Jesus as head of the household and directly responsible for her care.

✞

Andrew, Philip, Nathanael, James, and John all did their best to stay close to Jesus. I, on the other hand, was well content to follow at a distance. Too much was happening too quickly. I needed time and space away from this man. I just wanted to get back to my boat, my business, and my wife and leave all this prophet stuff to someone else. I felt suddenly trapped in a world I didn't understand and couldn't control. I needed to get back to real life. I needed to feel the spray of the sea on my face and hear the squawk of the gulls above my head. I needed to be free.

5

Jesus found a house in Capernaum for himself, his mother, and several other family members. Word of this fascinating newcomer swept through the city. His popularity increased daily as he taught publicly in the marketplace. Though he chose not to perform any additional supernatural acts during the days immediately following the incident with the wine, his teaching alone was more than enough to draw the crowds.

None of us had ever heard anything like it before. Our nation was well acquainted with the teaching of those within the religious mainstream. It consisted of little more than an ever increasing list of rules and regulations defining, expanding, and applying the law of Moses to the most intricate and obscure areas of daily life. How many yards could a person travel on a Sabbath day without it being considered "work" and thus violating the commandment? Was it necessary to count the exact number of mint leaves from each plant harvested and tithe exactly one-tenth of them, or was it permissible to simply count the number of whole plants in order to determine the required tithe? And they wondered why I had trouble staying awake!

The Prophet John, on the other hand, brought a dramatic contrast. His simple, clear, powerful call to personal repentance and submission to God deeply impacted those who heard him speak.

Jesus' teaching, however, was unlike anything we had ever experienced before. He didn't yell. He didn't plead or whine. He just talked, the way you would talk with a good friend in your own home. It was impossible for us to listen to him without feeling as if he was reading our minds. He knew what we feared. He knew what we lusted after. He knew all the things we were clinging to for security. He didn't excuse. He didn't condemn. He simply, powerfully pointed us back to the only source of true freedom, forgiveness, and security—to God himself. John was calling us to repentance before God. Jesus now called us to trust in God. And he did it in a way that made trust seem like the most natural, logical, reasonable thing a person could ever do.

I tried to stay away. I really did. There were so many obvious reasons why it would be ridiculous for me to get involved. I wasn't the student type. I didn't have the temperament. I had a family to support. I had a business to run. A disciple like me would ruin Jesus' reputation. I had a way of blasting and blundering that didn't work well in the religious world. Any further close personal involvement between me and this man was clearly out of the question.

Andrew, James, and John, on the other hand, lived for their times with Jesus. They were always pushing to bring the boats in early, and once the duties were done for the day, they nearly ran the few miles between Bethsaida and Capernaum. I encouraged them to do it. But not me. I could be an excellent support person for people like them who were more the disciple type. After all, somebody had to work. Somebody had to make a living. Somebody had to feed all of us. That was the best role for me. Of course I was impressed with the man. Who wouldn't be? But he surely understood why my pursuing any greater involvement with him was completely out of the question. It wouldn't be good for either one of us. And so what if I happened to go for a walk after the others left? And so what if I did happen to walk toward Capernaum? And so what if I did end up at the marketplace . . . at the back of the crowd . . . listening to this man? That proved nothing. Several hundred other men and women were doing the same thing. I simply wanted to stay well informed about the important events in our community.

I had no further direct contact with the Master for several days following our return from Cana. No, that is not precisely true. It would be better to say that it appeared as though I had no direct contact with the Master during those days. He and I both knew different. Take, for example, that thing with the little flower.

That particular day the fishing did not go well. We went out early, tried all our tricks in all our best locations with almost nothing to show for it. In the end we packed up and brought the boats in early. I told the others I'd finish putting things away so they could begin their evening sprint to Capernaum. When I arrived in the marketplace about an hour later, Andrew, James, and John had all squirmed their way up to the front of the group. I hung around the back of the crowd listening but trying to stay inconspicuous.

The Master was once again talking about the reasonableness of practical trust in God's care for us. Andrew piped up and asked him to explain what he meant. Jesus was sitting on a low stone wall as he spoke. He glanced down at the wall and noticed a tiny flower growing out of a crevice between two rocks. He reached over, cradled it in his hand, and said, "Do you see this tiny flower? It doesn't toil. It doesn't spin garments for itself. And yet Solomon at the height of his glory could not clothe himself like this little flower. If your heavenly Father dresses this forgotten little plant in such beauty, don't you think he knows your needs and cares about you?" Then he turned and looked across the several hundred people gathered around him, straight into my eyes.

That look jolted me like a sharp stick jabbed into my side. He knew the turmoil his entrance into my life was causing within me. He knew the fierce grip I maintained on my precious future. He knew I needed time to think, time to trust, time to let go. He didn't push. He didn't demand. But neither did he leave me alone. I heard him use that illustration numerous times during the next few years. That first time, however, he used it for me. He wanted me to trust him. He wanted me to trust God. And he wanted me to know that I could not do one without doing the other.

The annual Feast of the Passover was just a few days away. Andrew, James, John, Philip, and Nathanael made plans to travel with Jesus to Jerusalem for the celebration. I had never seen any of them so excited. The Passover in Jerusalem was always a great time, but Jesus' presence at the Feast this year created an even greater sense of anticipation. He was still unknown outside our immediate area, and this promised to be his first direct exposure to our nation's center of power.

I knew I was invited as well, but I just couldn't bring myself to join the party. Nothing had yet been resolved in my life, and I was in no mood to pretend. Watching the little group head out of town left me feeling empty and irritated. I couldn't stand not knowing where he was or what he was doing. I ran home and helped Ruth pack up the things we would need for the journey, and a few hours later we joined the growing stream of travelers heading south.

I didn't see Jesus again until after we arrived in Jerusalem. We found a place to stay for the celebration. Ruth renewed annual contacts with family and friends, and I took off on my own. Though I couldn't admit to myself that I was looking for the group, I did end up taking the most direct route I could find to the one place they were most likely to be—the temple.

By the time I arrived on the temple steps, the crowd was incredible. I inched my way along through the outer court where people were lined up to exchange their unsanctified Roman currency for the approved, holy temple currency they could then use to purchase the sacrifices they would offer in accordance with the law of Moses. Everyone knew that the exchange rates being offered by the money changers and the prices being charged for the "approved" sacrifice animals and birds were outright theft. But it was the way things were.

I tried to use my height to survey the sea of faces surrounding me, but any hope of finding Jesus in that mass of humanity was absurd. He had invited me to join him. I had refused. There was nothing I could do about it. As I stood there in the middle of the temple courtyard, with people pushing and bumping up against me from every direction, I felt lonely. I just wanted to get out of there as quickly as I could.

I couldn't have traveled more than a few feet when it happened. Suddenly the table of the money changer nearest me went flying up on end and then came crashing down on its side, sending a shower of coins in every direction. At first I thought a sacrifice bull must have broken loose. Then a second table went over, and a third, and a fourth, each time sending more coins flying and hundreds of men and women scurrying around on their hands and knees, clutching at the tiny rolling treasures.

Then I saw him standing there, a small whip in his right hand, his left hand clenched and raised above his head, an expression of controlled rage on his face. When the others around me also saw him and realized he was the cause of all the commotion, a silence filled the courtyard as people turned and stared in stunned disbelief at this stranger.

When he knew his voice could be heard, he looked first at the enraged band of money changers and then at the sacrifice sellers and commanded, "Take these things away; stop making my Father's house a house of merchandise."

The authority and intensity with which he spoke made it clear his request was not open to discussion. For a few seconds no one moved. Then Jesus brought his whip down hard on the table nearest him, splintering the wood and sending the money merchants scrambling for cover. Jesus then turned to the animal stalls, smashing cages and corrals, setting hundreds of birds free and sending bulls, sheep, and oxen charging in every direction. Some people cheered. Others ran. Still others just stood in amazed disbelief. The entire temple courtyard was in total chaos for nearly half an hour. No one dared challenge the Master—not with that whip in his hand.

When things finally settled down a bit and Jesus made it clear he had no intention of allowing business as usual to resume for the rest of the day, a group of six or seven distinguished-looking temple officials approached Jesus and demanded that he provide them with some sign, some evidence of his authority to do what he was doing.

His response came without hesitation. He drove his clenched fist into his chest and said, "Destroy this temple, and in three days I will raise it up."

At the time I remember thinking how unfortunate his response to those men had been. It seemed to simply confirm what they already believed, that an overstressed pilgrim had gone over the edge and run amuck. The whole group laughed in his face, and one of them responded by saying, "It took forty-six years to build this temple, and will you raise it up in three days?" It was not until after the resurrection that I recalled his statement that day and understood he had been talking about the only true temple in existence at the time he spoke, the one temple that literally housed God on earth, the temple of his own body. He understood, of course, that there was no acceptable sign he could ever offer those who had already chosen to reject his authority. It is not the validity of the message or the persuasiveness of the messenger that determines our response to God. It is the attitude of our heart.

6

And so Jesus introduced himself to the nation of Israel. It was an introduction made from center stage at a time and in a way carefully designed to capture the attention of the entire Jewish world. Jerusalem was packed with Passover visitors from every corner of our tiny country, and with several hundred witnesses eager to testify to what they had seen, the report of Jesus' temple confrontation spread throughout the city in a matter of hours.

But his introduction was not yet complete. Having introduced the people to his authority, he would now present them with his credentials.

I found Andrew and the others gathered in one corner of the courtyard. There must have been some discussion between them about the possibility of my coming, because as I walked up to the group I overheard James say to Andrew, "Alright, you win!" Then they both burst out laughing. I chose to ignore his comment.

Andrew gave me a punch on the arm and said, "Hey, brother! What a surprise!" Then he started giggling again.

Before anything further could be said about what we had just witnessed, Jesus looked our way and motioned for us to follow him. We had no idea what was coming next, but there was no way we were going to miss it.

Jesus walked out of the temple courtyard and down the steps leading to the street with us right behind and a multitude of curious onlookers behind us. The entrance to the temple was a favorite location for the beggar population of Jerusalem. Most of them were there because of some physical infirmity that prevented them from functioning as productive members of society. Some had severely deformed or missing limbs. Some were blind or deaf. It was a collection of the most pathetic and helpless in Israel. They lived off the occasional coin dropped into their hands by those coming to and from the temple.

The first beggar Jesus came to was a woman in her late thirties. She had a huge, hideous growth on her jaw and neck. Her deformity so distorted her appearance, I instinctively looked away in disgust. She sat next to the road, a little heap of pathetic rags, her eyes staring at the ground, her hands cupped in the hope of a coin cast her way.

The Master stooped, then knelt down on both knees in front of her. He reached out and cradled her face in his hands, then lifted her head until their eyes met. I could not hear what he said to her, but suddenly the growth was gone.

It took a few seconds before she realized what had happened. When the truth finally hit her, she grabbed her face, felt her neck and jaw, then began sobbing so hard she couldn't talk. She clutched Jesus' hands, then felt her face again, then clutched his hands, then again felt her face.

Jesus stood up and walked to the next beggar several feet down the street. He was a young man, barely out of his teens, with sunken hollows where his eyes should have been. This time Jesus placed his thumbs over the boy's eyelids, and when he removed them, the first thing that young man ever saw was his Messiah.

During the next two hours we watched as Jesus went from deformity to deformity and illness to illness, restoring and curing each one he touched. He did not stop until every beggar before the temple steps had been cured.

Those of us who knew the Master stayed as close as possible to him throughout the afternoon. Though the six of us formed the front row next to Jesus, the first few rows of the crowd behind us could see plenty, and those farther back were getting frequent, vivid accounts of what was happening.

The greatest impact of the healings, however, was coming from the testimonies of those who were being healed. Many were regular fixtures before the temple, well known by sight to the population of the city. Even before the healed person fully grasped the reality of what Jesus had just done, as Jesus would move on to the next sufferer, the crowd would squeeze in around the person and begin pumping him or her with questions. By the time Jesus finished, apart from the mob immediately behind us, there were numerous smaller groups up and down the street clustered around some excited individual, with everyone asking questions and straining to hear all at the same time.

His work completed, Jesus turned around and headed straight into the crowd with the six of us right behind him. Though the entire area was one solid mass of people, Jesus was still unknown by sight to any except those directly behind us during the healings and those who had seen him in the temple courtyard. By the time we wormed our way several layers through the crowd, the people we met did not realize the man they were bumping up against was the one who was causing all the commotion. Jesus led us outside the city to their Passover camp.

No one said much, even after we broke free from the masses and were able to walk next to each other. I think we were all in shock. Too much was happening too quickly. Changing water into wine at a private country wedding was one thing. But publicly declaring his authority over the greatest visible symbol of our God and our nation, then demonstrating his power to heal all kinds of physical diseases and deformities with nothing more than the touch of his hand . . . what was there to say? Now that I knew where the group was staying, I couldn't wait to get back to tell Ruth what had happened. I made arrangements to meet them in the morning and headed back to our camp.

The reports and rumors of Jesus spread through Jerusalem faster than I ever would have believed possible. By morning the entire city was talking of little else.

I found out later from John about a late-night visitor to Jesus' camp, a man by the name of Nicodemus. He was a person of tremendous influence in the nation's power structure. Unlike the temple rulers who had confronted Jesus earlier in the day, however, Nicodemus came with an open mind and an earnest desire to learn more about the Master. Their conversation together resulted in his becoming one of Jesus' fiercest allies within the establishment; Nicodemus openly defended Jesus even when the campaign to destroy him was at its worst.

Ruth joined me that second day, and together we followed Jesus through the most remarkable thirty-six hours we had ever lived up to that point in our lives. The Master returned to the temple, where he encountered an anxious temple guard and a mass of people filled with anticipation. This time, however, Jesus chose communication rather than confrontation.

He taught the people just as he had been teaching us back home. His words fascinated those who heard him, but they seemed to enrage the Jewish leaders even more than open confrontation. An overstressed, overcharged pilgrim going crazy in the courtyard could be handled. But a rational, deeply compassionate, insightful teacher speaking to the minds and hearts of the people was far more dangerous. Overturned tables could be uprighted. Smashed stalls could be rebuilt. But ideas that openly challenged the foundation upon which the nation's religious power structure was built could not be tolerated. Respected religious leaders repeatedly attempted to challenge the things Jesus was saying. Each time, however, Jesus' wisdom and insight into their underlying motives became abundantly evident to all who heard.

And then there were the healings. Everywhere he went the sick, crippled, and deformed followed. Each time he was confronted with their suffering, he touched and he healed.

Those of us from Capernaum stayed close to Jesus throughout his first public visit to Jerusalem. Though his instant popularity made any personal interaction with him almost impossible, he always alerted us to when and where he was going and made it clear he wanted us by his side. We helped a little with crowd control and kept things orderly when there were several sick seeking his attention.

Most of all, though, we learned. We learned that Jesus' compassion extended to every hurting human being he encountered. We learned it was impossible to intimidate the man. We learned that anyone entering into a battle of wits with him always went away looking like a fool. We learned that the public Jesus and the private Jesus were absolutely consistent. We learned that there seemed to be no limits to his healing powers. We learned that he brought with him no hidden agenda, no selfish or self-serving motivations. He did not seek to destroy the established authorities but rather to offer them a mirror in which they could see their own corruption. In every situation and every encounter, he simply, powerfully, irresistibly presented himself to each individual as accurately and effectively as possible.

If Jesus had remained in Jerusalem following that initial Passover presentation of himself, I believe the Jewish authorities would have sought his execution in a matter of weeks, if not days. They were far too threatened by his power and popularity. It was impossible for them to compete with this man, and submission to his authority was out of the question.

Following the conclusion of the Feast, however, Jesus shared with us his intention to travel south, into the Judean countryside. It was a move carefully designed to defuse temporarily the fear that Jesus' presence in Jerusalem was generating within our nation's leadership. The time would come when he would personally reignite that fear, driving those who held political power to fulfill the roles for which they had been appointed. But that time would be selected by no one but the Master himself, and that time had not yet come.

Judea would be safe and receptive to his message. Jesus had spent the first few months of his life in the small Judean town of Bethlehem, and there were those there who remembered well the miraculous events surrounding his birth. The Prophet John was also from that region. Judea was well prepared for the Master's arrival.

Jesus invited all of us to come with him. Philip and Nathanael accepted the offer immediately. James, John, Andrew, and I held a private conference to talk it over. By now it was obvious to all of us that we were in the presence of a divinely empowered and appointed prophet of God. It was obvious, too, that the hearts of my brother and my two best friends were wide open to this amazing man.

But with me it was not so easy. Submission, even to such a man as this, has never come easily for me, especially when that submission threatened the very foundations of my life. I just couldn't do it. I wished my friends a good journey, told them I would hold the fishing fleet together until they returned, packed up our travel gear and my even heavier load of unresolved turmoil, and headed back to Bethsaida with Ruth.

7

And so began the longest few weeks of my life. I tried hard to pour myself back into the business, but now it all seemed so hollow. Reports of Jesus' tremendous reception in Judea filtered up to us, making me feel excited and empty and irritable all at the same time. I should have been there with them. I knew that. Ruth knew that. In fact, Ruth knew that all too well. Each night she shared her home with a grumpy bear of a man consumed by his own stubborn will. She was so good to me during those days. Her exposure to Jesus on our trip to Jerusalem had produced in her a beautiful heart of openness and submission to the Master. She knew he was the one our nation was waiting for. She knew, too, I would never find peace with myself until I first found peace with the Master.

The skill with which she gently helped me move through my stubborn resistance to total submission to Jesus will forever be one of the greatest miracles in my life. Do you recall those words in my first letter to the churches? "In the same way, you wives, be submissive to your own husbands so that even if any of them are disobedient to the word, they may be won without a word by the behavior of their wives, as they observe your chaste and respectful behavior." I learned that principle through Ruth during my weeks of resistance against the living Word, Jesus. She knew how desperately I needed him. She knew I could never be happy without him. She knew, too, that I was fighting against him with everything inside me. But she never nagged. She never preached. She never said a word unless I brought up the subject first. And then she just listened and let me talk. I was miserable, and I made our lives miserable. But she never attacked me or blamed me. She knew she could not make my choice for me, and there was no value in forcing me to make it before I was ready.

Then came the terrifying news of the arrest and imprisonment of the Prophet John. John's recent bold public proclamations about Jesus had inseparably linked the ministries of the two men. When asked if he was troubled by Jesus' growing popularity, John described himself as the close friend of the bridegroom, who is thrilled at the sound of the bridegroom's voice. He understood his role perfectly, stating simply, "He must increase, but I must decrease."

If John had been jailed, could Jesus' imprisonment be far behind? And what would happen to those who were with him? What would happen to Andrew, James, and John?

Our whole household, in fact, our whole community, was deeply affected by the growing hostility of both our political and religious leaders against John, Jesus, and very likely all those who were closely associated with them.

Ruth's mom, who had been living with us since the death of her husband several years earlier, was so anxious about Andrew and the others that she literally worried herself sick. We woke one morning to find her soaked with perspiration, fighting a dangerously high temperature. Ruth immediately began a constant bedside vigil, doing what she could to help her mom fight off whatever disease was attacking her aging body.

Then word finally reached us of Jesus' return to Galilee. He was teaching in the synagogue at Cana. Two days later Andrew returned home filled with the most amazing account of his adventures with the Master. Judea had welcomed Jesus with open arms. News of his activities in Jerusalem had preceded him, and even in that remote rural region, crowds swarmed to meet him. They enthusiastically responded to his teaching, and of course his healing abilities drew every diseased and disabled person in the region.

Jesus' decision to return to Galilee was prompted by the arrival of several disciples of the Prophet John, bringing news of the prophet's imprisonment. Knowing the distress this turn of events would bring to the families of those traveling with him, and wanting to put a greater distance between himself and the political forces in Jerusalem, Jesus and his growing band of followers headed north.

Their return trip took them through Samaria, a region populated by the descendants of Jews who had intermarried with the Gentile inhabitants of the region. Though many still followed some of the customs of their Jewish heritage, their religious beliefs were mingled with the pagan worship of their Gentile ancestors, and they were viewed as a mixed race with a heathen core. Our nation's social and commercial relations with the Samaritans were limited to the smallest possible amount. They were not welcome in our synagogues, could not be called as legal witnesses in any of our court proceedings, and were not considered acceptable candidates for any type of proselytism.

Andrew shocked us with his report of Jesus' two-day stay in the region, which resulted in a large number of Samaritan men and women affirming their allegiance to the Master. The visit was apparently prompted by Jesus initiating a conversation with a Samaritan woman of questionable moral character.

$\sim$

And Andrew's amazing account did not stop there. He had broken away from the group to bring us word of what was happening, but he did not travel home alone. The previous day as Jesus was teaching in Cana, a court official from Capernaum forced his way to the front of the crowd and pleaded with Jesus to return with him immediately to Capernaum. The man's son was near death, and he hoped Jesus might be able to help the boy. Jesus told the man to return home, promising he would find his son well. Andrew and the man traveled back to Capernaum together. One of the man's servants met them on the road halfway home, bringing the news that the boy was well. When the man asked his servant what time the boy had recovered, he was told it was at the very hour at which he had been speaking with the Master.

The following day Jesus would travel to his hometown of Nazareth, where Andrew planned to rejoin him.

"You're coming back with me, aren't you, Simon?"

Andrew's simple question suddenly ignited the most explosive rage within me. "Look, little brother! Why does everyone always just assume that the only way to show support for Jesus is to trot along behind him everywhere he goes? Why don't people realize that we can't all spend the rest of our lives running irresponsibly around the countryside? If I wanted to be there, I'd be there. I happen to have a number of people relying on me to earn a living. I cannot afford the luxury of walking out on my responsibilities every time a new prophet comes to town. You go rejoin the faithful pack tomorrow, but leave me out of it. . . . I've got some work to do down at the boat. I'll be back in a few hours."

No one said a word when I returned. Andrew was busy putting together some things for the trip to Nazareth. Ruth was in with her mom. Her mom's condition continued to deteriorate to the point where we were deeply concerned about whether she would recover.

I felt so unsure of myself. What this family needed most of all was a man who could give strong, positive, supportive leadership at a time of real crisis and stress. What this family had was an angry, irritable, blundering fool whose presence caused more tension than it ever relieved.

"And you shall be called Peter"—ha! "And you shall be called Pathetic!" was closer to the truth. During the month after Jesus entered our world, I had witnessed numerous people whose lives had been transformed by the Master. But to be honest, all he'd brought me so far was chaos and confusion. Why couldn't I be like the woman in Jerusalem with the growth on her neck? Why couldn't Jesus just touch me and I would suddenly live happily ever after? Why couldn't I be like my beloved Ruth or like my little brother with a heart opened wide to Jesus? Why was I so afraid to trust the one person who was in every way more worthy of that trust than anyone else I'd ever met in my life?

I knew the answer, of course. It was a truth I learned first in my own life and then saw illustrated countless times in the lives of others in the years ahead. Jesus never demanded entrance into a person's life, but neither did he negotiate the terms of his entrance with those who chose to invite him. He did not want my endorsement. He did not want my approval. He wanted my life. He wanted me to choose to give him the right to take control.

The following morning Andrew returned to the Master, and I returned to my fishing. Everything in my life was falling apart. Ruth's mother was dying. I had driven a wedge between myself and my little brother so wide he didn't dare open his mouth around me for fear I would attack him again. My business partners had been gone for weeks and might now be gone forever. And worst of all, I was turning my back on the one person who could help me make sense of it all.

Andrew was not gone long this time. Two days later he came home announcing Jesus' return to Capernaum. James and John were also back.

The visit to Nazareth did not go well. The people there knew Jesus as a child, and now they refused to listen to him as an adult. At one point the people of the city became so hostile to his message, they dragged him to the edge of a cliff and tried to throw him over. He escaped, however, and left town with his disciples soon after.

With Andrew, James, and John all back home, we agreed to return to our much neglected nets early the next morning. Jesus was planning to remain at the house where he was staying in Capernaum for an extended period of time, so my three partners were willing to split their time between fishing and being with Jesus.

When I rolled out of bed the following morning, I assumed it was going to be my first somewhat normal day in weeks. The sun was shining, the four of us were returning to our nets together, and Jesus was busy doing what he did somewhere else. I was finally back in control of my world. I had no idea it was a world Jesus would bring to an end forever with just ten words in a matter of hours.

Andrew and I were on the beach early, fishing that morning from the shore of the Sea of Galilee. Nothing was really resolved in my life, but at least these things—the nets, the water, the fish, the work—these things I understood. James and John discovered their equipment had not been cared for well by the men their father had hired to fill in for them during their absence, so in the end they decided to spend the morning helping their father make some much needed repairs to their nets.

Less than an hour later I saw him. He was alone, walking toward me along the beach. And that, of course, was the point—he had been walking toward me since the day we met. A part of me wanted to drop my net and run to meet him. Another part of me wanted to grab my net and run away from him down the beach. In the end I just stood there waiting. As soon as Andrew saw him, he came and stood beside me.

When Jesus reached us no one spoke for a few seconds. Andrew just stood there with a big grin on his face, obviously thrilled to see him. I stood silent in a sort of terrified relief. I knew this was no chance meeting. For more than a month I had been running, hiding from this man, secretly hoping he would not give up his pursuit. I was tired of this horrible game, and no matter what he said to me now, at least I would not have to run anymore.

I stood silently, staring at his feet, waiting for his words of condemnation, anticipating his demand for an explanation of why I had stayed away from him for so long.

But the condemnation never came. He spoke just one word—"Peter!" When I looked up, I saw his smile, a smile of understanding and acceptance that instantly disarmed the terror within me. He looked first at me, then at Andrew, then at our nets and our little pile of fish. Then he said, "Follow me, and I will make you fishers of men."

He knew I understood what he was asking. He knew the time had come for me to choose. He was not asking me to follow him for the morning, or for the day, or for the week. He was asking me to follow him for the rest of my life. I could not have both *his* world and *mine*. I had to choose. I didn't know what "fishers of men" meant, but I knew it wasn't something I could do with the net I held in my hands.

When my decision finally came, it brought with it a sense of freedom and relief unlike anything I had ever known before. Jesus still wanted me, and I wanted him as I had never wanted anything else in my life. I wanted to be a part of whatever this man was doing. I wanted to be identified with him. I wanted to be on his side, his team. With every ounce of my massive hulk I wanted to do the one thing he was now asking me to do—follow him.

I didn't say a word. I didn't need to. He and my brother saw what no one had seen for more years than I could remember: they saw tears well up in my eyes and roll down my cheeks. And, of course, he understood. I dropped my net and waited for him to lead.

We walked with the Master along the shore until we reached the boat in which James and John were working. They were anchored to the shore. Jesus waded out to the side of the boat and spoke with the two brothers. We saw them look at each other, then at Jesus. Then they rose, jumped over the side, and waded ashore with their Master.

Together the four of us walked down the beach next to Jesus, heading toward Capernaum and toward a future that would change us, and eventually the entire world, forever.

8

My surrender to the Master left me feeling as though every troublesome issue in my life was instantly, eternally resolved. And in one sense, I was right. For the first time I knew I was on the right course, heading in the right direction. I was well pleased to spend the rest of my life following Jesus, getting to know him, trusting his lead. But submitting to his lead was only the beginning. Having accepted him as my goal, the Master now needed to introduce me to the only means by which that goal could be attained. And that learning process would take years.

And so the quake began. For several months our tiny nation had been feeling the Master's jolts and tremors. The pieces were now in place. He was ready to shake Israel as it had never been shaken before.

We walked with the Master back to the house where he was staying in Capernaum. People were already milling around the outside when we arrived. A few of the more aggressive ones were knocking on the door or peeking in the windows. As soon as Jesus appeared, the entire pack charged us. Some were sick, some crippled, some deformed. Others just wanted to meet this man who was causing such a stir.

The approach Jesus took with those people that morning established a pattern we saw repeated countless times as we traveled throughout the nation in the months ahead. He turned his attention first to those with physical needs. For those who hurt, entrance into the kingdom so often begins at the point of their pain. He healed and restored each sick and disabled person in the group.

Then he found a convenient place to sit and began to teach. Occasionally people would ask him a question. Sometimes he would ask the group or one individual within the group a question himself, using the response to help illustrate a concept he wanted to share with us. Always he talked about God, relationships, trust, and the world around us in a way that was absolutely consistent with real life. It was unlike anything any of us had ever heard before. And always we came away from those group teaching times feeling as if we had just finished a private conversation with the Master. That morning the people sat and listened, unwilling to move more than a few inches for fear they would miss something he said or risk losing their place. It was late afternoon before he finally dismissed the group so that we could return home to prepare for the Sabbath.

As Andrew, James, John, and I walked back to Bethsaida, we talked about what was coming. We knew our future was now bound up with Jesus. He would not remain in Capernaum long. When he traveled, we would travel with him.

It had been a long, intense day for me. I was tired. The feelings of peace and serenity that had been so intense on the beach that morning were being quickly eroded by what

I saw as the practical realities of life. I was a married man, the head of a household, with the responsibility to care for my family's needs. For the first time I wondered what Jesus did for money and even more how he expected us to meet our physical needs. We would not be able to fish during the days. But why couldn't we fish at night?

I suggested the idea to the others, and it met with no small resistance. They pointed out that it would be nice to sleep at night, and I pointed out that we had to do something to stay alive, and they pointed out that their needs had been well provided for by the people they met during their trip with Jesus to Judea, and I pointed out that eating a few meals in someone's house was a long way from providing for an entire household, and they . . . well, you get the idea. In the end they grudgingly acknowledged that some night fishing might become a necessity. Jesus was planning to attend the synagogue in Capernaum the following day. We would join him early, spend the day together, then begin our night job when the Sabbath ended.

Ruth could tell something was different the moment I walked in the door. Twelve hours earlier she had kissed a grumpy bear good-bye. Now the grumpiness was gone, replaced by an excitement she had not seen for weeks. We talked until late into the night. She understood my anxiety about how I was now going to earn a living given my commitment to the Master, but it didn't seem to concern her nearly as much as it did me. Her far greater and more immediate concern grew out of her mother's rapidly failing health. The previous twenty-four hours had been the worst yet. Her mom was now eating nothing at all. The fever raged unbroken. Though none of us dared put it into words, unless there was a dramatic change soon, it was obvious Ruth's mom would not last more than another day or two at the most.

"Simon, do you think Jesus would help her?"

Why is it always so much easier to trust the Lord for someone else's needs than it is to trust him for our own?

59

Perhaps for the same reason it is so much easier to believe he loves the person next to us more than he loves us. We know ourselves too well. We know all the reasons why we are unworthy of his involvement in our lives. It seems reasonable for him to miraculously intervene in the lives of Moses, and Elijah, and King David. But why should we expect him to do the same for us? That very day I had seen the Master heal a dozen helpless people. Yet, when Ruth asked me that question, I didn't know what to say. Certainly he could help her. But would he? All I could do was promise Ruth I would ask.

Andrew, James, John, and I left for Capernaum early the following morning. I wanted Ruth to join us, but her mom's condition made it impossible.

We joined Jesus just as he was heading into the synagogue. Everyone in the community knew he would be teaching, and the place was packed. He read a passage from the writings of the Prophet Isaiah and was beginning to comment on it when suddenly a man in the middle of the room stood up and let out the most hideous scream I had ever heard. Then he looked right at Jesus, thrust his finger as if he were trying to skewer the Master on the end of it, and cried out, "What business do we have with each other, Jesus, you Nazarene?"

The venom with which these words were spoken was unlike anything I'd ever heard before. It is true that Nazareth had a reputation in those days for being a rather ignorant, irreverent community, but this man made Jesus' hometown sound like vile, hideous blasphemy. Then the man's tone shifted from hatred to terror as he wrapped his arms around his face and whimpered, "Have you come to destroy us? I know who you are—the Holy One of God!"

That final phrase triggered an instant response from Jesus. "Be quiet! And come out of him!"

Jesus' double command brought an immediate reaction. The man suddenly crashed to the floor with such fury it

60

looked almost as if some massive invisible hand had picked him up and smashed him down. His entire body then contracted in a series of violent convulsions, followed by one final terrifying shriek.

For a few seconds the man lay motionless. I thought he was dead. Then he blinked, lifted his head, and rose slowly to his feet. It was hard to believe he was the same man. He looked at the stunned crowd standing around him, then turned his eyes to Jesus and spoke just two words: "Thank you."

The meeting ended early that day. As the man turned and walked slowly out the door, the entire congregation followed him. Some were walking beside him, asking him about what had just happened, while most of the others couldn't wait to get home to tell their family and friends about what they had seen.

Andrew, James, John, and I all grouped around Jesus, pummeling him with questions. What happened back there? How did you do that? What did it mean?

We talked for several minutes. Then, when a little lull came into the conversation, I blurted out my request. "Master, I need your help. Ruth's mom is really sick. I'm afraid she's going to die. Will you come?"

Why was that so hard? Why did it scare me so much to admit I needed him? Was it just my own self-sufficient pride? Or was it the fear he might not come or might not care?

Then I glanced up at his face and saw it once again—that look in his eyes. He knew already. He was simply waiting for me to ask.

I learned something important that day. During the next three years I would see Jesus intrude into thousands of people's lives with his miraculous touch, people he had never seen before, people who offered him no allegiance, no submission, people who often offered him no faith whatsoever. Some of them eventually bowed before him and called him Lord. Most simply took what he offered and went their way, never looking back again. With each of them, Jesus did what he did to present himself to the nation of Israel. He was their Messiah, and he came bringing his credentials for all to see.

But with those of us who were close to him, everything was different, and he wanted us to know it. The things we received from him were not given simply as one more item in his packet of credentials. They were given as the expression of his personal love for each of us. But we had to ask! Only then could we hear the love in his response. The world around us would share in the goodness of his presence simply because they happened to be near the one who is the source of all good, just as they shared in the benefits of the sun that rose each morning or the rain that brought life to their crops. With those of us who belonged to him, however, it was always intensely personal. We shared in his goodness not simply because we happened to be in the right place at the right time but because he loved us and willingly assumed responsibility for our needs. I knew now why it had been so hard for me to ask for his help. I was afraid—afraid he didn't know, or afraid he didn't care. Neither was true. The truth was he was simply waiting for me to ask.

I led the way home as quickly as possible. James, John, Andrew, the Master, and I all charged into the house. One look at the anxiety in my wife's eyes told me how her day had gone.

Her mother now lay near death, motionless except for her desperate, shallow breathing. Jesus entered the room where she lay and stood beside her bed. I stood next to him, watching, and Ruth stood next to me. The others gathered behind us. The room was dimly lit, hanging heavy with the odors of disease and approaching death. As I stood there, looking down at the fragile form before me, I was struck with the sudden terror that perhaps my plea for the Master's help was too late. Maybe this was beyond the Master's healing powers. If only I hadn't fought him for so long, if only I'd brought the Master earlier, if only . . .

What I saw next I had already seen in the lives of others. I would see it again thousands of times in the years ahead. Yet, for me, the Master's power to heal never lost its wonder. He did not approach disease or sickness or deformity as a doctor would approach it. He did not do battle with it. He did not conquer it with some mysterious potion. He simply forced the sickness to submit to his authority. He reached down, took my mother-in-law's right hand in both of his, and commanded her fever to leave. And the fever left.

She opened her eyes, looked first at Jesus and then at the room filled with people staring at her. She gave an embarrassed little laugh and said, "Oh! Dear me!" as if she had been caught sleeping in on cleaning day. Then she looked at Ruth and said, "Well! We must fix our guests some supper, my dear. Just give me a minute to get dressed, and we'll see what we can find."

The meal we all shared together that evening was the best I could ever remember. It wasn't the food, of course. It was the Master's presence, and the laughter, and the peace, and the realization that for the first time in a very long time everything was just the way it should be.

The Sabbath was over, but I chose to put off my night-time fishing scheme until the following day. For some reason, with Jesus sitting there with us, it just didn't seem appropriate to focus on my financial concerns. I wasn't altogether sure Jesus would understand. I saw no need for him to know about my little plan. Discipleship demanded sacrifice. I knew that. Asking Jesus to heal Ruth's mom was one thing. But asking him to feed my family was something very different. Besides, what could he do? He had no money. It was far better for me to take charge of the physical stuff and let him take care of the spiritual. We were fine for a few days. Tomorrow night would be soon enough.

How was I to know that the following night we would all be many miles away from the Sea of Galilee?

9

With sundown and the end of the Sabbath, our community underwent a dramatic transformation. The rumors of Jesus' healing powers had been circulating throughout the region for weeks. But his dramatic public confrontation with the demon-possessed man in the synagogue that morning finally ignited the explosion. The strict restrictions on Sabbath travel kept the crowds contained throughout the afternoon. But the instant the sun dipped below the horizon, every human being in the city suffering from any form of physical need imaginable made for the Master as fast as they could move. Those at the synagogue saw Jesus leave with me that morning, and word of his whereabouts spread quickly.

It was the noise that first alerted us to what was happening outside our home. At first I thought a neighbor was at the door. But when I looked out, what I saw sent a shock through me. Several hundred people were packed around the front of our house, with many more coming behind them. As soon as they saw me at the door, someone called out, "Is he here?"

I didn't dare answer for fear they would storm the house. I just closed the door, walked back inside, and said, "Jesus, what are we going to do?" By "we" I of course meant "you," and he responded immediately by opening the door and walking out into the middle of that mob. For the next five or six hours, Jesus touched, freed, healed, and released. James, John, Andrew, and I organized, directed, controlled, and reassured those waiting their turn. Finally, about one o' clock in the morning, the last suffering son of Abraham was sent home. We dragged ourselves inside and collapsed into bed. Jesus spent what was left of the night with us. I dozed off hoping for at least eight hours of uninterrupted sleep.

Less than four hours later the sound of voices outside our door jolted me out of a deep sleep. I've never been at my best when I first wake up and definitely not after half a night's sleep. I stumbled to the front door, peeked out, and saw a repeat of the night before. People! Hundreds and hundreds of people. Where were they all coming from? Now I knew what it felt like to be under siege.

I quickly closed the door and stumbled back into the house, looking for Jesus. It took only a few minutes to discover he wasn't there. Now what was I supposed to do? I got Andrew up and explained the situation to him. We both agreed we had to find the Master and find him fast. He couldn't have returned to his own place, or this mob would have already discovered it. We agreed to leave the house, head in separate directions so the crowd wouldn't think we were going to a rendezvous with Jesus, then meet at the boat and begin our search in earnest.

Our escape plan worked fine. When the people saw us leave without Jesus, they paid little attention and lost interest altogether when we split up. Once we regrouped on the beach, I suggested searching several secluded coves just outside of town.

He wasn't hard to find. He had been praying, and I felt embarrassed barging in, but I didn't know what else to do. When he looked up, I said simply, "All the people are looking for you." Neither my arrival nor my words seemed to offend him. He joined me, and we met Andrew and then James and John on the beach.

After greeting them Jesus told us he wanted to go to the towns nearby so he could preach there too.

He wanted to go immediately. I told the group I would let Ruth know we were heading out of town and then catch up with them in a few minutes. My return home seemed to cause more interest with the crowd than had my departure, especially because I was obviously in a hurry. I gave Ruth a quick update on our plans, told her I had no idea when I would be back, and attempted once again to stroll casually out the door. This time it didn't work. I was hit with a sudden urge to run. I wasn't exactly built for speed, though, so most of the mob had no problem keeping up with me. We must have looked ridiculous—several hundred frantic people thundering through town after a huge, red-faced, puffing, panic-stricken man. When I finally made it back to Jesus, I blundered into his presence with the whole multitude at my heels. Stealth and subtlety have never been among my stronger qualities.

Jesus was not harsh with those who were determined to claim him as Capernaum's private prophet and healer, but he was firm and direct. He assured them he would be back but also made it clear that his message and his work belonged to the entire nation. They were not to follow him but to wait for his return.

∝

His first extended trip through Galilee lasted nearly a month. Jesus went from village to village, town to town, teaching in the synagogues, proclaiming what he called "the good news of the kingdom of God." He healed every sickness and infirmity among the people he met and cast out numerous demons. News of his works went before him, and it wasn't long before each new village greeted him with a tremendous sense of anticipation. It wasn't unusual for us to be met at the outskirts of a community by a pack of excited children, placed there on watch for our arrival. As soon as we came into view, they turned and ran through the village, calling out, "He's here! He's here!" Their cries brought people from every corner of the community, all wanting to meet the amazing prophet with hands that could heal.

Though I didn't realize it at the time, Jesus used our early travels together to show us by example how we were to present him to the world in the years ahead. From the first moment I met Jesus, I knew he was unlike any other leader I had ever met before. You see, Jesus never attempted to win people to himself. Unlike all the other leaders I'd known, Jesus never attempted to create a following.

His approach to Israel was simple: He stepped into the center of our world. Through his words and his actions he enabled everyone to see exactly who he was and what he was like. Then he allowed us to decide for ourselves what we would do about it.

67

His use of his healing abilities is a good example. During the time of his public ministry, Jesus healed thousands of people. But not once did he use his healing powers as a hook with which to hold another human being. Never did he say, "If you follow me, I will heal you," or "Because I have healed you, I now expect you to follow me." He didn't "buy" people with his power. He didn't manipulate people with his persuasive abilities. He just stepped into their lives, allowed them to see him as he was, and then gave them the freedom to decide what they would do with what they had seen.

Most people were well pleased to take whatever they could get from the Master and then walk away. If they wanted healing, they would take healing. If they wanted entertainment, they would join the crowd, watch the show, and listen to the Master teach. Then, when the party was over, they walked away unchanged. My brother Matthew liked to call those people "the multitudes." It was a good name for them—an unthinking mass of humanity taking what came without charge, closing their eyes to the reality of what they were seeing and hearing.

Then there were some who hated Jesus from the moment he entered town because he threatened their power and control in the community. They challenged him whenever they could, they raised questions about the source of his power, they attacked and undermined his work whenever they had the chance, and they rejoiced when he walked out of town.

And finally, there were those of us who . . . well, those who entered into his love. There was only one requirement for this—we had to want him more than we wanted anything else. There were thousands and thousands who wanted what he could give. There were not many who wanted him. But something amazing took place in our lives when we reached that point. I can describe it only by saying he gave us himself. He allowed us to see his heart, and in so doing he created between himself and each of us a

68

depth of intimacy unlike anything else we'd ever known before. He ceased to be just the Prophet or the Healer or the Great Teacher and became our friend. He listened to us. He laughed with us. He lived with us. He opened his heart and his mind to us, and what we saw there changed everything forever because what we saw there was ourselves. *We* were in his heart, in his mind. Having seen that, life could never be the same again. Most of those we encountered, however, were never able to see his heart because they were never willing to give him theirs.

During the years since his departure, I have tried hard to duplicate the pattern Jesus modeled for us when he was here. It is not my responsibility to attempt to sell Jesus to the world or rally the masses to follow his teachings. It is my responsibility to present him as simply and accurately as possible and let people decide for themselves what they will do with the Master. The few who submit to him on his terms will know his heart and his love as I have known it. The rest will walk away. Or worse, they will attempt to use him for their own ends.

Already our Christian world is filled with those who are busy building their little empires in the name of Jesus. Brother Paul made a comment in one of the letters he wrote to the Christians in Corinth. He said, "We are not like many, peddling the word of God." And there *are* many. I can hear them now: "Who wants salvation? Who wants healing? Who wants peace? Step right up! Jesus can give you what you want." The focus, of course, is always on what *we* want, not on what *he* wants. And the result is an endless river of religious sewage, flowing out of the septic system of our own selfish pride.

That first teaching tour with the Master was a wonderful experience for me, with one significant exception. My anxiety over how I was going to provide for my family increased with every additional day I was away from home. My grand plan for night fishing was being postponed far longer than I had anticipated, and though I didn't dare discuss the subject with Jesus, I was a mess by the time we finally returned home.

We arrived back in Bethsaida in the early afternoon, exactly four weeks from the day we left. In some ways it seemed as if I had been gone a year. So much had happened since that morning when I peeked out on a sea of damaged humanity in front of our house. It was wonderful seeing Ruth again and telling her all about our trip. I was relieved to find out that friends and family who knew I was traveling with Jesus had met her needs during my absence. But it was also good to know I could once again take over that responsibility.

We were all exhausted from the trip, but I persuaded Andrew, James, and John that there was no telling how long Jesus would remain home. It was essential for us to implement our nighttime fishing strategy immediately. We rested a few hours, ate dinner with the family, and then headed to the boats.

I cannot recall a worse fishing experience in my life than the twelve hours we spent on the Sea of Galilee that night. The wind howled, making both the rowing and the fishing an agonizing experience. There was only a sliver of a moon, and the near total darkness made it almost impossible to position our boats accurately, to see where our nets had been thrown, or to see what was in them when we brought them up, though in truth we didn't need to see to know what was in our nets. Throughout the entire night we fought the waves, cast our nets, hauled them in, fought the waves, cast our nets, hauled them in, again and again, and never caught a single fish. We went from frustration, to irritation, to helpless anger, to despair. As the sun rose we finally folded our nets and fought our way back to the shore.

The scene that greeted us on the beach was almost more than I could handle. Word of Jesus' return home had spread quickly throughout the region. Jesus was standing at the water's edge with several hundred people packed around him. Many at the back of the crowd were attempting to squirm closer to the Master, which only caused the mass to pack in around Jesus more and more tightly. His feet were already in the water, but with none of us there to establish a perimeter around him, the crowd continued to surge forward.

We beached our boats a few feet on either side of Jesus with the hope of providing him with some measure of protection. James, John, and Andrew hopped out and tried to clear a little area around him, so he could at least stand up without being driven into the sea. I went to the back of our boat and began cleaning our nets. I was grumpy and exhausted and in no mood for yet another mob scene.

Then, as I wrestled with a tangle in one of the nets, I suddenly felt the boat shift under the weight of someone jumping aboard. I turned around and saw Jesus looking at me.

"Say, Simon, why don't we push out a few feet from the shore so I can teach without being driven into the sea in the process?"

He knew I was grumpy. He knew I was tired. He knew I had been out fishing all night. But he also knew I was finally ready for my first lesson in the difference between life in the flesh and life in the Spirit. He had me trapped, and he seemed to be well pleased with the arrangement.

Andrew gave us a push away from the shore, then jumped on board himself. We let the boat float out about thirty feet, then dropped the anchor. As soon as the crowd saw that no amount of pushing and shoving would get them near enough to touch Jesus, they settled down, then sat down on the beach.

Jesus sat at the front of our boat and taught for several hours that morning. He spoke on one of his favorite themes—the heavenly Father's willingness and ability to provide for those who trust him. His words *sounded* great, but everything he said just made me feel more grumpy. Talking about God's care and provision was fine, but after fishing for a full night without a single fish to show for it, the application part of this whole thing left something to be desired.

When he finished his teaching, he turned to me and said, "Now, Simon, put out into the deep water and let down your nets for a catch."

I couldn't let this pass without saying something. I was tired. I was hungry. I felt like I had just been preached at by a deeply sincere man who wasn't in touch with the practical realities of life. Maybe I didn't know as much about the sacred writings as I should, but I knew a whole lot about fishing, and I knew there were no fish out there—not today, not in this location. It was time to introduce Jesus to *my* area of expertise

"Master, we worked hard all night and caught nothing, but at your request I will let down the nets."

There! That was as tactful as I could be. If he wanted to go on a little fishing trip after his morning teaching session, I would do that for him, but he might as well know the truth right now—there would be no fish in the net.

Andrew and I pulled the boat out a couple hundred feet from the shore. We both knew it was a terrible location, but after last night we also knew it didn't really matter. This wasn't about fishing; this was about giving Jesus a relaxing little boat trip and escaping from the crowds for a few hours.

I must admit I became rather parental with Jesus at that point. If he wanted a fishing lesson, I would give him a fishing lesson. I went into great detail showing him how to correctly hold the net for proper casting, how to coordinate the back, leg, shoulder, and arm muscles to get good distance from the throw. After introducing him to the basics I gave a demonstration throw, dropping the net just where I wanted it to go. With one painful exception several years later, that was the last time I ever cast that net.

Few things in my life have impacted me more deeply than what took place during the next few minutes. Having completed Simon's little lesson in professional fishing, I started to pull the empty net back to the boat. Then, suddenly the water between our boat and the net began to churn and roll as if it were boiling. The turmoil under the surface was so intense it caused the boat to rock violently. The rope in my hand went instantly tight, and I braced myself and pulled with all my strength. At the same instant I saw what was causing the sea to churn—fish! Hundreds and hundreds of fish, more fish than I had ever seen in one place at one time in my life.

I called to Andrew for help, and he grabbed hold and pulled with me. As we strained at the ropes, I peered over the side and was shocked to see what appeared to be several thousand fish all attempting to pack themselves into our net at once. It looked as though they were fighting for the honor of being caught. The weight of the net was far beyond our ability to handle, and I turned my head to shore and bellowed for James and John to come help. By the time they reached us, Andrew and I had been able to bring the edge of the net up high enough so that we could scoop fish into our boat. We scooped and scooped and scooped and scooped until the boat was so low in the water I was afraid we would sink. And still the net was packed with fish. We maneuvered the other boat alongside the net and filled it as well, then rowed the boats to shore, dragging the half-filled net behind us.

The range of thoughts and emotions I experienced during that quarter hour of chaos was unlike anything I had ever known before. At the first sight of all those fish, my initial reaction was the kind of elated greed I always experienced with a great catch. But it wasn't more than a few minutes before it became obvious even to me that what was happening here had nothing to do with fish. At one point in the harvesting process, I glanced up into Jesus' eyes and saw once again what I had seen so many times before—he knew. He knew about my plan to live a double life, to be a disciple by day and a fisherman by night. He knew the plan was rooted in the great false foundation of my existence—my unquestioning confidence in my own natural abilities. He knew my commitment to him was deep and genuine, but he also knew my practical trust in him was almost non-existent. He knew I understood the world of the flesh perfectly and the world of the Spirit not at all. And in that instant I knew why I had fished all night and caught nothing. I caught nothing because he had told the fish to go away, just as he now told the fish to come.

I wonder if you can understand the terror that thought created in my mind. It shook the great pillars of my life. It meant that my effort, my abilities, my determination, and my physical strength were not and could not be my bottom line. It meant I was free to crank out as much effort and energy as I wanted to, but somehow this man could control what resulted from that effort. I felt suddenly, terribly ashamed—ashamed I hadn't talked to him about my worries, ashamed I hadn't trusted him, and ashamed most of all because he knew what was in my mind.

I waded through the fish to where Jesus stood, dropped to my knees at his feet, then blurted out, "O Lord! Stay away from me, for I am a sinful man."

I didn't deserve these fish. I didn't deserve his kindness. I didn't deserve his friendship or his involvement in my life.

Jesus reached down, took my arm, and brought me to my feet. He wanted to see my eyes; he wanted me to see his. He said simply, "Don't be afraid. From now on you will be catching men."

Don't be afraid. Don't be afraid of him. Don't be afraid of his ability to take care of my family. Don't be afraid of the future he has for me. Don't be afraid to walk away from the boat, the nets, and the illusion of security they provide. The issue was trust, of course—my willingness to trust him. It was just a beginning, but it was that. I had still learned very little about the difference between life in the flesh and life in the Spirit. But at least my double life ended that day. I ceased to be a disciple by day and a fisherman by night. From that day forward I became a full-time disciple of my Lord Jesus Christ. True, it was still a discipleship with deep roots in the flesh, but it was a start. And at that point it was all the Master asked of me because he knew it was all I was able to give. The teacher wanted my full attention, and now it was his. At last we were ready for class to begin.

_____ 1 0

It was now almost a year since the Master's entrance into my world, almost a year since he called me Peter, almost a year since he quietly dropped his net of love around me and began drawing me to himself. I had fought that net as I had never fought anything before in my life. I wanted so much to keep him at arm's length, to be objective, uninvolved. I could not deny his incredible authority, but neither would I submit to it. A year of fighting his gentle relentless pursuit left me exhausted. Now at last I was at peace. The quiet terror that had formed the backdrop to my life since the first day we met was finally gone, replaced by a vision of the most glorious future imaginable.

How could I have been so fortunate? Here I was, standing beside the man who was obviously destined to rule our nation, perhaps even to rule the world. Jesus had spent the previous twelve months assembling his team, introducing himself, his message, and his powers to Israel. Now at last the conquest could begin in earnest. The goal was obvious—the restoration of Israel to its former glory. The role I would play in that restoration was not yet clearly defined, but now that my total allegiance to the Master was certain, and my remarkable gifts and abilities were at his disposal, together we would find a way.

My heart was pure, but I had it all wrong—both the goal and the means. He knew, of course. He also knew if he had told me then that his goal was the cross and his means in all things was the Spirit of God, it would have sounded like gibberish to me. True, the hardest work was done; my spirit now belonged to him. But my confidence in my own abilities was still unassailable. He knew I would not let go of that confidence until I first placed all my hope in its sufficiency and then saw it fail me utterly.

∝

Though it didn't seem like it at the time, the Master's first year among us possessed an almost leisurely quality compared with the intensity of his remaining days on earth. His fame spread throughout the nation, and the understandable exuberance of some of those who were healed made life for the Master increasingly difficult. The impact of that fellow cured of leprosy was typical.

∝

We were on a short preaching tour in one of the villages near Capernaum when he approached the Master. As always the crowds were packed around Jesus, with everyone try-

77

ing to touch him, to hear him, to squeeze in a little closer to him. My brother and I were right next to the Master, doing our best with crowd control, when a commotion erupted at the back of the crowd. Then suddenly the mass of humanity in front of us parted, like the Red Sea before Moses, with people fleeing in every direction. They were pushing and shoving to get out of the way of whoever or whatever was coming toward us.

Then we heard a man giving the required warning to those who might be in his way: "Unclean! Unclean! Unclean!"

We all knew what it meant—a leper was coming. Few diseases create a deeper sense of fear and revulsion in our society than leprosy. Though not highly contagious, the disease can be contracted through contact with an infected person. There is no cure, of course, and once infected, the leper is compelled to spend the rest of his life in isolation and poverty. Though the disease can eventually cause grotesque and hideous external deformities in the infected person, the greatest pain comes from being compelled to live a life of endless physical and emotional separation from the world.

The man who approached us that day was as pathetic in appearance as any I have ever seen. His condition gave him a free ticket to a private audience with the Master. No one in that crowd would attempt to hinder his approach.

He walked straight up to Jesus and dropped to his knees before him. Andrew and I instinctively stepped back several paces, but Jesus didn't move. The man knew better than to risk touching the Master, but he looked straight up into his eyes. His nose was collapsed, and his lips and earlobes were enlarged and distorted into gruesome deformity.

The man's most distinctive characteristic, however, was not his appearance; it was his remarkable faith in Jesus. As he knelt in the dust before the Teacher, he said simply, "Lord, if you are willing, you can make me clean."

As I stood there staring at the pathetic wretch before us, I was struck with a sudden compulsion to protect the Master from the embarrassment of failure. I wanted to spring forward and say in a quiet, compassionate, yet authoritative voice, "I'm sorry, but we don't do leprosy. I'm sure you understand." The man's request was unreasonable in the extreme. He had been afflicted by this disease for years until his body was now a mass of horrible deformity. To ask the Master to halt the progression of the disease might have been reasonable. To ask for total cleansing with the obvious anticipation of complete restoration was absurd.

But before I could open my mouth, Jesus did what no other human being had done for more years than I even dared guess—he reached out and placed his hand on that leper's face. He was obviously deeply moved by both the faith and the suffering of the man before him. Not only was he not repulsed by the man's condition, Jesus actually seemed to be drawn to it. Then, with his hand still cradling the leper's head, Jesus said simply, "I am willing; be cleansed."

And cleansed he was! In an instant the creature before us was transformed from an ugly mass of deformed flesh into a man in his midforties with strong features and clear eyes that radiated an obvious love for life. For several seconds he just stared at his hands. Then he felt his face, sprang to his feet, wrapped his arms around the Master, and began bouncing around with Jesus, imprisoned in his bear hug. The healed man alternately laughed and cried and bellowed, "Thank you! Thank you! Thank you!"

When Jesus finally got the fellow calmed down a bit, he gave him two specific instructions. "See that you tell no one; but go to the priest, show yourself to him, and present the offering that Moses commanded, for a testimony to them."

The man did fine with the second part of the Master's instructions. The offering, of course, had to be made at the temple in Jerusalem, so the man set off immediately on the several days' journey he had before him.

But he failed miserably with the first part of the instructions. In fact, even before he was out of our earshot, we could hear him proclaiming to every person he met, "Look what Jesus did! Look what Jesus did! I was that leper you always ran away from. Now look at me. I'm whole, I'm cleansed, I'm free. Look what Jesus did!"

We found out all too soon he kept this up with every person he met throughout the entire trip to and from Jerusalem, creating a massive wake of people who were frantic to find the man who could perform such wonders. By the time the cured leper had finished his journey, the crowds seeking an audience with Jesus were so great, we could no longer openly enter the cities.

∞

On the surface it looked as if everything was progressing gloriously. Jesus was the hero of the masses as no one had ever been in the history of our nation. But, if you could have forced me to be honest during those early months of my second year with the Master, I would have told you that I saw him making what I believed were potentially disastrous tactical errors. Popularity was all well and good, but popularity did not bring about political power, and it was political power we needed if Jesus was going to move into the leadership position I had in mind for him. Certainly I didn't want him to compromise his values, but why did he have to intentionally make himself offensive to those who held the power?

The trouble began as the result of an incident that took place in Capernaum shortly after the leper was healed. Motivated in part by the leper's exuberant testimony in the temple, a number of key religious leaders from Jerusalem, Judea, and throughout Galilee came as a delegation, seeking an interview with Jesus. His popularity had increased to the point where he could no longer be ignored by those who held positions of power in Israel. This would be their first official contact with the Master.

The nature of the group and the prominence of those involved necessitated a closed meeting. The house being used by Mary, and by Jesus when he was in town, was the obvious place to have such a meeting. It was well suited for gatherings, with a large, open, central living area ideal for controlled meeting situations. The arrival of so many prominent men heightened the already intense interest of the local population, but only a select few were permitted inside, while the uninvited were forced to stand in the heat of the sun, peering in through the windows and crowding around the door.

I was a nervous wreck that day. I wasn't sure Jesus fully appreciated the importance of this meeting. These were the men who mattered, the men who possessed the power to move Jesus into a key leadership position. Their blessing and approval would do wonders for the movement. I wanted so much for everything to go well. I wanted them to like Jesus. I wanted them to be impressed with him. I wanted them to see his obvious potential for leadership.

I spent the morning trotting from visitor to visitor, finding places for them to sit, making sure everyone was as cool and comfortable as possible. The room was packed, but somehow we were able to get them all in. I kept watching the religious leaders to see how they were responding. I found it hard to read their faces, but as far as I could tell things seemed to be going pretty well. They were clearly interested in what Jesus was saying. If only we could pull this off . . .

Then a sudden commotion on the roof just above Jesus' head disrupted the meeting. The sounds of heavy feet and breaking tiles on the flat roof overhead echoed throughout the room. Bits of dirt, broken tile, and other roofing material

81

showered down onto the group, followed immediately by a sudden, brilliant blast of sunlight that caused us all to squint, making it impossible for us to see clearly what was happening just above our heads.

The commotion continued for another few minutes as the opening grew ever larger. Then, without warning, a stretcher suspended by two ropes dropped directly in front of Jesus. A young man, paralyzed from the waist down, lay on the stretcher, looking up at the Master.

As soon as the stretcher hit the ground, a silence and sense of anticipation more intense than the heat engulfed the crowd. This was what they were really here for. They had heard the rumors and the testimonies. Now they would see firsthand. Jesus would reach down, heal this helpless man with just a touch or a word, and victory would be ours. As I stood there next to the Master, waiting once again for the magic to happen, I wondered why I hadn't thought of staging something like this myself.

But the first words Jesus spoke to the man lying before him were not the words any of us anticipated. They were words I had never heard him speak before, words that sent a sudden shock through me and through every other person in that place. He said, "Take courage, my son; your sins are forgiven."

Nothing could have created a more disastrous impact on the group gathered before him than those eight words. With one sentence Jesus set the movement back by months, if not years. No man had the authority to forgive sins. Only God himself could do that.

A little rumble of guarded comments rolled through the men. No one spoke openly, but the word "blasphemy" could be heard from several sections of the courtyard. Jesus knew what they were thinking, of course. When the rumble finally quieted down, he put it into words. "Why are you thinking evil in your hearts? For which is easier, to say, 'Your sins are forgiven,' or to say, 'Rise and walk'? But in

order that you may know that the Son of Man has authority on earth to forgive sins," he turned to the paralytic, "rise,
take up your bed, and go home."

And the man rose and went home!

The crowd on the roof went crazy, cheering and praising
God for what they'd just seen.

Most of the men of power, however, reacted differently.
It was obvious to all that something supernatural had just
taken place. But it had happened in a way that made them
feel as though they were being publicly reprimanded by this
Galilean nobody. The meeting came to an abrupt conclusion. Jesus stood silent and alone at the front of the crowd,
watching his guests cluster in little groups as they made their
way outside. I did my best to patch things up, thanking each
of them for coming, wishing them all a safe journey home,
but my efforts did nothing to remove the suffocating tension throughout the crowd. The bits of conversation I heard
as the men left made it clear the meeting had been a disaster. They saw Jesus as a blasphemer empowered by Satan.
In their minds he needed to be silenced as soon as possible.

My hope, of course, was that the whole unfortunate incident would fade away in time and that Jesus would be given
another chance to prove himself to our nation's leaders. Not
only did the incident not fade away, the gulf between us
and them widened rapidly. From then on there were always
at least a few spies in the crowds, watching Jesus, challenging his teachings, seeking to discredit and undermine
his authority. They infiltrated every group, every meeting,
always on the alert for anything that might help erode his
popularity.

I had no idea how closely we were being watched until
a confrontation took place in the grain field a few days later.
It was the Sabbath. A group of us were walking with Jesus
along the edge of a grainfield just before the harvest. We
were talking as we walked along. As usual, I was hungry.
Without thinking I broke off a few heads of grain, rubbed

them in my hands to separate the kernels from the chaff, and popped them into my mouth. Andrew saw me chewing and asked me what I was eating. I told him, and he along with several others in the group followed my lead.

Then from out of nowhere an authoritative figure suddenly charged up to Jesus and bellowed, "Look! Your disciples do what is not lawful to do on a Sabbath." I recognized him as one of the Pharisees in attendance at the meeting in Jesus' home a few days earlier.

I felt like a fool. Without thinking I had led the whole group into a violation of the strict restrictions against harvesting on the Sabbath. I didn't really consider what we were doing to be "harvesting," of course, but I hated to be the cause of yet another open conflict between the Master and the Pharisees. I moved to the front of the group and was about to offer a repentant apology for my thoughtlessness when Jesus spoke. "Haven't you read what David and his companions did when they became hungry, how he entered the house of God, and they ate the consecrated bread, which was not lawful for them to eat because it was for the priests alone? Or have you not read in the Law, that on the Sabbath the priests in the temple break the Sabbath and are innocent? But I tell you that something greater than the temple is here. If you had known what this means, 'I desire compassion, and not a sacrifice,' you would not have condemned the innocent. The Sabbath was made for man, and not man for the Sabbath. For the Son of Man is Lord of the Sabbath."

It was a great response that left the accuser speechless and furious. I especially liked the part about the Sabbath being made for man and not man for the Sabbath. The problem, of course, was that rather than healing the rift between Jesus and the Pharisees, it intensified the battle. Within a matter of days he had publicly claimed for himself the authority to forgive sins, equated himself with King David, assumed rights given exclusively to the consecrated temple priests, announced that being in his presence was a greater honor than being in the temple of God, and declared himself to be "Lord of the Sabbath." I loved the things he was saying, but I wondered if he fully appreciated how destructive these kinds of comments were to our plans for his move into national leadership.

The third incident—the one that finally prompted me to take action—took place one week later. Again it was the Sabbath. We were in the synagogue listening to Jesus teach. The place was packed, with a large number of Pharisees scattered throughout the crowd.

In the front row at Jesus' feet sat a man with a withered hand. Jesus saw him. A number of the Pharisees saw him too. As soon as Jesus finished his teaching, one of the Pharisees popped up and asked Jesus a question.

"Is it lawful to heal on the Sabbath?"

The Pharisee's intention was obvious. God himself had called our people to the sacred observance of the Sabbath when his finger etched the Ten Commandments into the stone tablets given to Moses. Our nation's allegiance to the careful observance of the Sabbath was impenetrable. If this Pharisee could get Jesus to openly defy the authority of God himself as revealed through Moses, it would be a powerful blow to the Master's credibility.

The place instantly went silent. We all waited for Jesus' response to the question. He looked first at the Pharisee, then at the rest of us sitting in front of him, and finally at the man with the withered hand. Then he asked the man with the deformity to come forward.

When the man joined him, Jesus rested his hand on the frightened man's shoulder, then asked his own question of the Pharisee. "Is it lawful to do good or to do harm on the Sabbath, to save a life or to kill?"

The Pharisee saw the trap coming and didn't say a word. What could he say? With one remarkable question Jesus had once again placed morality above legalism, the heart's intent above external appearance.

When the Pharisee refused to respond, Jesus turned to the man beside him and said, "Stretch out your hand." As he stretched it out, we watched as the shriveled deformity was suddenly transformed into health and strength.

A silent rage came over the humiliated Pharisee. He and his companions exited immediately. If they could have found some way of turning the crowd against him, they would have attempted to execute Jesus that day for blasphemy. They were wise enough, though, to know the time was not yet right. They would be patient. They would wait and plot and watch for their opportunity.

At that point in my relationship with the Master, however, I was still optimistically hoping for some way to redeem what I saw as simply an unfortunate beginning in Jesus' relationship with Israel's political and religious leadership. Following what appeared to me to be three major public blunders in as many weeks, I finally felt compelled to speak to Jesus. Several days later, after carefully working out what I wanted to say, I found an opportunity to talk with him privately. I tried to impress upon him how crucial the endorsement of our national religious leadership was to the success of our program. I reminded him of the recent incidents that had generated so much tension between himself and the Pharisees. I suggested that if he would use a greater measure of tact and discretion in his future dealings with them, we might yet be able to redeem the situation.

He listened patiently to my little speech until I got to the part about "tact and discretion," at which point he began to chuckle. This was not the response I was hoping for. When I asked him what he found so amusing, he said something about how enjoyable it was to hear me share my insights on tact and discretion and how he wouldn't trade me for anything in the world. He didn't come right out and say it, but I couldn't help but think he didn't consider me to be the most reliable authority on the proper application of tact and discretion in human relationships. I found the whole conversation intensely frustrating, and I remember feeling as though he had failed to grasp the wisdom of what I was attempting to say.

∝

It is strange to look back on those days now, to remember how blind I was to him and to myself. That is the way of the flesh, of course, and I was always, only *flesh* at that time in my life. I saw only through the eyes of the flesh. I understood only the ways of the flesh. Jesus was a great prophet, empowered by God, destined to lead our nation to greatness. Our task was to move him into prominence and then a position of power. I knew Jesus would not use his powers to destroy his enemies, so our path to victory would be found in winning them over. Even now I can feel my face burning with embarrassment when I recall how I wanted to protect my Lord from failure, how I wanted to educate him in the ways of success. Such arrogance! Such blindness! Such pride!

And through it all he loved me, encouraged me, and fed me just as much truth as he knew I was able to swallow. My ignorance didn't bother him; he expected nothing else. My blindness didn't discourage him; he knew that only the Spirit could give me eyes to see. And my flesh-based approach to life didn't defeat him in the least, because he knew the only solution to the flesh was death—both his death, and the death of my confidence in the flesh. But those deaths were still several years away, and there was a great deal to be accomplished by him and in me before either of us was ready for that.

11

Though I could not see it at the time, the beginning of that second year brought with it the initiation of a radical new direction in the Master's strategy. I continued to cling to the hope that he would seek to build bridges of reconciliation with our nation's leadership. He and they, on the other hand, knew all too well that no such bridges could ever be built. They feared him as they had never feared anything or anyone else in their lives. He was truth clothed in power and compassion, and it terrified them. They had worked hard to build their power structure, dancing their intricate dance of corruption and compromise. They knew it was a dance he would not share. There was no place for him in their world. One way or another he would have to be removed.

And so began phase two of the Master's plan. Though he continued his public teaching and healing work among the multitudes in the rural areas, his primary point of focus was quickly redirected to those whom he once referred to affectionately as his "little flock." I think even then each of us knew who we were. Certainly he knew. We were the ones who had given ourselves to him. That doesn't say it well, but I don't know how else to put it. We were the ones who were drawn to him not because of what he said or because of what we got from him but simply because of who he was. We did not understand him, but we knew, too, that we could not live without him.

The Master's new strategy became evident to us all the day he designated the Twelve. I wonder if I can help you understand what that day was like.

It began, as most days did, with a group of us congregating at the house where Jesus was staying early in the morning. He was not there when we arrived, but we had grown accustomed to him slipping out before the sun was up to find a secluded place to talk with his heavenly Father. I found out later that this particular time he had been out all night.

By the time he arrived home, a sizable crowd was waiting for him. Many of the faces in the group were well known to me. Andrew, James, and John were there, of course, as were Philip and Nathanael, who preferred to be called by his family name, Bartholomew. There were a number of recent additions in the crowd as well, like Matthew. Until just a few days earlier he had been the collector of Roman taxes in the region. It seemed strange to see him there, standing off to the side by himself. I had spent most of my adult life hating the man for his shameless sellout to the Roman Empire for the sake of increasing the bulge in his wallet. But I was also standing next to the Master the week before, when Jesus stepped inside Matthew's office, looked into his eyes, and asked Matthew to follow him. I saw first the fear, then the shame, then the amazement and hope that passed over Matthew's face in his encounter with the Master. I had experienced this inner pilgrimage myself and had to admit Matthew might now be one of us.

As Andrew, James, John, Philip, Nathanael, and I stood there in our little group, waiting, watching for the Master's arrival, we had no way of knowing the significance of what was about to take place. The words spoken by the Master this day would alter the course of our lives, our nation, and eventually our world forever.

Jesus' appearance brought the same response it always brought; the crowd surged forward in excitement and anticipation. As always, everyone there brought with them their own private agendas for the Master. Some wanted healing, some had questions they wanted to ask, some came to attack or discredit him, and the rest of us just wanted to be where he was.

This day, however, the healing-teaching-discussion pattern with which we were so familiar did not occur. When Jesus saw the crowd moving toward him, he stopped, motioned for us to follow, and then led the curious procession to a grassy hillside outside of town. He asked us to sit, waited until the commotion quieted down, and then began to speak.

"This day I have chosen twelve men from among you to be with me as my disciples. When I call your name, I would like you to join me here at the front."

I had never seen a group of people become so quiet so quickly as did that crowd who heard Jesus speak those words. None of us knew what was involved in being designated as one of Jesus' disciples. We did know, however, that the designation carried with it an honor unlike anything we had ever known before. It was one thing for *us* to have chosen *him* as our leader—to follow him where he went, to listen to his teachings, to talk and learn and laugh with him each day. It was altogether different for *him* to choose *us*. As I stood there in the silence, waiting for him to speak again, I recalled my foolish antics on that first journey with the Master to the wedding in Cana more than a year ago. I remembered my frantic efforts to impress this man. I remembered thinking what a great addition I would make to his team. I remembered thinking how much he needed someone like me. The memory made me feel foolish. So many things had still not yet changed in my life at that point. But one thing certainly had. I knew Jesus didn't need me; I needed him.

To my credit, Jesus' announcement of his intention to name twelve disciples did not fill me with anxiety. I knew already he would call my name. How could it be otherwise? "You are Simon the son of John; you shall be called Peter." My future, my life, was bound up in this man.

The first six names he called came as no surprise to me. "Simon, Andrew, James, John, Nathanael, and Philip, will you join me up here?" We'd all been with the Master from the beginning. Our commitment to him and his to us was certain. The seventh name he spoke, however, took the crowd by surprise. "I would also like you, Matthew, to join me." No one was more surprised to hear his name than Matthew himself. He was sitting at the very back of the crowd, his eyes fixed not on Jesus but on the ground in front of him. When he heard his name spoken, he looked up, then looked around him, apparently curious to see the man who shared his name—the faithful, obedient, devout Matthew who had just been selected for this great honor. But when no one else stirred, Matthew looked at the Master. To his amazement, Matthew saw that Jesus, and indeed most of the rest of the crowd, was looking at him. For a moment he just sat there, his mouth hanging open in disbelief.

As I watched Matthew stand and then work his way to the front, I wondered at how such different paths could have led us both to this same spot. I had spent much of the past year dancing around in front of the Lord, frantically waving banners and carrying signs declaring, "Peter is your man!" My boastful flesh assured me that Jesus had indeed chosen wisely when he selected me, and he could certainly not do better than to choose others like me. Matthew, on the other hand, came forward in utter disbelief, still unable to accept what was taking place. His fearful flesh, combined with his sense of shame and failure over his union with the hated Roman Empire, made him feel as though Jesus was making a mistake. Even when he finally reached the six of us standing next to Jesus, he stood a few feet away. I looked over at him, saw the amazement and insecurity in his eyes, and in a rare moment of selfless compassion reached out and placed my hand on his shoulder. That was the first time I ever saw him smile. He took a step closer to the group and said, "I can't believe this! I can't believe he chose *me*." Silent tears were streaming down his cheeks.

The next two men named by the Master brought with them a greater history with Jesus than that of all the rest of us put together. They were Jesus' cousins, James, whom we called James the Less because he was a full head shorter than anyone else in the group, and his younger brother, Judas, or Thaddaeus as he preferred to be called to avoid confusion with the other Judas in the group. These two men had grown up with the Master, knowing him more as their older brother than as their cousin. With the exception of his mother, Mary, of course, James and Thaddaeus were the first and only members of Jesus' immediate family to follow him prior to his resurrection from the dead.

They were a great addition to the group. James was the most energetic, impish little fellow I'd ever known. His practical jokes and quick wit kept the rest of us forever on guard.

And his brother, Thaddaeus, brought with him a remarkable spirit of trust and obedient submission to Jesus. He was the youngest in the group, not yet out of his teens, having known the Master his entire life as his oldest and certainly most significant cousin. I don't know when he first began to view Jesus as more than just a good man, but I have often thought they must have shared experiences throughout his childhood that made it easier for him to follow now.

The tenth name Jesus called will affect you differently than it affected those of us who were there that day. "Judas Iscariot, I would also like you to join me."

Perhaps it is impossible for you to hear his name now without feeling a sense of revulsion. You know he is the one who would one day sell out the Master for a handful of coins. In your mind you might even picture the crowd sitting on that grassy hillside, wincing in disgust when his name was called. You could not be further from the truth.

Judas was the one disciple chosen by the Master who seemed "right" to all of us there that day. He was a likable, congenial young man, well known in our community and highly respected. He brought to the group a sharp mind, initiative, and an uncanny business sense. In the weeks ahead, as friends and followers of Jesus contributed money to help meet our needs, Judas was the unanimous choice for group treasurer. He had listened closely to the Master's teachings during the previous several months and brought with him an unshakable confidence in both the right and the ability of Jesus to lead the nation of Israel to greatness. He seemed to possess no reservations about linking his own personal future to the future of this miracle worker from Galilee.

The selection process was completed with Jesus' call for Thomas and Simon the Zealot to join the group.

It is difficult to imagine a more diverse collection of personalities than the ones standing next to Jesus that day. Whereas James the Less was a bouncing, bubbly, enthusiastic explosion of life, Thomas was serious and introspective, almost to the point of being morbid. He was a quiet, logical, brooding thinker who seldom spoke except to point out why some idea was impractical or why some scheme was destined to fail. His loyalty to the Master was undeniable, but his obsession with the negative in every situation made him a difficult comrade for me to relate to.

The Master's mosaic of contrasts was completed with Matthew's opposite in Simon the Zealot. While Matthew spent his former life in cahoots with the Roman enemy, Simon had invested his efforts in a frantic fight to free our nation from all Gentile oppression. Prior to his union with and submission to the Master, his determination to restore the sovereignty of the nation of Israel by any means, at any cost, made him one of the most outspoken and contentious members of our community. We never ceased to enjoy baiting Matthew and Simon into political debates that always ended with Simon being reduced to an irrational, frustrated, screaming rage.

Following the designation of the twelve of us, Jesus had us follow him up the mountain, away from the rest of the crowd. Once we were alone, he sat down with us and talked of his plans for us and for the future. Much of what he said that morning we did not understand until years later. One thing, however, was clear to me even then. From this time on training and equipping us would become his primary focus. For twelve months he offered his messianic credentials to the nation by teaching, touching, healing, discussing, debating, and almost constantly traveling throughout his beloved Israel. Those who held the political power had examined these credentials closely, understood all too well what they meant, and rejected them outright. From this time forward, though the offer of himself as the promised Messiah was never withdrawn, the focus of his work now turned away from the nation as a whole and toward equipping and educating the few who accepted him as their Master. He let us know that though he would continue to permit the masses to follow him and would continue to minister to their needs, from now on his example and his words were primarily for us.

As I look back now on the task our Lord was seeking to accomplish in us, I stand in awe at both what he did and how he did it. The task he sought to accomplish in the three remaining years he spent with us was challenging to say the least. Here we were, a group of mostly uneducated, selfish, stubborn, self-centered, strong-willed men with no idea who he was or what he was seeking to accomplish for the human race. Before his departure he would make certain he had equipped us with all the knowledge and tools we would need to continue the movement that would ultimately impact the entire world.

The Master knew how limited his time with us was. He knew, too, the great areas of ignorance and confusion that clouded our thinking. With his perfect, eternal understanding of all the sacred writings, I find it amazing that he seemed to put such a low priority on communicating specific content to us. Why didn't he sit us down for several hours each morning and instruct us in the Holy Scriptures? Why didn't he design a curriculum that would have led us systematically through the writings of Moses and the prophets and the history and poetry of our people? Why didn't he establish some sort of intense formal education process that would allow him to pass on to us massive quantities of knowledge?

Yet with so little time and so much to be done, all he asked of us was our willingness to build a friendship with him. He simply invited us to stay by his side, to eat with him, to walk with him, to camp out with him, to listen to him, to learn from his example, to build a comradeship with God in human form.

Jesus did not attempt to bring us to a point of competency in knowledge or techniques or programs. He simply sought to draw us into a depth of friendship with himself, a friendship that would ultimately become the driving motivation in every aspect of our lives.

When our little band came down from the mountain, we found the crowd still waiting, the sick still hoping for his healing touch. I never saw his healing powers more intense than they were that day. Hands reached out from every direction seeking to touch the healer. And everyone who touched him went away healed.

When all who had come for healing were cured, the Master led us once again up the hillside. This time, however, everyone was invited to join him. He found a spot that would accommodate all of us and sat down with his twelve immediately in front of him, with the multitude at our backs. Then he taught. Much of what he said that day I had heard him say before. But it was different this time somehow. Though hundreds of us heard his words that day, throughout the entire discourse his eyes were fixed only on us twelve. He talked for more than an hour. He talked about the rewards of discipleship. He talked about the importance of purity. He redefined love and humility in terms that created within me a hunger and a longing to be so much more and so much different than I was. He talked in painfully practical terms about the power money has to consume us, then went on to call us to a practical trust in our heavenly Father's willingness and ability to meet our needs. He talked with us about the destructive powers of lust and a judgmental spirit. He talked about the rich rewards that accompany purity and generosity. In simple, understandable words he revealed to us how life was designed to operate.

When he finally stopped talking, no one moved, no one spoke, no one took their eyes off the Master. Each of us felt as though this man had just opened up our hearts and revealed to all the world what was there. Yet, he had done it in a way that rather than flooding us with shame filled us with a hunger and thirst for righteousness unlike anything we had ever known before.

The only way I could bear the thought of that day coming to an end was by reminding myself that when I awoke in the morning, I would still be his disciple, and he would still be my Master. And, to be honest, it was this realization that sustained me every day for the next several years. It was all so good, so incredibly good, because he was . . . well, simply because he was, and that was all that mattered.

12

If the events of the months that followed are to make any sense to you, two things must be clear in your mind. First, you must understand what we the followers of Jesus were trying to accomplish. Second, you must understand what Jesus needed to accomplish within us.

For our part, the situation seemed clear. After more than four hundred years, a true prophet of God once again walked among his people. He was a prophet confirmed by God through miraculous healing powers. He was a prophet gifted with insights and teaching skills unlike anything any of us had ever seen. As with the prophets of old, this Prophet Jesus now gathered disciples to himself. Our role was to listen carefully to his message, learn it well, and apply it to our lives. We would then help him carry his message throughout the land. In time, no doubt, Jesus would follow the prophetic pattern and commit his message to written form so that it would become a part of our nation's heritage forever. Despite all this, however, it was understood that Jesus was just a man. He was a remarkable man. He was an amazing man. He was a man powerfully gifted by God. But, still, he was just a man. His absolute, total humanity was an unquestioned certainty of our relationship with him. We knew the woman who had given birth to him. We lived with him twenty-four hours a day. We saw him eat. We knew the scent of his sweat. We watched him, overcome with exhaustion, close his eyes and sleep.

Jesus, however, had a different agenda. He knew his ultimate destination was the cross. He knew, too, his remaining time on earth was measured better in months than years. And he knew that between the beginning of his public ministry and his departure, he would have to bring us from our comfortable, reasonable, logical belief in him as a mighty prophet of God to the discovery of his true identity. It would be nearly two years before he would ask us who we believed he was. During these two years he would make certain we had the knowledge we needed to answer that question.

As I write these words, I know my time is short. It would be impossible for me to attempt to walk with you through a detailed account of the months that followed. I do, however, want to share with you some of the turning points in my understanding of who this man was. Doctrine in its purest form is nothing other than our honest response to what God has chosen to reveal to us about himself. Following his designation of the Twelve and knowing he had our undivided attention, Jesus began to reveal himself to us in ways that kept us in a nearly constant state of thinking and rethinking and rethinking again our beliefs and assumptions about this man from Galilee. This mental stretching process began the following day.

～

We spent a night together at the house where Jesus was staying in Capernaum. It had been a wonderful day. It had also been a long day, an exhausting day. Following our evening meal together, we each found a corner in which to sleep. Sleeping has always been one of the things I do best. I closed my eyes and remembered nothing else until I woke to the early morning sun streaming in the window and the sound of Jesus seekers milling around outside the door.

There were always Jesus seekers outside the door, waiting for him to get up, waiting for him to come out, waiting for him to come back. This morning, however, there were several prominent faces in the crowd, leaders in our community, who brought with them an urgent request for the Master.

Rome maintains its iron grip over its conquered nations with the strategic placement of military garrisons throughout the empire. Though this hostile presence within our nation is a perpetual topic of complaint among our people, those of us in Capernaum knew we were more fortunate than many other Jewish communities. The Roman centurion in charge of the military post in our hometown was well known for his compassionate use of power and his genuine concern for the Jewish people under his control. He had been in our community for many years. He learned our customs and listened honestly to our concerns. Indeed, he personally financed the construction of our synagogue.

The Jewish leaders at the door came on behalf of this Roman military leader. He was well acquainted with Jesus' reputation in the community. Several times I had seen him standing at the stern of a crowd as Jesus taught.

This morning, however, the centurion did not come in person. He sent Jewish elders to ask the Master for help. A slave boy in his house lay in terrible agony, dying. Would Jesus be willing to help the boy?

Jesus set out immediately with the rest of us at his heels. There was something about this request that touched Jesus deeply. I think perhaps it was the obvious compassion of this Roman soldier. The boy was not his son. He was a slave. Yet the centurion cared deeply for the child. Jesus understood that kind of compassion perfectly. It was evident in his own eyes every time he touched the suffering in the lives of those around him.

The centurion watched for Jesus' arrival, and when he saw the Master coming, he quickly sent several close friends to meet Jesus in the street, bringing the message "Lord, don't trouble yourself further, for I'm not worthy for you to come under my roof; for this reason I didn't even consider myself worthy to come to you, but just say the word, and my servant will be healed. For I also am a man placed under authority, with soldiers under me; and I say to this one, 'Go!' and he goes, and to another, 'Come!' and he comes, and to my slave, 'Do this!' and he does it."

For a moment Jesus did not speak, but the expression on his face showed his obvious pleasure at the words he heard. Then he turned to those of us who were following him and said, "Not even in Israel have I found faith so great as this."

When the centurion's friends reentered the house, they found the slave boy standing next to his master, his little arms wrapped tightly around the man, tears streaming down his cheeks.

It is difficult for me to explain why that particular healing affected me so much more deeply than did most of the others. I found it altogether unsettling. My Jesus was breaking out of the boundaries I had carefully established for him. He was *our* prophet. He belonged to the nation of Israel. He was *our* hope, *our* future. He would deliver us from our oppression and reestablish us to the glory that was due the chosen people of God. Yet here he was trotting after the request of a Roman soldier, healing a Gentile child. Gentiles had *no* right to his kindness. They should have had *no* access to his power.

And then there were those words of praise for the centurion's faith. I was jealous. Why couldn't I believe like that? Why couldn't it have been me the Master held up before the world as a glowing example of faith-filled obedience?

And there was something else as well, something planted in the back of my mind as a result of the way in which that boy was healed. Prior to that event I saw Jesus as someone who possessed the ability to heal. I didn't know how he did it; I just knew he did. I saw it as a gift he possessed, given to him by God. In my thinking it was not unlike some of my own God-given talents and abilities. Obviously his abilities vastly exceeded mine, but still they were not fundamentally different in kind. They were abilities given to a man in order to equip him for the work God had for him.

But those words spoken to Jesus by the centurion bothered me. "For I also am a man placed under authority, with soldiers under me; and I say to this one, 'Go!' and he goes, and to another, 'Come!' and he comes, and to my slave, 'Do this!' and he does it."

He was suggesting that Jesus healed not because he had the ability to heal but rather because he had the *authority* to heal. But what man could claim authority over sickness and disease? Such authority did not belong to man. It belonged to God alone. It made no sense to me. And what we would witness the following day only intensified my confusion.

✂

Jesus left Capernaum immediately following his healing of the centurion's slave boy. The crowds now surrounding him everywhere he went made it necessary for him to spend most of his time either in the open fields away from the city or, more often, traveling to other communities throughout the region. Not that traveling helped a great deal. As Jesus walked away from Capernaum, several hundred people followed behind him.

We spent the rest of the day on the road, heading to the city of Nain near the southern tip of Galilee, about a ten-hour walk from Capernaum. We stopped a few hours short of the city and camped for the night, then completed our journey the next morning. Though we seldom knew in advance why Jesus was doing what he was doing, we grew accustomed to the knowledge that there was always a purpose behind his choices. This was his first visit to Nain, so we assumed this trip was simply part of his broadening exposure of himself to the nation. It was certainly that, but we soon discovered it was an exposure unlike anything any of us had ever seen before.

∽

We reached the city about midmorning. We must have looked strange to anyone watching our arrival—hundreds of people following in a huge procession behind a single man. As we approached the city gates, our procession was confronted by another procession coming out of Nain. This procession, however, was led by four men carrying an open coffin containing the dead form of a boy in his early teens. Alongside the coffin walked a woman in her mid-thirties, a woman consumed with grief. The agony in her sobs left no doubt about her relationship to the still form beside her.

Though Jesus was unknown by sight to the people of Nain, he was well known by reputation. When our two groups met, they merged into a solid mass surrounding the Master, the mother, and the undersized coffin. I could hear little ripples of "It's the prophet" and "It's Jesus" running through the crowd.

The Master's first words were directed to the mother. The intensity of her sorrow blinded her to what was happening around her. She didn't know and didn't care where all these strangers came from. She knew only that they were blocking the path to the open hole in the earth waiting for the body of her only son.

Jesus stepped directly in front of the mother, placed his hands on her shoulders, waited until she looked up into his face, and then said, "Do not weep."

He might as well have spoken to her in a foreign language. Indeed, his words must have sounded like utter nonsense to her. We would find out later her husband was dead. Now her only son was dead. Unending grief was all that remained. Out of respect for the prophet standing before her, she became silent, but it was a silence without peace, without hope.

Jesus then turned to the men carrying the coffin and instructed them to lower it to the ground. He walked around the still form until he was able to look directly down into the young man's face. Then he spoke again. "Young man, I say to you, arise!"

And immediately the boy sat up.

For several seconds no one spoke, no one moved. I don't think anyone even breathed. Then suddenly the boy broke into a huge grin, looked over at his mother, and blurted out, "Hey, Mom! I'm hungry! Hey! What am I doing in this thing?"

He jumped out of the coffin and gave his mother a big hug, and the crowd went crazy. They were clapping and cheering and yelling and screaming. Everyone talked at once, telling everyone else what Jesus just did.

The two processions became one as Jesus, the mother, and her son led the way back into the city. It would have been impossible for Jesus to design a more dramatic introduction of himself to the community. The city embraced him with a spirit of celebration beyond anything we had ever seen. By the time he departed from the community several days later, reports of his visit were spreading rapidly throughout the entire region.

I should have been thrilled, of course. My identification with the Master gave me a position of prominence unlike anything I had ever known before. Some of his glory spilled over onto me and the other disciples simply because we happened to be standing next to him. Outwardly I shared in the celebration, but secretly I found myself troubled by what I had just seen. Once again Jesus was forcing me to expand my concept of himself. To heal, to preserve life, to give health to the living was one thing. But to give life to the dead . . . that was something altogether different.

What did it mean? Could he, then, restore anyone to life? If so, why didn't he? If not, why couldn't he? Could he prevent his own death? Could he prevent mine? Was he immortal? And, most of all, what manner of man was this who could speak to the dead and summon them back to the land of the living?

∝

Then came the night of that storm.

It was weeks later, long enough for me to have successfully forced my troublesome questions about this man into the back of my mind. We were traveling a good deal during that time. As he had promised, his teaching was increasingly focused not on the masses but rather on us, his disciples.

It had been an intense day of teaching, a day in which we'd all been stretched to new limits in our thinking. It was the first day in which he taught exclusively in parables. The crowds loved listening to his fascinating little stories: "The kingdom of heaven is like a man sowing seed. . . ." "The kingdom of heaven is like a mustard seed. . . ." "The kingdom of heaven is like leaven. . . ." "The kingdom of heaven is like a treasure. . . ." "The kingdom of heaven is like a merchant. . . ." "The kingdom of heaven is like a dragnet. . . ."

They didn't understand what he was talking about, and at first neither did we. Still, they loved to listen to him.

Throughout the day he kept pulling away from the multitudes so that he could talk with us about the hidden meanings in each of his stories. He wanted us to understand. He wanted us to learn. With each new story we gained a new principle, a new insight into his kingdom. It was wonderful knowledge, but it was hard work too. When evening came, we were all exhausted, but the crowds kept pushing closer, demanding more.

Jesus was once again using our fishing boat as his teaching platform. He sat at the stern facing the shore with the Twelve of us at his back in the front of the boat. Late that afternoon he finally stopped teaching and turned away from the masses, talking privately with us about the parables. But it was obvious the people onshore had no intention of leaving him alone. *He* might have been finished for the day, but *they* certainly were not. With no other way of escape, Jesus told us to push off and set sail for the other side of the Sea of Galilee. We could not have been more than a few hundred feet from shore before Jesus stretched out at the back of the boat and fell into a deep sleep.

I have seen countless storms descend upon the Sea of Galilee in my lifetime but none like the one we encountered that night. We were perhaps halfway across the lake when the fury hit. Though it was still early evening, the sky came over as black as I have ever seen it. Then came the wind. Within a matter of minutes the gentle breeze we were trusting to power us to our destination turned first into vicious gusts and then into a ceaseless raging blast unlike anything any of us had ever known before. We dropped our sail as soon as the gusting began, but within minutes our

106

bare mast was no protection against the savage caldron in which we found ourselves. Massive mountains of water stood high above our little boat on either side, then suddenly plummeted down, thrusting us skyward. We rose and fell on the mammoth swells, blasted by the wind each time we reached another peak.

The gale intensified still more as the swells turned into immense foaming breakers crashing down on top of us. The crushing waves and howling wind made communication almost impossible. I kept screaming instructions to the others in the boat, but we all knew that no amount of skillful maneuvering would protect us from the tumult surrounding us.

For what seemed like hours we fought the storm. Our only hope was reduced to a frantic effort to bail out the water that kept crashing over the sides of our little craft.

It was not until I dropped to my knees, bucket in hand, scooping and dumping as fast as I was able, that I saw him there at the back of the boat, sound asleep. He was soaked from the spray and the waves sloshing around him, yet he slept. For just a moment I stopped, frozen in disbelief. How could he just lie there, unaware that in a matter of minutes our boat would break apart and we would all be dead?

The sight of him sleeping made me furious. I flung my bucket across the boat and worked my way to him. Then I grabbed his shoulders, shook him with all my might, and screamed, "Master! Don't you care that we are perishing?"

Jesus opened his eyes, looked at me and then at the world in chaos around him. By then the others were all grouped at my back, clinging to the boat, staring at Jesus.

Then he spoke, first to us, then to the wind and waves. To us he said, "Why are you so afraid, you of little faith?"

To the wind and waves he said, "Peace! Be still."

I know there is no way I can explain to you what it was like. In your mind, perhaps you picture the wind gradually subsiding, the fury of the waves slowly diminishing until eventually there was only a gentle lapping against the side of the boat.

If you see it that way in your mind, then you are wrong. The moment Jesus finished uttering the word "still," everything was. And I do mean everything. The sea immediately flattened out into a dead calm, the wind instantly ceased. There was no gentle lapping of waves against the boat. There was no gentle breeze blowing on our faces. There was nothing. Jesus spoke. The winds and the waves obeyed—not gradually, not partially, but totally, instantly, absolutely. And the silence that suddenly surrounded us was even more terrifying than the storm.

No one in that boat even remotely thought that perhaps I just happened to wake Jesus at the moment the storm began to subside. The storm did not begin to subside. The storm simply ceased at his command.

For a moment we all stood there in silence, him looking at us, us looking at him. Then he spoke again. "Why are you so timid? How is it that you have no faith?"

We had no answer, of course. And we knew none was expected. But it was not my lack of faith that troubled me that night. It was the unanswered question we kept asking one another but never dared to ask him. What manner of man commands the wind and the sea and they obey him? What manner of man takes upon himself the authority to forgive sins? What manner of man tells the dead to rise and they obey?

You may wonder why Jesus did not simply tell us in words who he was and what he was doing. Well, in the days and weeks just prior to his death, he did. Even then, though, we could not hear it. We could not hear what he was saying because we did not want to hear it. Acceptance or rejection of Jesus as God in human form has never been a matter of the evidence. Even at this point in our relationship with him, we had more than enough evidence. No mere man has absolute and instant authority over nature, commands the winds to cease, tells the sea to be still, and calls thousands of fish to cram themselves into a net. No man has the authority to forgive another human being's sins against God. No man has authority over all sickness, all disease. No man can, by his own act of will, bring the dead back to life. And, of course, it wasn't just what he did, it was the way in which he did it. He did not pray that God would heal. He did not pray that God would forgive. He did not pray that God would still the storm. He simply did it himself.

I think that's what scared me so much that night on the Sea of Galilee. If Jesus had stood up, raised his hands to God, and prayed, "Oh, great heavenly Father, deliver us from this storm!" and his prayer had been followed by that remarkable instant calm, I could have understood that. I could have accepted a prophet whose every prayer is instantly answered. But Jesus called upon no one. He didn't ask for help—he *was* the help. He sought no authority outside himself because he needed no authority but himself.

Nothing has changed, you know. In the end our ability to see Jesus correctly is never a matter of gaining sufficient evidence. The evidence is overwhelming. He has told us who he is with every action, with every miracle, with every word he spoke. But the only voice that has the power to confirm that identity must come ultimately from within ourselves. And that voice will speak only if we are willing to hear it, only when we are ready to listen. There are implications, you see, implications that can strike terror in our hearts, implications that will cause us to stop our ears, to blind our eyes, to put rigid limitations on what we will and will not accept.

At that point in our pilgrimage Jesus did not tell us who he was because he knew we were not yet ready to hear it, and saying too much would only drive us further away from him in confusion and fear. For now he would let his actions do the speaking.

We were not the only ones confused about what we were seeing. Even the Prophet John had questions. When he sent his disciples to Jesus, asking, "Are you the expected one, or do we look for someone else?" Jesus' answer emphasized not his words but his actions. "Go and report to John what you have seen and heard: the blind receive sight, the lame walk, the lepers are cleansed, and the deaf hear, the dead are raised up, the poor have the gospel preached to them. Blessed is he who does not take offense at me."

It was a terrible time for me. Though I could never have admitted it then, I wanted my Jesus to remain small. I wanted him to be just a prophet. I wanted him to stay within the boundaries I understood. I didn't know what to do with a Jesus who kept growing, a Jesus who kept expanding before my eyes. And my confusion would get far worse before it got better.

13

It's no wonder I was having trouble finding the right answers. For nearly two years I'd been asking all the wrong questions. How can I get this man to stop interfering with my brother and my career? How can I impress this man? How can I use his powers for my own profit? How can I get away from him? How can I continue to cling to my career goals and still follow him? How can I invest my talents and abilities into making him a success?

As we gently bobbed in the stillness of the silent sea, I finally asked myself the one question that really mattered. Who is this man, anyway? He's not just a prophet. He's far more than just a great teacher. He's certainly not a political leader. But then who is he? The first answer to that question came in a matter of hours from a most unlikely source.

⌒×

We spent the rest of the night in the boat on the Sea of Galilee. We were all exhausted, still several miles from shore, with no wind to propel us. I curled up in a corner of the deck and slept. When a gentle breeze returned with the sunrise, we set our sail and completed our journey to the eastern shore of the Sea of Galilee.

Following the Master's instructions, we put to shore a short distance from the Gentile fishing village of Gergesa. I think everyone on board wondered what we were doing in this Gentile region, but no one dared ask. It was a rugged, mountainous stretch of coastline, known to me only from the deck of our fishing boat.

We were still in the process of securing our boat on the beach when we heard the most hideous screaming coming from a cemetery on the hillside behind us. I turned around in time to see a man running among the graves. His long beard and hair were caked with filth and matted from neglect. He was completely naked. As soon as he saw us, he squatted down, scooped up a jagged chunk of rock, and sprang into a crazed run in our direction.

The sight and sound of that man screaming down the hillside catapulted me back into the fishing boat to find something with which to protect myself. I grabbed an oar and whirled around, ready for the attack.

But the attack never came.

Jesus stood silent on the beach, watching the creature racing toward him. He didn't turn away; he didn't run. He simply waited and watched. Then, when the attacker was close enough to hear the Master's words, Jesus spoke: "Come out of the man, you unclean spirit!"

The naked figure dropped to his knees and screamed out, "What business do we have with each other, Jesus, Son of the Most High God? I implore you by God, do not torment me!"

He spat out the words as a man would spit out a mouthful of filth. I'd never heard such terror, such rage in a human voice before. Following his short blast, he remained on his knees before the Master, looking more as if he had been forced into the position against his will than as if he had chosen it because of genuine submission.

I glanced around and discovered I was not the only one who felt more comfortable greeting our guest from the deck of the boat. Eleven other men, several of them also clutching makeshift weapons, huddled around me as we watched the scene in the sand below us.

Though no one moved for several seconds, there was clearly some sort of intense warfare taking place between Jesus and the figure kneeling in the sand at his feet. The next words Jesus spoke were certainly not what I was expecting.

He reached down, lifted the man's face, and said, "What is your name?"

The man responded, "My name is Legion; for we are many." His lips curled in a twisted smile as he spoke, and his tone communicated an arrogant defiance that sent a chill through my whole body.

Then their eyes met, and the naked creature once again dropped his face to the sand.

"Please! Please! We beg of you, don't send us into the abyss. You know it is not yet our time. Don't send us away from this land. Over there! That herd of swine. Send us into them. We beg you! You know our time has not yet come."

When he mentioned the swine, we all looked where he pointed and saw on the hillside several hundred pigs grazing in the morning sun.

For several seconds following the creature's pathetic pleading, no one moved, no one spoke.

Then Jesus broke the silence. "Go! Leave this man forever. You have my permission to enter the swine."

The man let out one last terrified scream, opened his mouth wide, and dug his long nails deep into his naked chest. Then he collapsed into a wretched heap. At the same instant we heard the sound of hundreds of pigs squealing as if they were being slaughtered. Then we watched as the entire herd thundered down the steep hillside, still squealing in terror, and straight into the water not fifty feet away from us. When the last squeal was silenced, we all just stood there frozen. The herdsmen silhouetted on the hillside looked down on the scene in terror, then headed into town as fast as they could run.

That moment of my life is forever etched into my memory—twelve men armed for battle, standing frozen on the deck of a beached fishing boat, a sea of lifeless swine behind them, with one man standing on the beach, and another huddled in a naked heap before him.

Slowly the crouching figure raised his head and said, "My Lord, please forgive my nakedness."

Jesus turned and said, "Andrew! See if we can find soap and some clothing for our friend. And perhaps we can provide him with a brush and razor as well." The man was big, nearly my size, so I told Andrew to bring the extra change of clothes I always kept on board.

We spent the next hour assisting him in his transformation. He spent more than half an hour in the water, laughing, talking, scrubbing, and thanking Jesus over and over again. Once he was dressed, we cut his hair and trimmed his beard. Then we invited him to join us for our noonday meal.

Our celebration feast was cut short, however, by the sudden appearance of a large delegation of local residents marching toward us along the beach. As soon as our guest saw them coming, he sprang to his feet, waving excitedly. He greeted a number of the newcomers by name and kept saying, "Look at me! Look at me! Look at what this man did!"

They looked all right, but they didn't look at him. They looked first at the now empty hillside, then at their motionless herd littering the shoreline, and finally at the Master. The apparent leader of the group spoke. "Please, sir, go away. Leave us alone. We don't know how or why you destroyed our herd. We only know you did. Now please just go away before you do any more damage."

Jesus offered them no explanation, no excuse. He certainly was not afraid of them, but neither would he force himself upon them. We gathered our things together in silence and were preparing to push off when our new friend grabbed Jesus and pleaded with him for permission to join us.

Jesus smiled at him, shook his head, and said, "No, my friend, I need you here. I want you to go home to your people and report to them what great things the Lord has done for you, and how he had mercy on you."

As we set sail for home, the man stood on the beach waving and watching us until we were finally out of sight.

It all happened so fast, I had no time to think about the events of that morning until we were once again on the open sea. Then those words spoken by the demons came back to me. "What business do we have with each other, Jesus, Son of the Most High God? I implore you by God, do not torment me!"

Jesus, Son of the Most High God! What did it mean? The demons inside that poor man seemed to know all about Jesus. They knew him, and they feared him. They hated him, argued with him, bargained with him, yet they knew they could not act without his permission. The terror with which they pleaded with Jesus not to send them into the abyss caused me to cringe once again as I recalled it. Twelve hours earlier I had seen Jesus exercise absolute authority over the physical world. Now I saw him accepting without dispute the title "Son of the Most High God," positioning himself as supreme ruler over the spirit world. He conversed with demons. He held their fate in his hands. He had the power to torment them, to act as their judge and executioner. And his jurisdiction was not limited to the nation of Israel. Even in the Gentile world, he reached out with the same healing, redemptive compassion he showed for the sons of Abraham.

There I was, in the center of a great drama being played out before my eyes. It was a drama with a cast of one and a script written from the foundation of the world. For reasons I have never fully understood, the Director of All Things honored me with the privilege of watching this drama unfold from center stage. I saw what was happening. I heard the words. I even held some of the props. But everything was backwards. The drama was the true reality, and I was the one playing a part. I was such a child, pretending the lines he spoke made sense to me, pretending I understood the flow and purpose of the plot as it unfolded. Of course Jesus was the Son of the Most High God. Of course he had authority over the Gentile world. Of course he had the right to send demons to the abyss. I even pretended I had a part in the drama. But he and I both knew differently.

The time would come when I would have a part. The time would come when I would understand. But not now. Now my only obligation was to watch, and to listen, and to seek to understand what manner of man this was.

14

To say that Jesus continued to provide us with evidence of his true identity in the months that followed is a little like saying the ocean contains some water or the sun gives off some light. Every relationship he entered, every attack he encountered, every question he confronted, every word he spoke only served to reaffirm his absolute authority over the world of man. He didn't *have* authority; he *was* authority. He defied all boundaries. He shattered all my preconceptions about the nature of true devotion to God. Prior to his appearance, the calling of the devout Jew was clear: learn the system and keep it faithfully. But such thinking just didn't work with Jesus. He knew no system. He lived on the basis of his own inner authority, an authority that enabled him to weave in and out of established religious customs, abiding by some while shattering others to pieces. In a subtle yet powerful way, he moved me ever closer to the realization that faithfulness to God and faithfulness to him were one and the same thing.

So many misconceptions had to be reworked within me. Jesus knew them all, and he knew, too, how to bring them out into the open so that I could see them in the light of himself. My misconception about his supernatural power was a prime example. In our early days together, when I still viewed him as just a great prophet of God, I assumed God was simply giving him the power to perform certain miraculous acts as part of his prophetic ministry. But with each new demonstration of power, I was forced to expand my understanding of the authority God was giving this man until I wrestled with the realization that somehow God had apparently given him dominion over everything.

But it was that incident in the street, when the woman touched Jesus without him knowing it, that forced me to see the flaw in my reasoning. Jesus was in Capernaum, teaching once again by the Sea of Galilee, when a man suddenly blasted through the packed bodies. He pushed, climbed, and clawed around and over anyone blocking his way until he reached the Master. It was Jairus, one of the officials of our synagogue. In a few short sentences, he told Jesus his daughter was near death and pleaded with him to help.

Jesus immediately set off with the man, as did the entire multitude around us. We disciples did our best to stay near him, but the mass of humanity packed around us made it almost impossible even to walk. Everyone wanted to be sure they didn't miss whatever it was the Master was about to do. As we reached the streets of the city, the throng surrounding us literally packed the roadway full of pushing, squirming, sweating human beings.

Then it happened. In the midst of this absolute chaos, with people squeezed up against one another so close it was difficult even to breathe, Jesus suddenly stopped and asked, "Who touched me?"

I heard the words, but they made no sense to me. It sounded as if Jesus was complaining. But Jesus didn't complain. It sounded as if Jesus was irritated. But that couldn't be. Jesus didn't get irritated. He didn't get grumpy. Sometimes he got tired. Sometimes he got angry. But he never got crabby or grouchy or sullen or cross. In fact, the human emotions that flow out of those situations in which we feel as though our rights have been invaded were simply not present within him. And yet now, in the center of this churning crush of human flesh, he suddenly seemed to be concerned because somebody had touched him.

For a moment we all just stood there, not knowing what to do or say. Jesus apparently was not moving another step until he got an answer to his question. But there were a dozen answers. I had just touched him. Andrew and James on his right had just touched him. Lots of people had just touched him.

It was an embarrassing situation. Everyone started denying that they'd touched him, even though lots of us were guilty of the offense. We all shoved our way back a step or two to be sure Jesus had plenty of room, but still the Master stood and waited for an answer to his question. I finally tried to smooth things over a bit by pointing out the obvious. "Master, you can see the multitudes crowding and pressing in on you, and you ask, 'Who touched me?'" I tried to make it sound like a joke, but it didn't work very well.

Then the Master spoke again. "Someone did touch me, because I knew that power had gone out of me."

For just a moment no one spoke. Then a woman standing directly behind me pushed her way into the little clearing in front of Jesus, dropped to her knees in front of him, and said, "I'm the one . . . I'm the person who touched you."

It was as if there was some sort of private conversation taking place between Jesus and this unknown woman. They alone seemed to understand the words while the rest of us just stood there ignorant and confused.

Then the woman explained. For more than twelve years she had suffered from what she described as "a flow of blood." She did not go into further detail, but I have always assumed it must have concerned a severe problem with her menstrual cycle. She was too embarrassed to approach the Master publicly and ask for his help with such a problem, but after watching Jesus heal so many others in the city, she knew he had the power to heal her as well. If she could get close enough to him to touch the fringe of his clothing, she just knew she would be healed. And the instant she touched him, her hope became a reality.

He reached down to the terrified creature before him, took her hand, and brought her to her feet. He smiled at her and said, "Your faith has made you well; go in peace."

Less than an hour later I stood next to the Master and watched as he restored Jairus's dead child to life. But that restoration, as dramatic and awesome as it was, did not affect me as deeply as Jesus' brief conversation with that terrified woman in the street.

Prior to that woman's healing I saw Jesus' power as being something he possessed. It was remarkable power. It was apparently limitless power. But it was simply something he had been given by God for his prophetic ministry. It was a tool he could choose to use or not to use, under the control of his will, requiring the active involvement of his mind.

But following the incident with that woman, I was forced to take a giant step forward in my understanding of this man. Power wasn't something Jesus had, it was something he *was*. This woman wasn't healed because Jesus chose to give her health; she was healed because Jesus was the source of all health. And because she believed he was the source of all health, she knew she could simply touch him, even without him knowing it, and be healed. She was made well not because Jesus possessed the power to heal but because he himself *was* health and power—they were woven into the very fiber of his being.

During his few years here on earth, Jesus chose to accept the limitations that come with a spirit's existence within a human body. His mind, like our minds, could focus on only one thing at a time. Because his mind was focused on following Jairus to his home, it could not at the same time be focused on the woman who touched his clothing. But the limitations of his physical mind did not in any way alter or impair the true identity of his spirit.

Step by tiny step Jesus was leading me ever closer to the one truth upon which all other truths must be built—this man, this person with whom I lived each day, was our Creator God in a human body.

15

Demonic spirits cowered in submission to his will. Storms ceased at his command. Dead bodies returned to life at his word. People touched his clothing and went away healed. Then came the day when he shared his power with the Twelve of us. It had been nearly two years since he first entered our world, nearly a year since he called twelve men to himself. Though the division between Jesus and our nation's leadership seemed to be widening, his popularity with the Jewish people was, understandably, at an all-time high. The only limitation he ever seemed obligated to submit to was the limitation imposed on him by time. Each of his days, like each of ours, had just twenty-four hours. The sun moved from east to west as quickly over his head as it did over ours. There were only so many people he could touch each day, only so many minutes he could talk, only so many questions he could answer, only so many times he could express his love to individuals within the endless sea of humanity surrounding him.

His decision to extend his impact on the nation through equipping us and sending us out in his name was certainly motivated in part by the time limitations he faced. We were all with him that morning, just a few days before he sent us out, when we woke once again from a few hours' sleep to find another crowd of desperate people packed around our door. As Jesus looked out the window, he said, "The harvest is great, but there are so few workers." Then he encouraged us to pray that the Lord of the harvest would send out more laborers into his fields. So many people, so little time. The overwhelming need in the lives of those around him was certainly part of the reason he sent us out.

But there was another reason as well, one I would not fully appreciate until the day of Pentecost following his resurrection. The Master was going to permit each of us to serve as channels through which his Holy Spirit could perform miraculous works. But he wanted us to know through experience the difference between this sovereign work of God, unrelated to any true change of heart within us, and the glorious infilling of the Holy Spirit that would come to every believer following his death and resurrection.

We knew something unique was about to happen the day he sent us out, but none of us were prepared for what it was. That day, rather than returning to the crowds waiting for his appearance, he took the Twelve of us away by ourselves. I loved those times when he did that. It always meant there was something special he wanted us to learn or do. Those times always involved a bit of a battle between Jesus and the people waiting for his appearance. Everyone had something they wanted, some urgent need they hoped the Master would meet. His telling them there would be no public meetings today was never well received.

We followed him out of town, down to the beach, then along the Sea of Galilee, until we found a place where we could meet in privacy. When we were all seated on the sand around him, he shared with us what he was about to do. He told us that this day he was going to equip each of us with the power and the authority to perform many of the miraculous works he was performing throughout Israel. He was giving us authority over unclean spirits to cast them out and the authority to heal all kinds of sickness and infirmity.

To say his words sent a shock through us doesn't begin to describe what we felt. For the past two years Jesus had formed the center of our world. He was the sun. He was the light. He was the power. He was the only one in the history of the world who possessed such gifts, such authority. These were not skills a person could learn. These were not techniques people could take and apply to similar situations in their own lives. King David couldn't do what this man did. Elijah never did once what Jesus did daily. The Prophet John, with all of his authority, all of his insight, and all of his faithfulness to God could not perform such works.

We all knew the great honor bestowed upon us when Jesus chose us for his disciples. It gave us the privilege of being with him, of learning from him, of growing under his personal supervision. But none of us held any illusions that we would one day be like him. I want very much for you to understand me here. There have been times in human history when God sovereignly selected a man to play a crucial role in his plan. Elijah was such a man. Samuel was such a man. Moses was such a man. The Prophet John was such a man, filled with the Spirit of God before he was born. But I was not such a man, nor was my brother, Andrew, nor my friends James and John. We were just ordinary people who somehow ended up standing next to the most extraordinary man who ever lived.

And yet now here we were, listening to Jesus tell us he was about to equip us to do the things he could do. Crowd control I understood. Following Jesus I understood. Listening and learning and living with him I understood. But working miracles I did not.

The Lord spent the rest of the morning instructing us on the proper use of the authority he was giving us. We were to go only to those he called "the lost sheep of the house of Israel." We were not to go to the Gentiles or even to the Samaritans. We would go out in teams of two, and our basic message was to be the proclamation that the kingdom of heaven is at hand. Jesus strongly impressed upon us that we were not to sell our healing powers. We could accept meals and housing from those who offered but nothing else in return for our ministry. We were to take no supplies with us but rather to trust God to meet our needs along the way. When we encountered people who resisted our message, we simply were to move on to the next village, shaking the dust from our feet as we left.

Jesus talked with us once again about God's deep love for us. He wanted us to know we did not go out *for* God; we went out *with* him. He told us God had numbered even the hairs of our heads, and we could trust his protection and his leadership as we went. I loved it when he said things like that. The idea of God numbering the hairs on our heads got us all laughing, especially because it was obvious God would have a much easier time with some of us than others.

As he talked with us that morning, I realized I didn't know this God the Master was talking about—not really. My God was a rather unpleasant being who demanded what I could not deliver and controlled through fear of judgment. He was a God created for me by the religious leaders in our nation, a God who kept track of every fish I caught and kept a record of every fish I tithed to make certain I was giving the required amount.

But a God who cared about me so much he numbered the hairs on my head was new to me. As the Master talked, I found myself longing for it to be true. I wanted such a God. I wanted to know him, to serve him. I wanted to learn how to love him.

If it was true, if what the Master was saying was really true, it meant . . . well, then it meant God was just like Jesus. It meant he delighted in me the same way Jesus delighted in me. It meant he valued my friendship the same way Jesus valued my friendship. It meant he loved me with a love that did not cease when I said it wrong or did it wrong or took years to understand what should have been obvious from the day I was born. It meant he didn't turn his back on me when I turned my back on him, when I let my flesh run wild or let my fears or my greed or my anger or my lust lead me into sin. If God was really just like Jesus, it changed everything forever. I suddenly wanted to ask the Master if this was true. But, when I formed the thoughts into words in my mind, it sounded stupid, and so I kept quiet. But oh! If only it could be . . .

The heart of our message was clear—we were going out to tell our nation about Jesus. We were to teach them what he had been teaching us. We were to point them to him, to create within them a hunger for him. Jesus told us that if we would confess him before our fellow men, then he would also confess us before his heavenly Father. And he linked us to himself in the most remarkable way. He said, "He who receives you receives me, and he who receives me receives the one who sent me."

Some of it I understood; some of it I only thought I did. At that point in my life, I assumed this was a brilliant alternative strategy for the Master. With all of us performing wonders and pointing the nation to Jesus, we would certainly create a groundswell of popularity so massive it would be impossible for the established Jewish leaders to prevent Jesus from rising to power.

Jesus divided us into six teams, pairing me with Judas. I was pleased with the match. Judas was a great conversationalist with a quick sense of humor and a keen mind. I knew he would be good company on our big adventure. We all shared a final meal together, made some decisions about who would go which direction, and then headed on our way by early afternoon. The excitement among the Twelve of us was intense. We had no idea what to expect, but we knew this would be unlike anything we had ever experienced.

It felt strange not having Jesus with us. Judas and I headed toward Chorazin, a small town several miles north of Capernaum. As we walked we fell into conversation about the Master, the movement, and the hope of bringing our nation under his leadership. At that point in our lives the two of us shared a great deal in common. We both believed Jesus was the obvious, the only, hope for Israel. We both believed the purpose of our mission was to help move the Master into some political or religious leadership position that would then enable him to restore Israel to its former glory. We differed in the details of how we believed this could best be accomplished but felt we understood perfectly the meaning of the message the Master had instructed us to proclaim: "The kingdom of heaven is at hand!" Obviously we were being sent out to herald the arrival of God's kingdom on earth and the presence of Jesus, God's designated king. And one other thing Judas and I agreed on— our personal futures, our hopes, our success depended on the success of Jesus.

Knowing now what I do about Judas and about his fate, I have thought back over those days and tried to see where he and I differed at that point in our lives. I certainly didn't see it clearly then, and perhaps not at all. But if I saw any difference at all between us, I would say that whereas Judas was wholeheartedly committed to the success of the movement, I was wholeheartedly committed to the success of the

Master. At the time, of course, we believed the two to be identical and saw ourselves as comrades in a common cause. It was not until very late in our relationship, when Jesus forced us to redefine the success of his mission in terms of the cross, and the crowds turned away from him in fear, or anger, or disgust, that the different allegiances of Judas and myself became evident. By then, however, my own world was in such chaos I could not see what was happening in those around me until it was all over.

We distracted ourselves with conversation as we walked the few miles to Chorazin, but inside I was so excited I felt as if I would explode. I couldn't wait to find someone who was sick so that I could try out *the power.* I was like a kid clutching the best birthday gift in the world, anxiously waiting for the party to end so that I could run outside and play with my new treasure.

I didn't have to wait long. We arrived at our destination by late afternoon and headed straight to the marketplace in the center of town. The daily business of buying and selling was winding down for the evening, but there were still a number of people in the area. And of course there were the beggars—the lame, the deformed, the crippled, the injured—hoping for a small gift from a compassionate merchant or customer.

I saw my target almost immediately. He was young, certainly not over fifteen or sixteen years old. He would have been a good-looking lad if a person's eyes would not have gone first to the little stubs protruding from where his arms should have been. I pictured him sitting in this same place as a child, his coin container between his little legs, calling out for kindness. I couldn't help but wonder if his success in competing with the other beggars for coins had diminished now that an insecure and awkward adolescent sat where a pathetic little boy once pulled at the hearts of those who passed by.

He looked up when I approached, and the sadness in his eyes jolted me out of my self-centered excitement. This wasn't a target. This wasn't a test case. This was a real, hurting human being before me. For a few seconds I just stood there, staring at the lad, not saying a word. A rare bout of self-doubt flooded over me. What if this didn't work? What if nothing happened? What was I doing here without Jesus? What if I ended up looking like some sort of sadistic fool? Then I heard Judas's voice beside me. "Go ahead, Peter! Do it! He said we could. Give it a try. We'll never know if we don't try."

Now I understood why Jesus sent us out in twos.

I knelt down in front of the boy, reached out and put my hands on his shoulders, and said, "Be healed!"

Instantly two little stubs of flesh were transformed into strong, young, whole shoulders, arms, hands, fingers, and thumbs. To this day I'm not sure which of us was more surprised. For a few seconds we both sat frozen in position, staring at the transformation in his body. Then the boy sprang to his feet and began waving his hands wildly in the air. As soon as I stood up, he grabbed me, wrapped his two new, miraculous arms around me, and gave me the first hug of his life.

The boy's yelling and waving and bouncing around the market attracted the attention of everyone within hearing distance. Judas and I looked at each other, and above the boy's squeals of delight, I heard Judas say, "It works! It really works!" As the crowd gathered around us, I saw Judas reach down and touch the eyes of an old blind beggar and restore his sight.

For the next half hour, the two of us moved throughout the marketplace touching and healing every disease and deformity we encountered. By the time we finished, most of the community was packed around us watching in stunned amazement. When we finally ran out of candidates for healing, I jumped up onto a wide stone wall, held up my hands for silence, and then began to speak.

It was the greatest moment in my life up to that point. Never had I experienced such a sense of power. As soon as the people saw I was about to speak, silence filled the marketplace. The sun was setting behind me. It was the time of day when most people would have been heading home to their families. But not today. Not now. Not with me standing on that wall before them. I knew already what my first words would be.

"My fellow Israelites, THE KINGDOM OF HEAVEN IS AT HAND!"

I must have stood on that wall for more than an hour talking to the people before me. I told them we were disciples of the man they had been hearing about, Jesus of Nazareth. I told them he had given us the ability to perform these great works. I told them about his work, about his message, about his powers. I told them he was the great hope and future for our nation. I finally stopped when it grew too dark for them to see me. My young friend with the new arms stood directly beneath me throughout my lecture. As soon as I jumped down from the wall, he grabbed my arm and urged Judas and me to come to his parents' home for the night.

For the next two weeks Judas and I traveled from village to village healing, preaching, proclaiming the arrival of the kingdom of heaven, and pointing people to Jesus. Never had I known such power, such popularity. Never had my flesh known such a glorious time. This was the life I was meant to lead. This was the place in society I truly deserved. Nothing would stop us now. Nothing could. With Jesus leading the way and the Twelve of us filled with his power, no force on earth could rob us of victory. The nation was ours. The Roman Empire was ours. The world was ours for the taking.

130

The only way I can explain that phase of my life is to say that for a brief period of time, my Lord allowed me to know what it was like to express the power of God with the mind of the flesh. The time would come following the resurrection of our Lord when for the first time in the history of the human race, every true child of God would be filled with the Spirit of God. Our great burden of sin would be placed upon the shoulders of Christ, and he would carry it away from us forever. He would then create within each of us a new heart, a pure, perfect heart, a heart that loves him and longs to serve him. With that new heart within us, and his Holy Spirit working through us, he would then be freed to reshape our minds and our emotions into greater and greater conformity with his own glorious image, while daily expressing himself through our personalities in ways perfectly matched to the unique people he designed us to be.

But that was not what was happening at this point in my life. This was not the infilling of the Spirit of God given to every Christian. This was not the outflowing of the life of God from a heart in submission to him. This was simply the specialized gifting of the Holy Spirit, equipping us to perform acts of healing for the purpose of powerfully proclaiming the person of Christ throughout the nation of Israel. It had little to do with us. It certainly had nothing to do with the quality of our lives or the purity of our hearts. As Judas and I traveled together, I watched the power of God performing mighty miracles through him. And yet, in a matter of months he would sell out the Master for a few coins, and I would recall the words of Jesus: "Many will say to me on that day, 'Lord, Lord, didn't we prophesy in your name, and in your name cast out demons, and in your name perform many miracles?' And then I will say to them, 'I never knew you; depart from me, you who practice lawlessness.'"

I wonder if you have read the account of the life of Samson. Have you ever wondered how a man so obviously filled with the power of the Spirit of God could remain so enslaved to his own fleshly lusts? I understand Samson. He and I were both gifted by God with limited supernatural power to accomplish God's sovereign purposes among his people. Samson had supernatural strength. I had the ability to heal. Both of us exercised those gifts from fleshly minds for selfish purposes. I didn't know it was selfish at the time. I honestly believed I was fighting for the success of the Master. What I could not admit, though, was that it was not his success I really wanted—it was my own. I loved the Master, but I was still a man driven by the flesh, deeply in love with my own fleshly goals, and if I could have been honest, I would have admitted that most of all I wanted Jesus to succeed by my terms because I knew his success was the key to my own.

It was an incredible fleshly ride. Everything seemed to be going so perfectly. And then we received news that sent a sudden jolt of terror through us, news that brought our fling to an abrupt end and sent us scurrying back to Jesus. The Prophet John had just been executed.

16

Kill the leader and the movement dies. Men of power have known this simple truth for as long as there have been men of power. If Herod could execute the Prophet John, then Herod could execute Jesus, and Herod could execute us. There was an unbroken line between the Prophet John and Jesus and Jesus' twelve disciples. Every public message John gave in the weeks prior to his arrest and imprisonment pointed directly, specifically to the Master: *"He must increase, but I must decrease."* Though none of us spoke about it openly, I think we all anticipated John's release from prison as soon as Jesus' power and popularity grew to the point where Herod would be forced to comply with Jesus' demands.

With the whole nation following this miracle worker, how could Herod risk doing anything else?

But Herod had moved too quickly. We were not yet strong enough, not yet big enough, not yet organized sufficiently to make our demands. Our world is governed by tiny men who live in fear and use their power to protect their little empires. And now suddenly we lived in fear as well. Given the tragic news of John's execution, I suggested to Judas that this might not be the best time for us to be seen proclaiming our union with Jesus in front of large public gatherings throughout Israel. He saw the wisdom in my words, and we headed back to Capernaum.

We were not the only ones who thought it wise to return home. Every one of us arrived back at Jesus' house the same afternoon. It was an incredible reunion—twelve men all talking at once, louder and louder, blasting each other with vivid accounts of the amazing events of the past two weeks. The spirit of one-upmanship escalated throughout the afternoon, with everyone "sharing" their most dramatic healings and their most enthusiastic crowd responses, until some of the later accounts truly did stretch the limits of credibility.

Jesus said very little as the rest of us babbled on. At the time I remember thinking his silence must be the result of his concern over John's execution. Perhaps he feared for our safety as well, or for his own. Certainly he grieved deeply over the loss of his friend and comrade. But I now know his silence that day had nothing to do with anxiety over our safety. I believe it was produced most of all by the overwhelming depth of our ignorance and arrogant pride. The gift of God being wielded by the mind of flesh is such an ugly thing. Given where we were mentally, and given what we could not know about him or about ourselves until after his death and resurrection, he was certainly not discouraged. But I am certain he could not help but long for the time when our minds of flesh would be replaced by the mind of the Spirit.

We were understandably excited, but we were also exhausted. And to make matters worse, news of Jesus' return produced an instant multitude seeking the Master. By early evening the place was packed with several thousand people waiting outside the door. We didn't even have time to eat. Late that night we finally pushed the last Jesus seeker out the door and collapsed for a few hours.

Just before sunrise the following morning, I felt Jesus shaking me. When he had us all awake, he told us to head quickly and quietly down to our boat. We needed a rest, and it was obvious we were not going to get it here. And so began the two most remarkable days I ever spent with the Master prior to his crucifixion.

‿✕

Our attempted escape was well intended but futile. I think we realized that even before we pushed off from the shore. Thirteen men quietly attempting to slip away unnoticed was a joke. We had to step over sleeping pilgrims just to get to the road. By the time we untied the rope and pushed out to sea, there was no small congregation gathered on the beach, watching our departure. Before we were out of earshot I heard several voices on the shore calling out, "They're heading north! They're heading north!"

We planned to sail to a secluded spot a few miles up the coast from Bethsaida. We knew that section of the coastline well and felt confident we could make our escape before our pursuers found boats in which to follow us. It wasn't long before we were out of sight with no one in pursuit.

It was a beautiful morning—warm, with just the slightest breeze pushing us along. Progress was slow, but we already had what we were looking for; the absence of clamoring crowds was like heaven. I don't think anyone spoke more than a dozen words the whole trip. It was so wonderful just to curl up on deck, soaking up the warmth of the sun, dozing off and on, knowing no needy human being could get to us.

It was midmorning before we reached our destination. As we turned toward shore, I wondered what that noise was coming from the beach. I knew this section of land was uninhabited, several miles from any houses. And yet there was definitely some sort of movement on the shore and a noise I couldn't quite place. Then suddenly it hit me—it was voices, hundreds and hundreds of human voices. The beach was packed with people, all pointing and waving at our little boat. That mob we left behind at Capernaum had run along the shore, picking up more and more people along the way, arriving at our destination ahead of us.

As soon as I saw them, I started to turn the boat around and head back out to sea. Jesus saw what I was doing, smiled at me, shook his head, and nodded toward the shore. So many desperate, hurting people . . . he said they were just like sheep without a shepherd. And so ended our great escape.

The rest of the afternoon was like so many other mornings and afternoons and evenings with the Master. Jesus healed those who were sick, answered the questions people asked, and taught until late afternoon. There were several thousand on the beach when we first arrived, but the crowd kept growing throughout the day until some of those next to the shore were being pushed into the sea. The whole scene became unmanageable, and Jesus finally led the mob away from the beach and up onto a grassy hillside a short distance inland from where our boat was beached. The crowd grew until there must have been nearly five thousand men, women, and children spread out across the grassy slope. It was the largest public meeting we'd ever held.

Jesus finally finished his discourse and sat down. It was obvious that he was finished teaching for the day, but no one moved. Rather than gathering their families together and heading home, they all just sat there—an endless sea of humanity spread out before us. Apparently they had no intention of leaving unless they saw Jesus himself depart. The whole situation became rather awkward, and we disciples grouped around the Master, not knowing exactly what to do. I finally took it upon myself to speak to Jesus. I pointed out the obvious: we were miles from the nearest village, it was getting late, these people were hungry, and they all needed either to go home or find temporary lodging for the night. I encouraged Jesus to send the people away.

Jesus looked up at us hovering around him and said, "They don't have to go away. You give them something to eat."

We looked at the crowd. Then we looked back at Jesus. Then we looked at the crowd again. This time I kept my mouth shut. I'd been here before. I was hearing Jesus speaking words, but the words made no sense.

Finally Jesus broke the silence. "Philip, where can we buy bread to feed these people?"

I was thrilled it was Philip he singled out for the test. I didn't know the answer to this one. Philip did some quick mental calculations and stated what we already knew. It would take more than half a year's wages to buy bread for this mob.

Silence reigned once again in our little group.

Then my brother spoke up. "There is a lad here who has five barley loaves and two fish, but what are these for so many people?"

I looked over at him and saw Andrew standing with his hand resting on the shoulder of a boy perhaps ten or eleven years old. The boy was holding a small lunch basket, neatly covered with a white cloth. I remembered seeing Andrew sitting with the boy throughout much of the afternoon. Apparently the little fellow had been playing outside when the crowd passed through his village in pursuit of Jesus that morning. He begged his mom for permission to join the

137

group. She learned their neighbors were going, so she quickly packed him a little lunch and sent him off in their care. In the confused transition from the beach to the hillside, the young fellow had been separated from his neighbors and found himself all alone in that multitude. He was safe enough but a little scared. Andrew had a way of picking up on those things. He saw the boy standing by himself, struck up a conversation with him, and offered to keep him company until they located the boy's neighbors.

Andrew told me later how that lunch basket ended up in the Master's hands. Throughout the afternoon the little fellow kept glancing at the basket sitting next to him. He felt uncomfortable eating his lunch when he knew those around him had none. When Jesus finished his teaching and sat down, for a few minutes neither Andrew nor the boy spoke. It was apparent to Andrew that the lad was deep in thought about something. Then he turned to Andrew and asked, "Do you know if Jesus brought a lunch with him today?"

Andrew said he knew Jesus had not brought a lunch and, in fact, had not eaten anything since early morning.

The boy was silent again for a few minutes. Then he turned again to Andrew and said, "Do you think Jesus would like to have my lunch?"

Andrew suggested they go up and ask him.

The events that followed are no doubt well known to you. Jesus sent Andrew and Matthew back to the fishing boat to get the large baskets we kept on board for sorting and storing our catch. He told the rest of us to divide the crowd into groups of somewhere between fifty and a hundred people in each group. As I headed out into the crowd I glanced back and saw the boy sitting on the grass next to the Master. He was laughing at something Jesus was saying. The lunch basket sat unopened on the grass between them.

138

As soon as Andrew and Matthew returned, Jesus stood, offered a prayer of thanksgiving for the little basket of food, then pulled back the cloth cover, removed the contents, and began breaking pieces of fish and bread into one of the baskets. In just a few seconds the basket was filled, and he told us to bring it over to the first group of hungry listeners. The next basket he filled was the boy's little basket. He filled it until it overflowed, then handed it back to the lad. The boy sat next to Jesus with the basket on his lap and ate his lunch. But his eyes were glued to the miracle taking place in Jesus' hands.

For the next several hours we toted and dumped and toted and dumped basket after basket of food. As fast as we brought them back Jesus refilled them.

Everyone ate until they could eat no more. When they finally finished, we gathered up the uneaten food and found we had twelve baskets full of leftovers . . . one for each of us.

The crowd's response to that feast exceeded my wildest expectations. Someone began chanting, "KING JESUS! KING JESUS! KING JESUS!" and it wasn't long before thousands of voices joined in. At last we had the power of the people behind us. Surely nothing could stop us now. Nothing, that is, except Jesus himself. Rather than seizing the moment and acknowledging their nomination, he told us the meeting was over and ordered us to return to the boat immediately and head back to Capernaum. Once again I felt he was making a tragic tactical error, turning his back on this tremendous momentum, but he made it clear his instructions were not open for discussion. As we shoved off from the shore, I could hear the Master telling the multitude to return to their homes. When I looked again, he was nowhere to be seen.

What a day! At last we had the masses on the move. Our victory could not be far away. And it wasn't over yet. For me the best was yet to come.

Our return trip was nothing like our leisurely escape from Capernaum that morning. The sky remained clear, with nearly a full moon for light, but we no longer bobbed contentedly along in a gentle breeze. The wind, now blowing straight into our bow, increased in intensity throughout the night until our only hope of forward progress meant pulling at the oars with all our strength. After three or four hours of this agony, we were all exhausted and still several miles from Capernaum. I wasn't really concerned about our safety; I was just tired and wanted to get where we were going. Whitecaps broke on top of rolling swells as we rose and fell with each new wave sweeping under us.

Then I saw something, two swells over, moving our direction. The human mind does not adjust easily to the impossible. We were in a boat, several miles from land, at three o'clock in the morning. Something tall and thin was protruding from the sea about fifty feet from our boat. It couldn't be a rock, because it rose and fell with the waves. I thought it must be a log of some sort. But then why was it floating on end? . . . And why was it wrapped in a robe? . . . And why did it appear to be walking? . . . And why did it have arms . . . and a head . . . and a face?

I dropped my oar and stood up for a better look. As soon as I rose, the others followed my gaze. I heard James put into words what everyone was thinking. "What is that thing?"

Then, as the "thing" rose high onto the churning swell directly across from us, we all recognized him at the same time. It was Jesus . . . walking toward our boat . . . on top of the water. Someone behind me muttered, "It's a ghost! It has to be his ghost."

As soon as the word "ghost" was mentioned, we all pulled back from the side of the boat. Even in the full moon it was difficult to see clearly whatever was coming toward us, and no one was volunteering to be official greeter. It looked like Jesus, but with the waves splashing up against him and his hair and clothing whipping about in the wind, it was the most frightening Jesus we'd ever seen.

Then he spoke. "Take courage, it is I; don't be afraid."

Even in this wind I knew that voice.

Rarely have I troubled to think before I speak, and that night was certainly no exception. I took a step forward, leaned over the side of the boat, and bellowed back, "Lord, if it's you, command me to come to you on the water."

It all took place so fast, I didn't realize what was happening until after it was all over. As he looked at me, clutching the side of the boat, I saw that incredible, contagious smile spread across his face and heard him speak just one word, "Come!"

And I did!

To this day I don't know what got into me, apart from just being my normal, unthinking, impetuous self, but as soon as he said the word, I sprang over the side of the boat and dropped to the water below. I remember hearing my feet hit. They hit with a thud rather than a splash. It was the strangest sensation. The water gave firm, solid support, and yet the surface on which I stood kept moving up and down with each new wave passing under me. Even with the sea providing firm footing, I should have been flung off balance immediately by the violent movement of the churning breakers. But my muscles seemed to know instantly how to flex and bend with the fluid chaos under my feet.

Jesus stood waiting for me about thirty feet away. I let go of the side of the boat and took a step toward him . . . then another . . . and another. I was doing fine until I took my eyes off of where I was going and looked back at where I'd come from. I saw eleven anxious faces staring at me in concerned disbelief. No one else was following me. If anything, they appeared to be clinging to the boat even more tightly, obviously glad I was out on the water and not them.

Faith by majority vote is never a safe path for the child of God. Rarely does our Lord give others faith for the work he seeks to do through us. In looking back I allowed the others to vote on the wisdom of my trust in the Master. The vote was eleven against one. When I turned back to Jesus, I no longer saw him; I saw the storm. I no longer heard his voice saying, "Come!" I heard the wind blasting around my ears. I no longer felt the solid footing under my feet. I felt the spray of the sea soaking my face and legs and arms and hands. And a great wave of terror flooded over me.

My muscles went rigid. The waves that just a few seconds earlier had been rolling harmlessly under my feet now smashed against my legs causing me to lose my balance. I knew I was going down and reached out instinctively to break my fall. As I went down I caught a breaking wave full in the face, and my arms plunged deep into the churning caldron around me. I couldn't breathe, I couldn't see, and my waterlogged clothing wrapped itself around me in a sort of cocoon that made swimming impossible. I was going under—I knew it! At the top of my voice I let out one great, terrifying wail. "Lord! Save me!"

Immediately I felt his strong grip on my right forearm. I closed my fingers around his arm in response as he lifted me effortlessly back up on top of the waves. He wrapped his left arm around my back, and together we walked to the boat. Until my left hand touched wood I didn't realize how tightly I was gripping the Master's arm. I flopped onto the deck, still spluttering the water I'd inhaled. Then Jesus climbed in next to me.

As I lay there on the deck, feeling foolish and relieved, he knelt beside me and said, "O you of little faith, why did you doubt?" As soon as the words left his mouth, the wind stopped, and the violence around us ceased, leaving a small fishing boat bobbing gently under a full moon shining down on the night sea. On deck, eleven men grouped around a twelfth man lying on his back with his Savior kneeling beside him.

Perhaps to you, not hearing his tone or seeing the expression on his face, the words Jesus spoke to me on our boat that night might seem like words of condemnation. They were not. Jesus knew I would doubt before he ever called me onto the water. The title he gave me as I lay there before him was accurate; I was a man of little faith. It was not a condemnation; it was a statement of truth. The great gift he gave me that night was not the thrill of accomplishing the impossible. It was not the honor of being the only man other than himself to have ever walked on water. The great gift he gave me was that single question with which the episode ended: "Why did you doubt?" It was this question that Jesus wanted me to ask myself, and keep asking until I knew the answer.

Why *did* I doubt? He had already given me proof of his faithfulness. I was already walking on the water. The storm had not intensified. The waves were not increasing in size. My circumstances had not changed. And yet one minute I was walking on the sea, and the next I was being destroyed by it.

The twofold answer to the question was obvious. I took my eyes off my Master, and I focused instead on where I was coming from and what was going on around me. The illustration of that night has become a lifelong part of my walk with the King. I now know where doubt comes from. I know where fear comes from. It does not come from seeing the storm around me; it comes from not seeing who stands beside me. I have certainly not lived a life of flawless faith since that night on the water. In fact, all of my greatest blunders were yet to come. But the principle Jesus gave me through our water walk together is now a solid anchor for my life. When I fear, when I doubt, when I allow my past to define my future and feel the stress and anxiety it brings, whenever I feel myself sinking once again, I know I am not seeing my Lord correctly.

Why did I doubt? I doubted because I took my eyes off the only true source of hope and security in this world. I took my eyes off my Lord Jesus Christ.

Even the greatest days must come to an end. When we finally stepped onshore back at Capernaum, the adrenalin high of the past eighteen hours was wearing off, and I slept the instant I closed my eyes. But I slept knowing we finally held victory in our hands. I slept knowing thousands upon thousands of people now stood behind us, cheering us, ready to crown Jesus king. I slept knowing all we needed was one well-organized march on Jerusalem, and the nation was ours. I slept knowing there were no limits to what the Master could do.

The one thing I did not know was how quickly our popularity would come crashing down around us.

17

I woke to the Sabbath-morning sun streaming in through the window. My muscles ached from our late night and early morning adventure, but even before my mind remembered why, I felt a sense of excitement. Then it all came surging back into my consciousness. The chanting crowds . . . the calls for "King Jesus" . . . the raw excitement and enthusiasm of that cheering congregation . . . there were good things coming.

Of course Jesus had been right to send the crowds away the night before. We needed time to organize, time to plan, time to devise the most effective strategy. Should we march on Jerusalem? How would Rome respond? Should we set up our own alternative power center here in Galilee and let the nation come to us? Jesus would know. Surely he already had it all worked out. This was what we'd all been waiting for. Watch out, Israel! Here comes your king!

Following our morning meal together, we walked to the synagogue with Jesus. His presence at these weekly gatherings always brought a tremendous sense of excitement among those present, and never more than on this particular Sabbath. When we boarded our boat the night before, our departure generated little interest because the one the people wanted remained with them on the beach. But following his instructions for them to return to their homes, Jesus quickly eluded his pursuers. After searching for him in vain, a number of them retraced their journey along the shoreline back to Capernaum. They knew he would be at the synagogue if he was in town on the Sabbath, and the throng surrounding the building upon our arrival was thrilling.

The normal Sabbath synagogue routine never happened that day. Jesus' arrival prompted a flood of questions. When did Jesus arrive in Capernaum? How did he escape his pursuers the night before? Why did he leave them? How did he get back to the city?

And so began what at the time I viewed as the most disturbing and disappointing interaction between the Master and the mob since his public ministry began. Jesus ignored the direct questions about his return to Capernaum altogether and responded instead with a statement that could not help but offend a number of his listeners. "You don't seek me because you saw signs, but because you ate of the loaves until you were full."

His meaning was obvious—you don't seek me because of who I am, you seek me because you want another free meal.

The brutal public revelation of their true motives clearly irritated the crowd. But then he went on to make a statement that seemed to renew their hope of common ground. "Don't work for the food which perishes, but for the food which endures to eternal life, which the Son of Man will give you, for on him the Father, God, has set his seal."

This was better! Jesus was talking about food again. *Food* they understood. That stuff about "enduring to eternal life" was all a blur, but the part about the Son of Man giving them this wonderful food was clearly worth examining more closely.

The self-appointed spokesman for the group put into words the question they really wanted Jesus to answer. "What do we have to do so that we can work the works of God?" The intent of the question was obvious to everyone: "Can you teach us to make food from nothing too?"

It was obvious to everyone, that is, except Jesus. His response suddenly caused the discussion to head a direction no one else wanted it to go. He said, "This is the work of God, that you believe in him whom he has sent."

That was all well and good, but somehow Jesus was missing the point. A second spokesman took up the challenge. "Then what will you do for a sign, so that we can see, and believe you? What work will you perform?" And then, with skillful verbal maneuvering, he turned the conversation back to the real issue of the day. "Our fathers ate manna in the wilderness; as it is written, 'He gave them bread out of heaven to eat.'"

The man's words prompted a rumbling murmur of approval throughout the crowd. The reference to Moses and manna and the quotation from the Prophet Nehemiah about bread out of heaven brought the discussion right back on target.

At first Jesus' response seemed to be staying with the crucial issue. "It is not Moses who has given you the bread out of heaven, but it is my Father who gives you the true bread out of heaven. For the bread of God is that which comes down out of heaven, and gives life to the world."

Whether it was Moses or whether it was God working through Moses really didn't matter in the least to those listening. The important thing wasn't who gave it but rather what he gave. If Jesus wanted to play theological word games, they would gladly concede their error just so long as this fellow was willing and able to come up with a lot more of that life-giving bread from heaven.

Jesus' apparent offer to once again produce the goods brought an emphatic, enthusiastic response. "Lord, give us this bread forever!"

Let the party begin! Who has a lunch for the Master to multiply? What size groups would you like us to divide into today? Can you do anything else besides fish and bread? Can you hold off long enough for me to run home and get my family? Would you prefer to be addressed as "king," or will "Lord" be acceptable?

Then came the blow from which the crowd never recovered. Jesus said, "*I* am the bread of life; he who comes to me will not hunger, and he who believes in me will never thirst."

The whole dialogue was so strange. It was like listening to actors attempting to perform a scene in which the director had mistakenly given them scripts from two totally different plays. The questions and the answers didn't match. With every additional word the Master uttered, I saw another chunk of our support base crumbling. Yesterday Jesus provided these people with an apparently endless supply of free food. Today they returned with a polite request for a second serving only to find Jesus telling them he himself is the only bread they really need.

Most of them never heard anything else Jesus said that morning. They didn't hear because they didn't want to hear. They brought their agenda to their God and skillfully sought to maneuver him into fulfilling that agenda. When he refused to comply with their wishes, they had no more use for him.

As I stood there watching the growing tension between Jesus and the crowd, hoping this time Jesus would finally rally his troops, fearing he would not, I recalled the words I'd heard him speak a few weeks earlier. "But to what shall I compare this generation? It's like children sitting in the market places, who call out to the other children, and say, 'We played the flute for you, and you did not dance; we sang a dirge, and you did not mourn.'"

It was all so confusing to me. Though I wisely kept my mouth shut throughout the subtle verbal warfare raging between Jesus and the crowd, I knew my own hopes and desires seemed to align far more closely with the mob than with the Master. They wanted to crown him king; I wanted to crown him king. They wanted him to lead our little nation; I wanted him to lead our little nation. They wanted the things only he could give; I wanted the things only he could give. True, they were things that would make life better for us, easier for us, but what was wrong with that? He was the one who offered free food in the first place. Why offer it one day and then refuse to do so the next? Jesus obviously cared deeply for each of us. He loved us. He had the power to give us everything we thought we needed for a fulfilling life—health, food, safety, protection. Then why wouldn't he do it?

My questions would not find answers until the Master finally crushed my heart of flesh just prior to his crucifixion. At present I was still doing what I had been doing since the first day Jesus stepped into my life. I was staring at the world of the Spirit through the eyes of the flesh, wondering why nothing seemed to make sense. There are some among us who think the mind of the flesh sees only the world of the flesh. That is certainly not true. The mind of the flesh may see the world of the Spirit with vivid clarity, but it sees it as a means, a resource through which the goals of the flesh can be achieved. The flesh can pray. The flesh can call upon God. The flesh can cry out to its Creator. But it does so with the hope that it can enlist the power of the spirit world for its own fleshly goals. I longed for the supernatural, as did this crowd standing before Jesus. But we longed for it only as a means through which we could more effectively achieve our selfish, self-centered little fleshly ends.

It all seemed so complicated, so confusing back then, like pieces of a puzzle I could not fit together. It was complicated because the one piece onto which all the others fit was still missing. It was standing right in front of me, and yet I could not see it. I like the way my brother Paul said it in that letter he wrote to the church at Corinth. He said, "But I am afraid that, as the serpent deceived Eve by his craftiness, your minds will be led astray from the simplicity and purity of devotion to Christ." There we all were, several thousand hungry, greedy, selfish people seeking what only Jesus could give. And that, of course, was the heart of our problem. We thought we needed what he could give. What we really needed was him. We thought God could provide the things that would fill our spirits and make our lives worth living. We could not see the truth. The only thing that could ever truly fill our spirits and make our lives worth living was God himself.

I now understand, of course, that Jesus was not playing verbal games with his audience that day. He answered their questions with razor-sharp precision. They came telling him they hungered, asking him for help. He responded not with far less than they asked for but with far more. He said in effect, "I know you hunger, and I know, too, that what you truly hunger for is me." He said it so perfectly, so beautifully that day. "I am the bread of life. Your fathers ate the manna in the wilderness, and they died. This is the bread which comes from heaven, so that one may eat it and not die. I am the living bread that came from heaven; if anyone eats this bread, he will live forever; and the bread which I will give for the life of the world is my flesh."

He spoke the truth. We could not hear it. When he talked about eating his flesh, the discussion disintegrated completely in a matter of minutes. I heard one of the group's leaders who turned to another standing next to him and said, "How can this man give us his flesh to eat?"

Jesus' final words of response brought the meeting to an abrupt end. "I tell you honestly, unless you eat the flesh of the Son of Man and drink his blood, you have no life in yourselves. He who eats my flesh and drinks my blood has eternal life, and I will raise him up on the last day. For my flesh is true food, and my blood is true drink. He who eats my flesh and drinks my blood abides in me, and I in him. As the living Father sent me, and I live because of the Father, so he who eats my flesh, he also will live because of me. This is the bread which came down out of heaven; not as the fathers ate and died; he who eats this bread will live forever."

Even I had to admit that it sounded as if Jesus was losing touch with reality. the Twelve of us stood silently behind the Master and watched as several thousand disgruntled former followers of Jesus finally dispersed in frustration, irritation, and bewilderment.

Then I heard Thomas's voice saying quietly, "Well, that didn't go well, did it?"

I responded, "No, and for obvious reasons."

Though none of us wanted to come right out and say it, we all felt as though the Master could have handled the situation far better. Less than twenty-four hours earlier we had a small militant army behind us ready to crown Jesus king of Israel. Now we had Jesus and the Twelve of us and maybe half a dozen others still in the group. Perhaps it would be best to postpone that march on Jerusalem for a few weeks.

Jesus knew we were frustrated and confused. He turned to us and said, "Does this cause you to stumble? What then if you see the Son of Man ascending to where he was before? It is the Spirit who gives life; the flesh profits nothing; the words that I have spoken to you are Spirit and are life."

This was awful. He might feel as though his words were life, but they certainly seemed to be the death of the King Jesus Movement. He made a few more comments to us, then for a few seconds we all just stood there, huddled together in silence. No one knew what to say. We felt as though we'd just witnessed our best friend bungle the most important public address of his life. For some reason it didn't seem to trouble him, but it devastated us.

Then Jesus spoke again, not a statement this time, but a question, a question possessing the power to bring peace and renewal and, in the most amazing way, hope to my heart. He said, "You don't want to go away too, do you?"

In that instant I saw the great divide between us and them. Jesus' words that morning had brought pain and frustration to everyone who heard them. But there was a difference. They brought pain and frustration to the mob because they knew they could not follow Jesus. They brought pain and frustration to us because we knew we could not leave him. I wonder if you can understand how Jesus' question gave me hope. Of course I had my agenda. Of course I wanted him crowned king so that I could serve as his right-hand man. Of course I wanted his fame and fortune and success, knowing my fame and fortune and success were inseparably linked to his. But if I could not have the fame, if I could not have the fortune, if I could not have the success, if we lost it all in an instant, I still wanted *him!* I wanted *him* more than I wanted anything he might bring me. If the movement collapsed, and the crowds never returned, and we all died in obscurity on the back side of the desert, it would still be worth it all, because what I wanted most I still possessed. I was still his friend, and he was still mine, and it was enough.

The words I spoke that day in response to that question were, I believe, the first words the Spirit of God ever spoke through me. "Lord, to whom shall we go? You have the words of eternal life. We have believed and have come to know that you are the Holy One of God."

As is typical with the working of the Holy Spirit, I spoke more than I understood. I have quoted those words to myself countless times since that day, savoring their truth, drawing strength from the security they bring. I did not understand the man standing before me. To be honest, I did not yet understand most of the things he said. But one thing I did understand—he was Truth. There was no place else to go. If there was no Jesus, then there was nothing. When Jesus asked if we too would leave, his question forced me to recognize I already had what I wanted most—I had him. And he was enough.

18

It is painful for me to recall those months immediately following the feeding of the five thousand men and their families. The memory of it makes me feel embarrassed even now. I wonder if you have had such a time in your own life—a time when you look back and marvel that you could have been so blind, so completely consumed with yourself, so totally immersed in your own fleshly, selfish little goals. My devotion to the Master and my desperate need for him remained as intense as ever. But that just made it all the worse.

You see, Jesus wasn't behaving correctly from my perspective. He wasn't doing the things I knew he should be doing. I know now why he concluded that hideous day following the great feeding by asking me that question, "You don't want to go away too, do you?" He knew the power of speaking the truth, the tremendous value of forming it into words and articulating it to others. He knew I needed to face the next few months having reaffirmed to myself and to my world the only truth about him that I was certain of. Even if he did it all wrong from my perspective, even if I could not understand what he was doing or why he was doing it, even if I knew in my heart that his way would lead us to disaster, still there was no place else to go, there were no other answers. Either there was Jesus or there was nothing.

Having watched the Master turn his back on what at the time I believed to be our greatest open door to success, rather than regrouping our forces and rebuilding our power base, he then chose to invest huge blocks of time with individuals and groups who were powerless to help him reestablish the throne of David and the righteous, sovereign rule of Israel. Timing was crucial. Momentum was essential. And yet Jesus seemed to be either blind or ignorant of the strategies that were so obvious to me. There were days during that period when I wanted to grab him and shake him and scream, "What are you doing with our lives? What are you doing with your own? We are not where we should be, and we won't get there heading the way you're taking us!"

Accounts of Jesus' most recent miraculous works traveled throughout the nation more quickly than I would have believed possible, each new account inciting our political leaders to more intense resistance against him. With his name now firmly established at the top of their "Most Hated" list, Jesus remained in the north, well away from the national power center in Jerusalem. That much of his strategy, at least, I agreed with. He was certainly not in hiding, but neither was he ready for direct confrontation in what our nation's leaders believed to be their home territory. At the time I assumed he simply wanted a few more months in order to regain our momentum and rebuild our forces. I now know the truth. He did need more time. But it had nothing to do with rallying the masses. It had everything do with the things he still needed to accomplish, both in us, his "little flock," and in those who were bent on destroying him.

A few days following Jesus' rejection of the mob's offer to crown him king, another delegation of Pharisees and scribes arrived from Jerusalem. By now all pretense of politeness was gone. The Pharisees pounced on any apparent offense they could find that might help discredit the Master in the eyes of his followers. This time they lunged at him for not adhering to the proper form of ritualistic purification. Our traditions held to rigid divisions between places, people, and things we considered to be "clean" and those we considered to be "unclean." Following even casual contact with anything on the "unclean" list, it was necessary for a person to adhere to a clearly established pattern of ritualistic cleansing in order to restore proper personal purification. Some of the Pharisees caught us ignoring this purification ritual and accused Jesus of failing to follow and teach the highest standards of our people.

Their words were barely out of their mouths when Jesus responded with the most direct and unqualified condemnation I'd heard him deliver up to that point. His words carried a ring of unquestioned and uncompromising authority. "You hypocrites! Rightly did Isaiah prophesy of you: 'This people honors me with their lips, but their heart is far away from me. They worship me in vain, teaching as doctrines the precepts of men.'"

Using the words of Isaiah as an attack weapon against them enraged this self-righteous flock of Pharisees. Their entire lives were based on creating the appearance of absolute adherence to the writings of Moses and the prophets. Nor did it help when he equated their attitude toward him with their attitude toward God himself. A few seconds of stunned silence followed his rebuke. He then added a few more words of direct condemnation for their behavior before turning his attention to the onlookers observing this heated exchange, warning them about the dangers of the hypocritical teachings flowing from the mouths of the Pharisees. Nothing could have more completely or more quickly alienated these Jerusalem visitors. Not only did Jesus not honor them for their piety, he actually held them up as the worst possible examples of true righteousness, men whose approach to God was to be avoided at all costs.

The crowd loved it, but the tension and hostility between us and the Jerusalem leadership surged to new heights. The following day Jesus took us out of town for a while—way out of town. We headed north to the shores of the Mediterranean Sea and the Gentile regions of Tyre and Sidon.

At the time I felt as though Jesus was running away. Except for the obvious advantage of keeping us out of Jerusalem's reach, our journey north was a puzzle to all of us. With his own people so close to crowning him king, why turn now to the Gentile world? An occasional gesture of kindness to a Samaritan or prominent Gentile leader was fine. But why suddenly fling wide the offer of his love and kindness to those who had no claim to it? There were so many things I did not understand at the time. How could I, with my narrow, selfish little goals? Most of all I did not understand the absolute perfection with which Jesus was orchestrating not only his own actions but also the actions of all those who were to play a part in this supreme drama scripted by God himself from before the foundation of the world.

Each step of the way he told us what he was doing, but we did not have ears to hear. He told us why he was taking us north. "I have other sheep, which are not of this fold; I must bring them also, and they will hear my voice; and they will become one flock with one shepherd." Most would not

157

respond to his voice until after the resurrection, but at least he wanted a few of them to hear it and to taste just a little of the sweetness of his love.

✂

Even in this Gentile region, Jesus' reputation preceded him. A few healings, a few acts of deliverance, and the Gentiles followed him with the same fervor and devotion as did many of the Jews. In fact, in some respects the Gentiles' response surpassed that of their Jewish counterparts because the Gentiles brought no rigid religious standard with which to measure the Master. It wasn't long before his Gentile followers gave him their own special title. To them he was "the man who does all things well."

We spent several weeks in that Gentile world with Jesus' popularity growing daily in numbers and intensity. They knew nothing of a promised Messiah. When Paul wrote that letter to the Ephesian Christians, nearly all of whom came to Christ from the Gentile world, he described their condition well when he reminded them that prior to their submission to Christ, they were separate from Christ, excluded from the Commonwealth of Israel, strangers to the covenants of promise, having no hope and without God in the world. That says so well what we saw in the lives of those we encountered throughout our northern journey. And yet they were hungry, desperately hungry for hope, for him.

I must admit that throughout the entire trip I fluctuated back and forth between resentment and envy. I resented their intrusion into our lives, seeking a claim in the riches flowing from *our* prophet, *our* messiah, the hope for *our* nation. And yet I envied them as well. I envied the simplicity and purity of their devotion to the Master. They brought no tub full of intellectual questions, no troublesome passages from ancient writings. They brought no intricate religious agenda with which to test the Master. And because they brought no agenda, their spirits were freed to drink of his kindness and his love in great, greedy, guilt-free gulps. It was a tiny glimpse into what we now see in such vast numbers throughout the Gentile world. At the time, however, we could only assume Jesus was laying the groundwork for good relations with those who would border him on the north when he finally established his kingdom in Israel. No other explanation made sense to us.

By the time we turned back toward Israel, our tiny band had once again grown into a massive throng. Thousands of Gentile followers refused to let Jesus out of their sight. Many wanted healing, of course, but most just wanted to listen to him talk. This man understood life. He wasn't pushing some new religious fad. He didn't want them to join anything. He wasn't after their money. He simply wanted to love them, to touch their lives, to meet their needs. Jesus fed their spirits and gave them hope.

The size of the group forced us to spend our final few days out in the uninhabited regions of the Decapolis, along the eastern coast of the Sea of Galilee, miles from any cities or towns. The Gentile tour culminated with a mass meeting in which Jesus taught all afternoon. There were about four thousand men with at least twice that many women and children. Many had been with us for several days.

When Jesus finished his teaching, he asked the Twelve of us to join him at the front. He told us he didn't want to send the people away hungry and asked what food we had with us. Our own supply was down to nearly nothing—just a few small loaves and fish.

I know what you're thinking. You're thinking we'd been here before, and surely we'd get it right this time. I'll admit the thought crossed my mind, but I wasn't about to speak up, nor did any of the others. You see, in our minds the situation was not at all the same. These were not Israelites. These were pagans, Gentiles with no right to his gifts. Surely he would not feed them. Even our presence with them

159

made us unclean. And then, too, we remembered vividly what happened the last time someone asked Jesus to do a repeat of his magic food trick. That was the day his refusal made everyone so mad they turned away from him. No, it was better to say nothing and let the Master do whatever he was going to do.

It could not have been a more glorious conclusion to our Gentile tour. For a second time we watched as he took our few loaves and fish and fed us all—not just a bite or two but heaps and piles of food from which we all ate until everyone was stuffed. The crowd's response was understandable. With their minds filled with truth, their spirits filled with hope, and their tummies filled with fish and bread, "the man who does all things well" could not be allowed to leave. Jesus made it clear his visit was now over, but in the end we found it necessary to recruit the help of a sympathetic fisherman who provided us with his boat and an escape route across the Sea of Galilee. As we set sail for home, I hoped things had settled down in our absence and that we would be able once again to get the movement moving forward.

✣

Looking back, I can't help but wonder how many spies Jerusalem had scattered throughout Galilee in those days, watching for Jesus' return. Rather than sailing back to Capernaum, we put in at Magadan, a tiny fishing village on the coast of the Sea of Galilee a few miles south of Jesus' hometown. Under normal circumstances it would have been the last place we would have encountered a group of big-city religious leaders. But our world was not operating under normal circumstances. There was a war raging in our little nation. On the surface it was a war between Jerusalem and Jesus. But that was only the stage, the external facade. Just under the surface a much greater war was raging, a war involving the supreme forces of good and evil, a war with eternal consequences for both the victor and the vanquished.

We were still standing on the beach, securing our boat, when the delegation arrived. Jesus faced them, waiting silently for their attack. I stood beside him, my heart pounding with anticipation. How could we ever hope to regain our following when our every move was watched and our every conversation was dominated by these men?

The attack took a different bent this time. The leader of the pack demanded that Jesus show them a sign.

Show them a sign! I couldn't believe it. For nearly three years Jesus' life had been one endless stream of signs and wonders and miraculous works. And now these men came pretending to be, what? Earnest seekers? Confused followers? Troubled disciples? Perhaps they had some trap in mind, or more likely they just wanted to control the conversation. They wanted to control him. What their arrogance would not allow them to accept, and what my ignorance at the time would not then allow me to see, was the absurdity of any human being ever seeking to control the one who by his very nature possessed absolute control over all that is.

The guarded roar in the Lion of Judah's reply was evident to all. "When it's evening, you say, 'It will be fair weather, for the sky is red.' And in the morning, 'There will be a storm today, for the sky is red and threatening.' Do you know how to discern the appearance of the sky, but cannot discern the signs of the times? An evil and adulterous generation seeks after a sign; and a sign will not be given it, except the sign of Jonah."

The sign of Jonah (a lone prophet calling to repentance a nation steeped in wickedness) was not the sign these men sought. But this day it was the only sign they would be given. The interview ended as abruptly as it had begun. The Master turned and boarded the boat once again, and we went away.

161

Following the attack at Magadan, we returned to Bethsaida, where Jesus limited his ministry to quiet interactions with specific individuals. He continued to heal those who came to him in private, but when they left, he consistently asked them not to tell anyone what he had done for them. Though the forces in Jerusalem might have allowed themselves to believe they were now gaining control, driving the Master into hiding, in truth they controlled nothing whatsoever. Jesus alone controlled his own agenda and did it with absolute precision. It served his purposes better at this point in his ministry to become less visible to the masses. When he knew the time was right, he would initiate the final campaign that would culminate in the supreme event of human history. But there were several intricate threads still to be woven into his tapestry, a process that would require a little more time and a few more carefully controlled confrontations with his Jerusalem adversaries.

We spent the next several days at my home in Bethsaida. Then, just prior to the Feast of Tabernacles, we all returned to Jesus' mother's house in Capernaum. Mary was there, as were several of his younger brothers. It was an awkward time in his relationship with his family. The Jewish leaders had been working hard throughout our absence to discredit the Master, and their efforts were bringing results. Prior to his resurrection, his mother was the only one in his immediate family, apart from James and Thaddaeus, of course, who recognized him as the promised Messiah.

Jesus' family was leaving the following morning for Jerusalem, where they would celebrate the Feast of Tabernacles. It was the most popular national holiday of the year for our people. The Feast came immediately following the fall harvest, intended in part as a celebration of God's bountiful provision for our physical needs. But it was far more than just that. The Feast had its roots in the events surrounding the nation's great exodus from Egypt and return to the land of Israel. The celebration lasted a full week, and each family was required to live the entire week in a makeshift temporary dwelling, or "tabernacle," made from branches and leaves. It was to be furnished with just the bare essentials. Part of the dwelling had to be open to the sky so that those within could see the sun, the clouds, and the moon and stars at night. These dwellings were intended to remind our people of God's deliverance from their houses of bondage in Egypt and of his fatherly care throughout the journey in the wilderness.

People from throughout the nation flocked to Jerusalem for the celebration. For those involved in agriculture, it provided a week of rest and enjoyment in the big city following the intense labor of the harvest. The adults loved the opportunity to reunite with family and friends, and the children delighted in the fun of having the whole family crammed into the little stick structures, with Mom cooking over an open fire and Dad forever fussing and fumbling with his crumbling construction. It was a powerful and treasured annual tool for building a strong sense of family unity.

This year, however, in at least one Galilean family, the Feast of Tabernacles was having the opposite effect. As Mary and her children prepared for the trip south, Jesus' brothers began goading him about his plans for the Feast. "Aren't you coming down with us, Jesus? What's the matter? Are you suddenly afraid to be seen in public? Surely you want your disciples to see the works you're doing. No one does things in secret when he wants to be known publicly. Why don't you come on down to Jerusalem with us and show yourself to the world?"

They knew all too well the level of tension that now existed between Jesus and the Jewish leaders. I think they just wanted to see what would happen if Jesus made a grand public entrance into the city.

I wonder if perhaps one of the most painful aspects of Jesus' time on this earth was his knowing that no one understood him and his plan, and there was no way they could understand prior to his resurrection. In response to his brothers' continued harassment, Jesus said, "My time is not yet at hand, but your time is always opportune. The world cannot hate you; but it hates me because I testify its deeds are evil. Go up to the feast yourselves; I don't go up to this feast because my time has not yet fully come." Then, having said these things to them, he stayed in Galilee until after the family departed. We, of course, stayed with him.

"My time has not yet fully come." He knew his own plan. He knew his own time. He knew his own future. And he knew there was no way any of us could understand until it was all over.

Two days following his family's departure, when those traveling to the Feast were well on their way and the roads were once again quiet, Jesus told us we would now go to Jerusalem. He knew it was necessary to intensify his adversaries' feelings of hostility and desperation. Only through cultivating in them a sense of helpless rage would they be fully prepared for the role assigned to them. But his purposes could best be accomplished at this point not through a grand public spectacle but rather through several carefully controlled, more private confrontations.

His first such confrontation came in the form of a sudden powerful presentation of himself in the temple, proclaiming that his teaching was not from himself but from God and that if anyone truly had a desire to do the will of God, that person would know that his teaching was from God.

His words were not well received. It was no giant mental step from Jesus' words to the obvious conclusion that anyone who did not accept his teaching did not have a heart for God. It was enough. Before the situation could escalate, he dropped once again out of sight.

Twice during the week he used others to provide him with the platform for the fulfillment of his purposes. At one point, when the religious leaders spotted him teaching in the temple, they suddenly burst into his presence, dragging a woman caught in the act of adultery. With the pathetic creature cowering in shame at his feet, they demanded his opinion of what should be done with her. The law of Moses was clear; such a one should be stoned. In a brilliant response to their attempted entrapment, he confronted the accusers with their own sin. "He who is without sin among you, let him be the first to throw a stone at her." For obvious reasons the execution never took place. In silence the woman's accusers melted into the crowd. When they were gone, he turned his attention to the terrified woman before him and said simply, "From now on sin no more."

A few days later he enlisted the help of a man born blind. After Jesus restored his sight on the Sabbath Day, the man's bold proclamation of gratitude triggered a theological debate between him and the Pharisees that once again enraged Jesus' accusers and, in the end, made them look absurd. They were determined to force the formerly blind man to admit Jesus must be evil because he accomplished this wonder on the sacred day of rest. The man's response to their theological stupidity has been quoted and requoted countless times since that day: "Whether he is a sinner, I do not know; one thing I do know, that though I was blind, now I see."

But my favorite memory of the Master from that week in Jerusalem took place on the last day, the great climactic day of the Feast. The entire city was talking of little else but Jesus. Who was he? Was he of God? Was he from Satan? Was he the promised Messiah? Could he really do the things people said he could do? With the whole city talking about him, watching for him, wondering about him, he suddenly positioned himself at the top of the temple steps and raised his hands. As soon as the crowd saw him, absolute silence filled the courtyard. The words he then spoke left little doubt about his claim to leadership over the people of God. "If anyone is thirsty, let him come to me and drink. He who believes in me, as the Scripture said, 'From his innermost being will flow rivers of living water.'"

On the day of Pentecost, when the Holy Spirit was poured out upon us, I recalled that proclamation of the Lord's and understood what he was talking about. That day at the Feast I could not say I understood, but I loved the sound of it.

It was enough. Having accomplished his purposes, Jesus then pulled us back out of sight once again. We returned to Galilee for the next two months and avoided all public meetings and open confrontations with the Pharisees.

✺

Two months later we made one final visit to Jerusalem prior to the visit that culminated in Jesus' crucifixion. It was December, the Feast of Dedication, the annual cleansing of the temple altar and the rededication of the building for the coming year. His conversation with the Jews in the temple on that occasion was calculated to leave no question in their minds about his identity or his claims.

This time the Jews brought no veiled request for "a sign." They came right out and asked him, "How long will you keep us in suspense? If you are the Christ, tell us plainly."

And the Master's response was just as direct and to the point. "I told you, and you don't believe; the works that I do in my Father's name testify of me. But you don't believe because you are not of my sheep. My sheep hear my voice, and I know them, and they follow me; and I give eternal life to them, and they will never perish; and no one will snatch them out of my hand. My Father, who has given them to me, is greater than all; and no one is able to snatch them out of the Father's hand. I and the Father are one."

Their choice was clear: accept him as the Messiah, or stone him for blasphemy against the Most High God. Immediately they looked around for stones.

When I saw the stones in their hands and the hatred in their eyes, I was as terrified as I'd ever been—terrified and angry. I was terrified of the Jews, of course, but I was angry at the Master. How could he have brought us to this point? Why did he intentionally enrage these men? How could he possess so much power, so much wisdom, and yet fail to understand the techniques necessary to move himself into leadership over our nation?

His debate with his enemies continued a few minutes longer. Then, when he had accomplished what he wanted, we left. The stage was now ready. The key players had just received their final instruction. With two rows of men standing on either side of us, their fists clenching the largest stones they could find, the Master walked out of the city with us following close behind. No one threw a stone, no one spoke another word, not because they didn't want to but because they had yet to be given permission to do so by this man who did all things well.

19

Yes, I know the Master called me Satan. I know he told me
to get behind him. I also know he told me I was a stumbling
block to him. But it was really a very good day for me . . .
a very good day indeed! Let me share with you the events
that led up to that exchange between Jesus and me, and I
think it will help you better understand.

Following our dramatic exit from Jerusalem, we em-
barked on a journey that would take us more than a hundred miles away from our nation's capital and culminate
more than a year later with the Master's great pre-Passover
reentrance into the city just a few days prior to his crucifixion. That final year was a year Jesus reserved mostly for

us, his twelve, and the relatively small band of other faithfuls who continued to travel with us. It was a year when he taught us how to think as his church, how to function within society as his victorious minority. At the time we could not hear what he was saying, because we did not want to. Our minds were still fixed exclusively on the here and now. He knew that, of course. But he also knew his Spirit would bring his words back to us following his departure, and then the principles he communicated to us during those final months would become the pillars upon which he would build his church.

Rather than returning home following the Feast of Dedication, Jesus took us east to Perea and the region beyond the Jordan where the Prophet John's ministry had begun. It was a wonderful few weeks. It brought back memories of our earliest days with the Master. In that isolated region the people's attitudes toward Jesus had not been corrupted either by the selfish greed of so many in Galilee who now viewed Jesus as their own private resident miracle worker or by the vicious hatred of the Jewish national leaders. They simply welcomed him, trusted him, loved him, and bathed in his unending compassion and kindness. Though the days were long and the masses always with us, the absence of manipulation and hostility from the people around us made our tour throughout the region seem almost like a vacation. For one of our last extended times together, we were doing what we all did best—introducing people to the Master and helping them gain access to his love.

Over the course of several weeks we followed the Jordan River north through Perea and the Decapolis, then along the eastern edge of the Sea of Galilee, and finally into the villages surrounding Caesarea Philippi. We were now at least 120 miles north of Jerusalem. A number of our Jewish countrymen were once again traveling with us, and even in this distant Gentile region, Jesus' reputation preceded him. Then, just a few days following our arrival in the area, an event took place that in retrospect marked the most dramatic change we ever witnessed in Jesus' earthly ministry prior to his crucifixion. And it was an event in which I became a key player.

Of course I didn't see it coming at the time. I was excited about the success of our most recent campaign and the resurgence of Jesus' popularity. We were regaining momentum after several unfortunate setbacks and, from my perspective, some regrettable miscalculations on the part of the Master.

It is strange to remember myself back then. I knew so much and understood nothing at all. I had amassed a greater accumulation of facts about Jesus than nearly any other person alive at the time. Inside me, though, was a great chasm between the facts and the truth. It was a chasm created by my own selfish, stubborn will, a chasm I guarded and protected because I still believed I desperately needed Jesus to be what I wanted him to be. But my Lord is so good to me. While I was busy guarding and defending that chasm, he was busy building for me a bridge between the facts and the truth. Such bridges often take time to build. In my case it had taken three years, and even then it was not a solid, sturdy bridge. It was more like a rope sort of thing. It got me over to the truth, at least briefly. But it left me feeling shaky, unstable, longing for the familiar side of the chasm where I could once again pursue my own agenda. Is it surprising that following that first crossing into the truth, I almost immediately retreated once again to the other side?

It was early morning. We were getting ourselves up and going for the day. Jesus was once again in prayer a short distance from camp. Then we heard him calling for us to join him. We assumed he wanted to alert us to his plans for the day. No one anticipated the question he asked once the Twelve of us were gathered around him.

"Who do the people say that I am?"

It's funny how it was with him sometimes. As soon as he asked the question, we all knew he had a reason for asking, a reason that went far beyond the obvious desire for our input. We'd been with him much too long for any of us to have any hesitation about answering his question honestly. We told him the things we were hearing—the rumors, the theories, the guesses. "Some say you are the Prophet John risen from the dead, and others say Elijah; and others say that one of the prophets of old has risen again."

As we reported to him the things we'd been hearing, he just sat in silence, listening. Some of the suggestions he found amusing; none of them seemed to trouble him. He knew how people loved to talk. He knew, too, that the entire nation was talking about little else than the miracle worker from Galilee.

But even as we shared with him, we knew there was more to come. And it came with tremendous force in the next eight words he uttered.

"But who do you say that I am?"

And there it was, all of the sudden—the question each of us had been asking ourselves for the past three years, the question upon which everything else rested, the question we knew could have only one correct answer, but the question we were so hoping he would answer for us rather than asking us to answer for him.

Though on that particular morning, with the Twelve of us gathered around Jesus, my relationship to that question was totally, intensely personal, in the years since I have marveled at the power and simplicity of that one question. "But who do you say that I am?" There is a frantic, desperate, driving part of us that longs to answer that question with "prophet . . . teacher . . . wonderful, wise, and remarkable man." Those responses carry limited implications for ourselves. I can learn from a teacher. I can respect a prophet. I can admire a wise and wonderful man. I can take what he offers and integrate it into my own life as I see fit. But what

171

if he is more? What if he is someone to whom I owe submission, to whom I must relinquish my own agenda? What if the correct answer to that question requires not just my mind but also my will?

I don't think the Twelve of us had ever been so silent for so long in the presence of the Master. I too sat in silence. Under normal circumstances I would have instantly begun jabbering on about how he was the most incredible, remarkable, wonderful human being in existence. But something was happening within me that day, something I knew very little about. The Spirit of God was active within my mind, giving me the ability to think before I spoke. It was a strange sensation for me. And the Spirit's work did not stop there. Having gotten my attention, he then opened my eyes to see and to know with absolute certainty the truth in which I had been immersed since the first day I met the Master.

"You are the Messiah, the Son of the Living God."

It wasn't a guess. It wasn't an attempt to impress Jesus. It wasn't the first of several possible suggestions I had to offer in response to his question. It was the truth, and I *knew* it was the truth.

And a gleaming ray of hope pierced the darkness.

My little brother had been pierced briefly by that ray the first time he met the Master. But this was different. This was not simply an expression of hope and faith. This was truth based on knowledge. This was the first time a human being affirmed Jesus' true identity in his presence, based on the evidence, with absolute certainty that it was the truth. The mind of man could understand. The Spirit of God could break through the fear, the pride, the arrogance, and the selfishness surrounding our hearts and give us eyes to see. It took the Master three years just to bring us to this moment and this understanding. It was not enough to call him rabbi, teacher, prophet, healer. Unless we understood who he was, it was of little value for us to know what he said or what he did. His greatest work was yet to come. But unless we understood who was doing it and why, he could not accomplish in us the work he must accomplish.

At the time I did not understand even a tiny fraction of the significance of the words I spoke. I did, however, know the words were truth. And I knew, too, they were words that obligated me not simply to respect but to submission. I could not have this Jesus on my terms. I could not shape him into the man I wanted him to be. This was not simply a great prophet. This was the Christ—the Savior of our nation, the Son of the Living God. I could only accept him or reject him for who he was.

You don't understand why this was such a revelation to me, do you? You can't figure out why, with all his miracles, and all his power, and all his authority, it took me three years to see the truth. Well, you see, it was because . . . because he *liked* me, and because I *liked* him. I knew Messiah was coming. I knew Messiah was the hope of our nation, the hope of our world. But who could have guessed that Messiah would be my best friend? Who would have guessed that Messiah would love me and that I would love him? Who could ever have imagined that Messiah would laugh at my stupid jokes, and sit and talk with me for hours about nothing, and clearly delight in my friendship and my presence with him? Messiah was not supposed to like me, and me like him. Messiah was supposed to rule and conquer and judge and command great armies. Messiah was supposed to be absolute power. But no one had expected him to be nice, to be kind, to be gentle. Of course Messiah would care about *the nation,* but how could I have known he would care about me?

And if you were not one of the few who were there with us in those days, I think you may have to fight this battle from the other way around. For those of us who were there, we found out Jesus was nice and that he cared about us and that he really, truly loved us before we discovered that he was Messiah. You, on the other hand, may have already accepted him as Messiah, but you have not yet allowed yourself to believe that he loves you personally, deeply, eternally. You cannot imagine that he delights in your friendship and cherishes your sense of humor and values his communication with you as much as the communication he shared with King David. If so, then you also have before you a pilgrimage, a bridge to cross. Only, when the Spirit finally leads you to the other side, and the Master asks you, "Who do you say that I am?" your great and glorious breakthrough will not be, "You are Messiah," it will be, "You are my friend."

You think perhaps I had a head start, beginning with the knowledge of his love as I did. You are wrong. I did not have a head start; I simply had a different start. Having begun with the knowledge of his love, I then had to grow into the knowledge of his deity. You, perhaps, will begin with the knowledge of his deity and then must grow into the knowledge of his love. Both pilgrimages are filled with pitfalls. Neither can be successfully accomplished apart from the leadership of the Spirit. But neither, I think, is easier than the other. And both lead us in the end to the same amazing truth about the same amazing God.

When I spoke on behalf of my fellow disciples that day, I knew I spoke the truth. And it was that certainty, that conviction within me, that brought about the Lord's immediate response. "Bless you, Simon Barjona, because flesh and blood did not reveal this to you, but my Father who is in heaven. I also say to you that you are Peter, and upon this rock I will build my church; and the gates of Hades will not overpower it. I will give you the keys of the kingdom of heaven; and whatever you bind on earth shall have been bound in heaven, and whatever you loose on earth shall have been loosed in heaven."

I had never felt so wonderfully affirmed in my life as I did at that moment. I loved what he'd just done with my name and my testimony and that whole rock thing. It was such a powerful contrast for those of us who were there. Always he crafted his words with such power and precision. The name the Master gave me, Peter, does mean "rock," but it is a little rock, a rock a person can pick up and throw. But the word he used for the rock upon which he would build his church was altogether different. It meant bedrock—a massive, solid slab of immovable stone. The little rock referred to me, the one who spoke. The bedrock referred to the truth I had spoken. It was this truth—the truth about his real identity—upon which Jesus would build his church. His little rock had just been used by the Holy Spirit to communicate the bedrock upon which his church would rest. And it has been that way ever since. His little rocks—his living stones—continue to proclaim the bedrock truth upon which our hope and our salvation rest: Jesus is the Christ, the Son of the living God. I like the way my brother Paul said it in that first letter he wrote to the Christians at Corinth: "For no man can lay a foundation other than the one which is laid, which is Jesus Christ."

There was so much in those few words he spoke that morning. It was the first time we ever heard him speak of his church. At the time we had no idea what it was. The nation of Israel we understood. His kingdom we thought we understood. But what was his church? Was it us—the special group of his faithful ones within the Jewish people? Or was it something else? At the time we had no idea. But one thing we did understand: a dramatic transformation was taking place in the Master's teaching.

We were hearing words we'd never heard before. We were being given concepts we couldn't even begin to grasp: "I will build my church . . . the gates of Hades shall not overpower it . . . I will give you the keys of the kingdom of heaven . . . whatever you shall bind on earth shall be bound in heaven, and whatever you shall loose on earth shall be loosed in heaven." This was not Jesus the wise teacher sharing important principles for successful living. This was not even Jesus the great prophet drawing people to God. This was Jesus the Messiah, the Son of God, boldly proclaiming a mighty new work of God among men. He was imparting to us, his disciples, an authority that would be affirmed and secured by God himself. It was the first of many church principles Jesus would share with us throughout his final few months prior to his crucifixion. We did not understand them at the time, but following his departure, his Spirit brought them all flooding back to us, providing us with tools with which he built his church through us.

∞

It was a remarkable experience. I had been used by the Spirit of God to speak the truth. I didn't know what to do next. True, the Spirit had been able to briefly speak to me and through me, just as he had once spoken through Balaam's ass. But I was still fundamentally a creature of the flesh, and having ventured briefly into this strange new land, I quickly retreated once again into my familiar, ego-driven world of self-glorification and selfish goals for the Son of God.

My affirmation of the Master's true identity provided Jesus with the opportunity for which he had been waiting. He immediately began to prepare us for the final phase of his earthly visit. He wanted us to know exactly what was going to happen to him. He wanted us to know that *he* knew exactly what was going to happen to him. He wanted us to know that his approaching death would not be the result of bad timing or bad luck or bad choices. It would be the crowning culmination of his brief visit among us, a visit in which everything, including his death, would be accomplished by his choice, in his way, in his time. He told us he was going to return to Jerusalem. He told us he would be subjected to great suffering at the hands of the elders and the chief priests and the scribes. He then told us this suffering would culminate with his own death, but three days following his death he would rise again.

His words brought a sudden surge within me. Bolstered by the memory of my recent glowing success, I once again felt strange forces within me prompting me to speak. And speak I did! I stood up, placed my two huge hands on the Master's shoulders, and with all the boldness and confidence within me, I bellowed, "God forbid it, Lord! This shall never happen to you."

His condemnation of my lie came as quickly as had his confirmation of my truth. "Get behind me, Satan! You are a stumbling block to me; for you are not setting your mind on God's interests, but man's."

Do you think his words to me were harsh? I want you to know that what happened at that moment in my life was among the greatest expressions of kindness and love the Master ever showed me during his time among us. In those few minutes that morning, he provided me with a truth I never would have believed had I not experienced it myself, a truth that has delivered me from disaster more times than I can count in the years since the Living Word walked among us. The truth is not complicated. It is simply this: Apart from the Word of God, it is impossible for a human being to distinguish between the voice of the Holy Spirit and the voice of Satan. Twice that morning I had experienced a strong prompting from the spirit world causing me to speak. The first time that prompting had been from God himself. The second time it was from Satan. Both were real. Both had the appearance of truth to my mind. But one was consistent with the living Word of God. The other was not. One was from heaven; the other from the pit of hell.

Human flesh is so arrogant. We think because we sense the presence of the spirit world, because we know it is real, because it touches our minds and emotions, we can then distinguish between the Spirit of God and the spirits of the Evil One. The truth is, only the Word of God can give us the

177

ability to tell the difference. My Lord gave me a precious gift that day. He freed me forever from my arrogant assumption that I can accurately discern between the multitude of voices in the spirit world seeking access to my mind and my emotions. It does not matter how good it feels, how right it seems. If the voice I hear deviates in any way, at any point, from the revealed truth of my God, I know I am being deceived.

From that day forward the Master's teaching changed dramatically not only in his private communication with us but also in his public teaching. Later that afternoon he gathered together the whole group of us who were traveling with him. He talked with us about "taking up our cross every day and following him." It was another first, this reference to the cross, a reference that made no sense to us at the time. He told us if a person was determined to save his life, he would lose it, but if he was to lose his life for Jesus' sake, he would save it. He talked about a time when he would come in the glory of his Father, with his angels, and render judgment upon the whole world.

His words were as thrilling to us as they were mysterious. The time of his departure was approaching rapidly. He was not rushed. But neither was he distracted from his purpose. There was an intensity to his preparations for the final events of his time with us, an intensity evident to all of us. There were things he wanted us to know. He knew we would not yet understand, but the knowledge must be communicated and confirmed. And a few days following my confession of his true identity, he arranged for James, John, and me to receive a confirmation so dramatic, it reduced me once again to a babbling fool.

20

"Wake up, you big lug! Jesus wants us to go with him."

I opened my eyes to find John kneeling beside me. His pathetic attempt at a pleasant whisper was not my idea of the best way to greet a new day. The sun wasn't up yet, and I wasn't sure I wanted to be either. I could see Jesus and James moving around in the semidarkness. The rest of the camp was still sound asleep. I felt my strong natural aversion to morning wrestling with the exhilarating prospect of some new adventure with the Master. In just a few minutes the exhilaration won out, and soon Jesus, James, John, and I were walking out of the silent camp in the half-light of the early morning.

We walked along in silence for a while, bathing in the gentle splendor of a sunrise that promised a glorious day ahead. We had no idea where we were going. After three years with the Master, I knew he wouldn't tell us even if we asked. It wasn't his way. And I knew it didn't matter anyway. If I was going with him, I knew I was going where I wanted to go and would end up where I wanted to be.

It had been nearly a week since my identification of Jesus as the Messiah. We had been working our way farther north each day until our camp was now located at the base of Mount Hermon. The mountain was by far the highest peak in all of Palestine, towering more than nine thousand feet above the Sea of Galilee. The winter snows were now gone from its peak, but the sheer majesty of the massive mountain dominated the world in which we walked. It quickly became evident that Jesus intended to lead us at least part way up the mountain.

We hiked for several hours, picking our way upward through the dry, rocky terrain. As the sun grew warmer, beating down on my back, I found myself increasingly grateful for the early morning departure that now enabled us to climb for several hours in relative comfort. When we finally reached our destination, I was soaked with sweat, puffing, panting, and exhausted. The others seemed to have survived the climb in a little better shape than I did. I comforted myself with the thought that I had been carrying at least thirty or forty pounds more muscle up the side of that mountain than any of them. The view from our ridge made it more than worth the effort, though. James, John, and I plopped down on the ground and drank in the wonder of the world spread out before us. Jesus stood in silence at our side.

The warmth of the sun on my face felt good after the climb. I wasn't going to sleep, of course, but just a little rest in the warmth and the quiet seemed only natural. As I stretched out on my back, I noticed James and John following my lead.

I'm not sure what it was that woke us. It may have been the noise. It may have been the light. But whatever it was, I came out of a deep sleep knowing something was different. The sun was still shining, but the scene before us made our sunlit surroundings seem pale by comparison. Just a few feet away from us Jesus stood talking with two other men. The first and certainly the most dramatic aspect of the scene was Jesus' appearance. I can only describe him by saying that he was clothed in light. It wasn't just that he was glowing. It certainly wasn't as if a brilliant light was being pointed at him. It was more as if he had become light himself. We could still see his clothing, but his entire being was bathed in a radiance unlike anything I had ever seen before. I have seen the metal craftsmen heat iron and bronze until it glows white-hot. It was something like that without the heat or the fear of injury.

For several minutes we sat in silence listening to the conversation taking place before us. The two men were also clothed in light. Jesus addressed them by name as they talked—Moses and Elijah! They were talking about the preparations being made for what Jesus referred to as his "departure from Jerusalem" in the near future.

It was the strangest sensation, sitting there, listening to them talk. Have you ever seen a child attempt to converse with a group of adults, believing in his childish mind that he is communicating on their level, being accepted as an equal in their eyes? As I listened to Jesus speaking with Moses and Elijah, I suddenly felt like that child. For the past three years, I had been talking with Jesus, living with Jesus, offering him suggestions and advice. I knew we were not really equals, but I allowed myself to believe we were not far from it. Had he not chosen me to be with him? Had he not equipped me with the ability to do some of his works? Did he not genuinely delight in my friendship? And yet now, watching Jesus engaged in conversation with these two supernatural personalities, discussing issues I could not even begin to grasp, cloaked in some sort of heavenly brilliance, I suddenly saw my own infinitesimal stature next to the Master.

We listened to Jesus' conversation with his visitors until it ended and Moses and Elijah departed. The silence following their departure was more than I could take. I don't do well with silence. Jesus said nothing. James and John just sat there in silence. It was up to me to fill the void.

I sprang to my feet and babbled, "Master, this is great! If you want, we can make three tabernacles here: one for you, and one for Moses, and one for Elijah."

Even as I was speaking, a sort of radiant cloud suddenly appeared just above our heads, blocking the sun while at the same time filling our world with light. It dropped over our heads, swallowing us instantly in its heavy, glowing interior. Though we were only a few feet apart, I could no longer see Jesus, James, or John. We each found ourselves in total isolation, and yet I had never felt less isolated in my life, for the cloud itself contained a presence that somehow communicated itself to every sense and sensation of my being. It was at the same time terrifying and thrilling, as if I was somehow being immersed in an endless sea of liquid *life*. I dropped to the ground and buried my face in the dirt.

Then a voice came from the midst of the cloud. Have you ever heard thunder? I mean really heard it—heard it explode just above your head, causing the ground to shake under your feet, obliterating all other sounds and senses? Now can you imagine what it would be like for that thunder to suddenly form itself into words and speak? If so, then you have some sense of what we heard.

The words and their meaning were unmistakable. "This is my Son, my chosen one; listen to him!"

Then, as quickly as it had come, the cloud departed, leaving us in absolute silence. This time, though, I had no desire to speak. Everything that needed to be said had just been said by God himself. For several minutes we continued to lie there, our faces to the ground. When we finally looked up, we saw only Jesus standing next to us, looking as human and safe and wonderful as we'd ever seen him.

It changed me, of course, that morning on the mountain, but not in the way you might think. When it was all over, I was still just "Simon Peter," the man. In fact, even more so, if you know what I mean. Having entered into the very presence of God himself, and having heard him speak to me in audible words, with a voice that could create or destroy anything, everything at will, I came away profoundly aware of my own finite humanity. Until that day I had spent my life comparing myself to others, using what I chose to see in them to feed my own pride and arrogance. Look at my strength! Look at my skill! Listen to my bellowing voice! I am great among men!

But those few seconds in the presence of God provided me with a mirror in which I caught a fleeting glimpse of my real self. For the first time I understood Isaiah's agonized cry when he too entered into the presence of God. "Woe is me, for I am ruined! Because I am a man of unclean lips, and I live among a people of unclean lips; for my eyes have seen the King, the Lord of hosts." Isaiah came away overwhelmed with his sinfulness. I came away overwhelmed with my arrogance. It wasn't that I saw myself as having no value. Indeed, it was exactly the opposite. Everything that happened that day between myself and my Creator confirmed my incredible value to him. But it was a value absolutely unrelated to anything I had ever done or ever could do. I had value to him simply because I had value to him, and nothing I could ever do or not do would alter that reality. I left the mountain that morning knowing I was a tiny speck of God's infinite creation yet a speck who had incomprehensible value to him.

Those few minutes in the presence of God provided me with another gift as well. Having seen the real thing, I can now so easily recognize the counterfeits. There are so many games used by Satan to cheat and rob the people of God. One of his most effective seems to be inviting God's people into a kind of spirit-world communication that plays on their egos and bolsters their pride. He feeds them messages and offers them experiences that seem to confirm for them an elevated status in the family of God. They come away feeling as though they have become skilled in the ways of the spirit world, qualified to interact with the presence of God at will.

To those who have been so deceived, let me speak the truth. Entrance into the presence of the real God, the living God, is the most humbling of all human experiences. If you find yourself coming away from spirit-world exploration focused on yourself and what you've learned and what you've experienced, seeing yourself as a select member of a privileged few within the family of God, then you have simply been deceived into playing ego games with the devil. For, you see, when we enter into the real thing, with the real God, we do not come away focused on ourselves. We come away overwhelmed with *him*, and with his Son, Jesus Christ. And if we see ourselves at all, we see only our unworthiness and the inexplicable wonder that he loves us as he does.

⸎

The three of us bombarded Jesus with questions all the way down the mountainside that day. What did this mean? What did that mean? What did he want us to do with what we had just experienced?

Many of his answers made no sense to us at the time. Until we finally were able to understand his departure, none of the other pieces seemed to fit. One thing we did understand, however. For now he wanted us to keep silent about what we had seen. He told us we were to say nothing to anyone until after he rose from the dead. When we pressed him further about what he meant by "rising from the dead," he simply assured us that when we saw it, we would know.

184

21

I have heard the throbbing cadence of the taskmaster's drum pounding out the rhythm for those chained to the oars on the Roman galleys as they glide past on the Great Sea. There was such a cadence to our final months with the Master. Though in truth it had always been there, it was far beyond my range of hearing until the morning I called him "Messiah." And even then I could not yet hear it with my mind. But I believe my spirit sensed it—a distant, steady, relentless rhythm being drummed by an Almighty Hand upon the foundation of the world with two massive rough-hewn timbers formed in the shape of a cross.

The rhythm marked our pace and our destination—a hill just outside Jerusalem, a hill called Golgotha. Each step the Master took coincided perfectly with the cadence. With each step the volume increased a decibel or two. And each step brought him closer to the fulfillment of the purpose for which he came. I can hear it now, looking back with the mind of the Spirit. At the time I refused to accept the reality of its existence until I stood before that cross and felt the earth shake under my feet, saw the sun driven from the sky, and heard the hammered blows driving nails through the flesh of the Son of God.

But that day was still several months away, and Jesus had much he wanted to accomplish in those final months. The following day we packed up our camp and headed back to Galilee. He kept us close to himself as we traveled south, but his conversations with us were unlike the ones we were accustomed to. He wanted us educated. He wanted us prepared. He wanted us equipped with the truth. "Let these words sink into your ears; for the Son of Man is going to be delivered into the hands of men, and they will kill him, and he will be raised on the third day."

It was hard stuff for us, in fact, impossible stuff at the time. It grieved us deeply to hear him speak this way. We found it impossible to think of Jesus dying. Though I kept my mouth shut, every one of those reaffirmations of his approaching death brought within me a renewed determination to make certain no such thing would ever take place. He would live or I would die attempting to save him.

Our return to Capernaum was unlike any we had known before. The miracle worker from Galilee was not open for business as usual. Another Passover Feast came and went during our travels in the north. Jesus' absence from Jerusalem at the feast, combined with his suspension of any additional mass meetings throughout Galilee, helped lull his enemies into believing he was complying with their wishes while at the same time provided Jesus with the time he needed for his final preparations.

For the next several weeks he spent a great deal of time with us alone in his house or walking with us by the sea. The masses were gone now, but there were still several hundred loyal followers who stayed close to us. Together we listened and learned. We heard and remembered his words to us then, though we did not understand them until after his departure. He was giving us the mental pillars for life in the Spirit. Who is greatest among us? It is the one who serves. Entrance into the kingdom comes only through humbling ourselves and entering as little children. We are the salt of the earth. Our Lord seeks us as a loving shepherd seeks his favorite little lamb lost on the mountainside. How often should we forgive? (I thought perhaps as many as seven times. He thought perhaps seventy times seven would be better.) If your brother offends you, go to him in private. Forgive others as we ourselves have been forgiven by our heavenly Father.

He was redefining our understanding of success and failure. Success in the kingdom of God came not from fighting for myself and my supremacy, it came from fighting for my brothers and sisters, fighting for my relationship with them, fighting for their health and strength and survival. He was teaching us how to act toward one another as he himself was acting toward us. He was teaching us what it means to love.

Following our several weeks of semiseclusion in Galilee, we returned to Perea beyond the Jordan for one final public teaching tour in that area. The people were thrilled at his return and responsive to his ministry beyond even our high expectations. They loved him, they honored him, they listened to him, and they reminded all of us just a little bit of what he could have given to our nation if only our hearts had been open to him.

∽

Then, from Perea, he turned his face one last time toward Jerusalem. The Lamb of God was coming, at the time and place chosen by him, to offer himself as the perfect sacrifice for the sins of the world. He would stage his final entrance in the city of David in such a way as to generate blinding terror in our nation's leadership. He would drive them to perform their role in his death at a time and place they never would have willingly selected for themselves. Jesus' offer of himself would be no hushed-up, hidden, convenient removal of an unsubmissive country rebel. His death would be a noisy, bloody, brutal affair, witnessed by thousands, reported in vivid detail throughout the land.

What would it take to create such terror in his enemies? What if they witnessed what appeared to be the entire nation marching alongside the Master as he entered Jerusalem, flinging their clothing on the ground before him, proclaiming him their rightful king? What if his name and his praises flowed from the lips of every pilgrim in the city at the great annual Feast of the Passover?

Jesus' preparations for his final entrance into the city of David began with the most highly organized and structured teaching tour of his earthly ministry. He began by designating and educating thirty-five teams of two. He equipped all seventy of us with the ability to heal and with authority over the demonic world. He then assigned each team to specific towns and villages throughout the nation, even providing us with the words we were to speak. We were to be his heralds, proclaiming the coming of the king, promising his personal appearance, and presenting the people of Israel with a taste of what he would bring when he came.

It all looked so different to me at the time, of course, seeing only through the eyes of the flesh. I saw the surging wave of Jesus' popularity in response first to our arrival and then to his. I heard the open calls for his kingship. I felt the resurgence of my own hopes for Jesus' rise to political power. It all seemed so right, so powerful, so unstoppable.

Even as he placed the final touches on his public popularity, he continued to equip us with the truth. He was going to Jerusalem. He would be killed when he arrived. Following his death he would come back to life. But with such a wave of popularity surrounding us, his words seemed like foolishness. What he was prophesying simply could not happen. It was obvious to all of us. After nearly four years of careful preparation, the nation was finally ours for the taking.

⌒×

We all went out. We all met with spectacular success. And we all came back filled with jubilant optimism for ourselves and for our future with the Master. Following our return Jesus departed with us almost immediately on his final great tour throughout the nation. I will never forget the words with which Jesus began that final tour. They were words spoken by him before but never with such urgency. They were words chosen to publicly proclaim his heart's longing for his beloved Israel. "Come to me, all who are weary and heavy-laden, and I will give you rest. Take my yoke upon you and learn from me, for I am gentle and humble in heart, and you will find rest for your souls."

And come they did, by the thousands! His public teaching throughout those final weeks captivated our nation as never before. He taught us from the example of the good Samaritan. He showed us how to pray. He blasted the unresponsive multitudes in those cities where his greatest works had been done. He warned us repeatedly of the contagious corruption of the religious spirit within the Pharisees and Sadducees. He promised special recognition for those who confessed him before men and warned us that the message of himself would sometimes bring great divisiveness between people. He told us the story of a second son who squandered his inheritance, of a father who waited eagerly for the son's return, and of an elder brother who hated the wayward boy's reconciliation with the father when it came.

With parable after parable and teaching after teaching, he fed us sweet, rich gulps of truth. Some of it was designed to equip us for what would shortly take place in Jerusalem. Some of it prepared us for the life we now live in his Spirit. Some of it even offered us a glimpse into the events surrounding his future return.

Some of it, however, was designed to inflame and infuriate our nation's religious leadership. When a group of scribes and Pharisees came asking for a sign from heaven, Jesus' response left no room for misinterpretation: "An evil and adulterous generation craves for a sign; but no sign will be given to it except the sign of Jonah the prophet; for just as Jonah was three days and three nights in the belly of the sea monster, so the Son of Man will be three days and three nights in the heart of the earth." He then went on to tell them that, at the final judgment, the men of Nineveh and the Queen of the South would stand up and condemn this generation because Nineveh repented in response to Jonah's preaching, and the Queen of the South came from the ends of the earth to hear the wisdom of Solomon; and yet something far greater than Jonah or Solomon was here.

When another Pharisee challenged him for failing to follow the ceremonial cleansing ritual before eating, Jesus responded with a swift public rebuke condemning the Pharisees for their careful cleaning of the outsides of cups and platters while their own hearts were filled with robbery and wickedness. He said they carefully tithed exactly 10 percent of the little plants growing in their gardens yet disregarded justice and the love of God. He then went on to condemn them for their love of public praise and affirmation, warning his listeners that these men were like "concealed tombs," filled with death and decay.

And so the battle raged on. The lines between the two sides were clearly drawn. There could be no compromise, no reconciliation. With blow after blow Jesus drove his adversaries deeper and deeper into their rage and terror. And all the time his popularity with the masses intensified.

Then came that day—the incredible, amazing, glorious day of Jesus' return to Jerusalem. Can you understand what it was like for those of us who were there? This was our ultimate victory. This was the fulfillment of all our hopes. Never had I known such unbounded exhilaration. Everything I wanted, everything I longed for, everything I knew I needed for happiness and success and total fulfillment seemed suddenly within my reach. Of course I knew those who held political power hated Jesus. But I knew, too, the power of the multitude surrounding us. And I certainly knew the power of the Master himself. Why, just a few days earlier, had we not all stood outside the tomb of Lazarus, a fellow disciple dead and buried four days earlier, and watched Jesus call his friend back to life? Who could contend with such power, such authority? Who would dare try?

But let me back up a step and walk with you through that day. The Passover Feast was now just six days away. People were pouring into the city by the thousands. It is impossible for me to adequately describe the sense of anticipation surrounding the Master at that point in his ministry. Our final extended sweep throughout the nation, combined with the rumors and testimonies of the thousands whose lives had been touched by Jesus during the past four years, made him the supreme topic of conversation throughout

Israel. And the tension was only intensified by the public proclamation of the chief priest's warning to the people about Jesus, demanding that anyone who knew where he was should report it to him immediately. The entire nation waited, and watched, and wondered if he would come.

We spent the night in Bethany, a village about two miles outside of Jerusalem, at the house of Simon the Leper. We still called him "Simon the Leper" even though several years earlier Jesus' healing touch made the title untrue. Simon himself loved the title. Indeed, he refused to let it go because it provided him with an ever present reminder of the life he would have led had it not been for the Master.

Lazarus was with us, as were his sisters, Mary and Martha. Word of Jesus' arrival spread quickly, and a private supper soon turned into a grand public celebration. The house was packed with disciples and pilgrims and neighbors and friends. The food and laughter and festivities went on until late in the night.

The only blot on the evening came when Judas lashed out at Lazarus's sister, Mary, because she anointed Jesus with a costly, fragrant ointment partway through the evening. He wanted to know why this ointment had not been sold and the money given to the poor. At the time it sounded like a genuine expression of compassion. For the past three years, Judas had been our group treasurer. I don't know when he first began stealing from the donations entrusted into his care by the faithful followers who supported the Master's work. None of us were aware of it until after his death. Nor do I know to what degree his lust for money was intensified by his frustration over the Master's refusal to pursue Judas's personal program for success.

The awkwardness was soon put to rest, however, by Jesus' strong words of affirmation and appreciation to Mary for her expression of kindness and love. He did say her anointing was in preparation for his burial, but we all once again tactfully refused to respond to what at the time we saw as yet another reference to an event that could not and would not take place. Within a few minutes the festive atmosphere resumed and, apart from the unnoticed absence of an angry and humiliated Judas, continued for several more hours.

We all got to sleep late but rose with the sun a few hours later. This was the day! We all knew it. This was the day Jesus would enter Jerusalem. We didn't know what to expect. But we knew it had to be good. Even here in Bethany several hundred Passover pilgrims waited, refusing to complete their journey into the city until they could complete it with the Master.

Following our morning meal we gathered our belongings together and began walking the few remaining miles into Jerusalem. When we moved, so did those waiting for Jesus' departure. The road was packed with travelers, though, and it wasn't long before Jesus was lost to sight by all but those of us immediately surrounding him.

We walked for less than an hour, stopping just outside Bethphage, the last small community before entrance into the city. We could now feel the warmth of the morning sun on our faces. Jesus pulled us out of the stream of travelers and gave Andrew and James some private instructions. They left the group, and the rest of us sat down by the side of the road and waited.

Within a few minutes Andrew and James returned leading a donkey, followed by her colt. When I asked Andrew where they got the animals, he told me they were tied in the exact spot the Master told them to look. Jesus wanted no misunderstanding. There was no chance, no luck, no accident in what was about to take place. It had all been planned, prepared beforehand by the Father.

We placed our outer garments on the colt. Then Jesus mounted the makeshift saddle, and we resumed our journey into the city, leading the donkey so that the colt would follow.

I'm still not sure why Jesus' appearance on that colt caused the people to respond the way they did. Part of it, of course, was simply the fact that he now sat elevated above his fellow travelers, and they could see him. Part of it, too, was the pent-up anticipation of his arrival. But it was more than that. For the first time since King David himself, our nation finally had the hope of a leader who came from our world, who understood our lives, a man who rode on a little donkey. He was not high and lofty and elevated in his royal carriage, surrounded by guards. He was right here with us, next to us, in the same dirt and dust and odors and heat in which we lived. Here at last was a man we could trust, a man we would follow. Here at last was a man worthy of our adoration. In a matter of minutes, people were flinging their clothing in front of the colt and ripping branches from the trees to pave his way. Cries of "Hosanna! Praise him who comes in the name of the Lord, the king of Israel!" ran through the crowd.

The road between us and the gates of the city was already one solid mass of humanity. But as the cries of Jesus' approach flew ahead of us, all travel stopped in anticipation of the coming king. What began as a caravan suddenly transformed into a parade. Thousands of Israelites moved to the sides of the road and waited for the arrival of the great man astride his tiny mount. Hands reached out to touch him from all directions as we passed. The shouts and cheers and affirmations of praise thundered around us: "Save us, Son of David!" "Praise him who comes in the name of the Lord!" "Hosanna in the highest!" "Praise to the coming kingdom of our father David!"

The procession came to an abrupt halt when several irate Pharisees blasted through the throng and blocked the pathway before us. For a few seconds they glared up at Jesus, waiting until they could be heard. When the crowd recognized that some sort of confrontation was taking place, silence quickly spread throughout the mob. When the leader of the delegation knew he could be heard, he spoke, rage and indignation oozing from his words. "Teacher, rebuke your disciples!"

The thought of Jesus receiving and accepting such proclamations was more than they could take. Jesus must be stopped. This mob must be silenced.

The crowd strained to hear Jesus' response. Would he submit? Would he dismount? Would he apologize? Even now, as I recall the Master's response, I can feel the thrill of it running through me. "I tell you," he responded, "if these become silent, the stones will cry out!" Jesus' thinly veiled reference to Habakkuk's prophetic promise of what would happen if truth and righteousness were not affirmed within the nation of Israel brought a deafening explosion of jubilation from the multitude. In that same prophetic passage, Habakkuk went on to say, "For the earth will be filled with the knowledge of the glory of the Lord, as the waters cover the sea." These Pharisees knew their prophetic writings, as did many of the rest of us. We knew the passage, we knew the promises, and we felt the first mighty wave of that knowledge pouring over us, bathing us in hope while drowning these Pharisees in terror.

The Pharisees crept aside; the procession resumed once again. Andrew led the donkey; I marched by the Master's side drunk with the exhilaration of what was happening around us. Nothing would stop us now. How could I ever have doubted the Master's wisdom? How could I have doubted his flawless sense of timing? This was the perfect moment, the appointed time for Jesus' ultimate victory. It was all I could do to maintain the facade of reserved, dignified detachment I considered appropriate for the king's second in command. I longed to grab palm branches in both hands and lunge through the crowd, screaming, "WE WIN! WE WIN! WE WIN!"

The procession was slow, but what did it matter? We were crowning the new king of Israel. If it took all day to do it, what difference did it make? As long as the cheering continued, as long as I held my place by the Master's side, my flesh wallowed in it all.

At one point Jesus stopped the procession and stared for several minutes in silence at Jerusalem spread out before him. Tears streamed down his cheeks as he looked at the city in which he would soon be crucified. I knew the Master well enough to know he was not attempting to "stage" anything. The tears were real. The pain was real. He hurt for those he loved. At the time, however, I do remember thinking what a great added touch this was to Jesus' overall image. Here was royalty, humility, and now deep, rich compassion all combined in one perfect person. The words he spoke as he sat there, looking over the city of David, disturbed me, but I took comfort in knowing only a few of us were able to hear them. "If you had known this day the things which make for peace! But now they have been hidden from your eyes. For the days will come upon you when your enemies will throw up a barricade against you, and surround you and hem you in on every side, and they will level you to the ground and your children within you, and they will not leave in you one stone upon another, because you did not recognize the time of your visitation."

These were not the words of a king riding to his coronation. Indeed, they sounded very much like a prophetic curse placed upon a city that had rejected him. But where was the rejection? Certainly not here, not now. I dismissed his words as misguided pessimism, just as I had dismissed his persistent proclamations of his own approaching death. It was time Jesus faced the truth. Couldn't he hear the cries of those around him? Didn't he understand? This crowd was his. This city was his. This nation was his. And soon this Roman Empire would be his as well. Speak what he would, there could be no denying the obvious reality of what was taking place around us. Stand back, world! Here comes your king!

22

It was a week unlike any other, a week in which victory and defeat, heaven and hell, exhilaration and utter despair stood side by side and marched against me. It was a week in which the world I wanted seemed at last within my grasp, a week in which my flesh guzzled sweet, rich gulps of hope, staggering under its intoxication. It was a week in which blinding light turned to blackness and despair. It was a week in which everything I longed for, everything I sought, everything I trusted surged into my life in one great, glorious climax and failed me utterly. It was a week in which the Master plunged his hand deep within me, grabbed my heart of flesh, and crushed it in his almighty grip. It was a week I would not exchange for all the wealth in the world, nor choose to live again for the same compensation.

$\backsim$

Jesus' dramatic entrance into the city turned out to be an all-day affair. The entire city knew of our arrival long before we passed through the gates. Not since King David himself returned victorious from battle had such unbounded exhilaration filled these streets.

Jesus instructed us to lead his mount to the temple. By the time we finally arrived, however, it was late afternoon. None of us knew what the Master would do. In the end, however, he simply dismounted and did nothing. For a few minutes he stood in silence at the base of the temple steps and looked up at the structure before him. Then he turned and led us out of the city and back to Bethany for the night.

For my part it was enough. Of course I was hoping for some sort of glorious final coronation ceremony to culminate the day. But I was content. A great barrier had finally been breached. For the first time since his public ministry began, Jesus not only accepted but encouraged the people's acknowledgment of his rightful kingship. He knew what they wanted. He heard their words, "Blessed is he who comes in the name of the Lord, even the king of Israel!" He alone selected this time and staged this entrance into the city. Having acknowledged their nomination, could his coronation be far behind? It had been a good day. The Master was meeting my expectations. I would allow him the right to coordinate and finalize the remaining details in his great victory.

Conquering a nation, even without violence, is exhausting work. We closed the doors that night, ate our evening meal, and then dropped our weary bodies into bed for a few hours' sleep.

The Master was up with the sunrise, and then so were we. Following our morning meal we once again reentered the city. This time we all traveled on foot, however, without the public procession and recognition. It was mid-morning by the time we reached the temple courtyard. The grounds were once again packed with pilgrims busy about the business of exchanging their Roman currency for temple money, purchasing their "approved" sacrificial animals, and arranging for the sacrifices to be offered by the priests. As I inched my way through the crowd, trying to keep an eye on the Master ahead of me, I couldn't help but recall the last time I'd been in this situation. Had it really been three years since the day I saw the Master explode in anger against these money changers? I was still fighting him then, terrified of his intrusion into my life. How could I have changed so much? And how could these people around me have changed so little? The money still clinked. The stalls still held the overpriced animals. The gleam of greed still glowed in the eyes of those who stole from their countrymen in the name of God.

Then, without warning, it happened again. A table upended, crashing to the floor. Money rolling everywhere, people screaming, pushing, crawling, grabbing, shoving little treasures into their pockets. A second table and a third came crashing down. Terrified money changers ran for cover. Excited pilgrims clutched and cheered. Animal cages flew open. Birds and bullocks and goats added to the chaos.

This time, however, as the circle widened around the Master, giving him room for his work, there was a difference. This time everyone knew who he was. I heard delighted comments buzzing around me. "Jesus is doing it to them again!" "He's back! And look at the cowards run!"

There was no question whose side the crowd took. And there was no question about the terror in the eyes of the temple leadership. Three years earlier the wrath of a country nobody being poured out on their greed was a temporary, irritating inconvenience. Now, with his name and his praises flowing from the mouths of every pilgrim in the city, Jesus was a significant threat to their very existence.

When the confusion finally subsided enough for Jesus' words to be heard, he looked directly at the cluster of the temple merchants cowering in one corner of the courtyard and said, "Isn't it written, 'My house shall be called a house of prayer for all the nations'? But you have made it a robbers' den."

No delegation attempted to pacify him this time, however. No soothing voice tried to reason with him. They all knew this was open warfare, and the cheering multitude on the Master's side gave him a temporary advantage. Business was over for the day. In fact, business was over for the week. Following his temple cleansing, Jesus claimed the courtyard for himself. He spent the rest of the day teaching the people until late in the evening.

It was dark when we finally made it back to Bethany for the night. Once again I gave the Master acceptable marks for the day. I did feel as though he was not using the power of the people to his greatest advantage, and he had yet to level a decisive blow against those who held political power. But there was still time. The city would be filled with Passover pilgrims for another week. Perhaps he was planning his final attack for the feast day itself.

$\backsim\!\!\!\times$

If I had the time, I would walk with you through every detail of those final few days. I would let you listen with me to the helpless frustration of those who attempted to engage the Master in open debate as he taught in the temple throughout the week. I would share with you his public proclamations warning all who listened to beware of the scribes and Pharisees, calling them hypocrites, serpents, the offspring of vipers. I would share with you the remarkable prophecies he shared with us concerning the future of Jerusalem and the signs surrounding his own return. If I had the time . . . but the time allotted to me is now nearly at an end. Besides, my dear brother Matthew, the meticulous Dr. Luke with all his notes and interviews and research, and my frequent traveling companion, Mark, have already written excellent accounts of those final days.

It is better for me to limit myself to the events that bear directly upon the Master's work within me. It is a tiny part of the whole, I know, but it is the part assigned to me, the part I know the best.

My frustration with the Master continued to increase throughout the remainder of the week. Rather than capitalizing on the surge of popular support surrounding our entrance into the city, Jesus spent much of his time publicly humiliating and attacking his enemies. At the time it appeared to me to be the worst possible strategy. By the end of the week Jesus had successfully driven them into a terrified, blinding rage, while at the same time doing nothing to remove them from their positions of power. By the time we gathered together for that final Passover meal, I urgently hoped the Master would allow us to use this private meeting to develop an effective strategy for defeating our foes.

I was not the only concerned member of the group. The truth is, all twelve of us went into that supper bickering over the merits and difficulties of a dozen different possible schemes for moving the Master into power. The debates degenerated into heated arguments over who had the greater claim to leadership within the group. By the time we all sat down to eat, we were a gathering of grumpy, stubborn men using surface irritation with one another to mask our much deeper frustration with Jesus for his refusal to use his powers and charisma to catapult us into victory.

I was sitting between James and John, still arguing with them about my obvious, rightful role as Jesus' second in command, when it happened. I was completely unaware of the growing silence in the room until I suddenly realized my voice was the only one left still blasting forth. Even then, in my arrogance, I at first assumed my fellow disciples were finally submitting to my leadership, heeding my words. Then I turned and saw him, a towel tied around his waist, his hands resting on a bowl of water, as he knelt before Andrew at the end of the row of his disciples.

We all watched, dumbfounded, as Jesus removed Andrew's sandals and gently placed each foot into the water, washed it thoroughly, then dried it in turn. He then moved to the next man in line, and the next, and the next.

No one spoke a word. Here was our Master, our King, scooting along on his hands and knees, fulfilling the role in our society reserved for the most lowly household servant. For several minutes the only sound in the room was the gentle lapping of the water in the bowl as foot after foot was placed in, cleaned, removed, and carefully dried, followed then by the sound of Jesus shuffling along the floor to his next disciple.

When he finally came to me, I could stand it no longer. As he knelt before me, I reached out, placed my hands on his forearms, and said, "Lord, are you going to wash my feet?"

He knew it was not a question so much as it was a challenge. This was terrible. The thought of him serving me in this way went against everything I thought I wanted him to be. I wanted my King to go forth in his almighty power, conquering his enemies, with me by his side. I wanted lightning bolts flashing around him, with the multitudes kneeling before him in submissive adoration. To see him now, kneeling before me, a bowl of muddied water in his hands, a soiled towel around his waist, struck at the cornerstones of my existence. I had no way of knowing that in less than twenty-four hours, he would be offering himself not just to me and to a handful of other disciples but to the entire human race, presenting not just a bowl of water but his own blood, seeking to cleanse not just the dust from our feet but all the accumulated moral filth and sewage of the ages from our lives.

He looked up at me and said simply, "You do not realize what I am doing now, but the time will come when you will understand."

His answer didn't satisfy me, and I drew back my feet as I bellowed, "You will never wash my feet!"

The words he spoke in response, however, caused me to recant instantly. "If I don't wash you, you have no part with me."

There it was, the central message of his life in a single statement: "If I don't wash you, you have no part with me."

I didn't understand it at the time, of course, as my response made abundantly clear. "Lord, don't just wash my feet, but also my hands and my head."

His face broke into a grin, and he said, "He who has had a bath only needs to wash his feet to be completely clean; and you are clean." He paused for a moment, then went on to say, "But not all of you."

I know now his final statement was a reference to Judas. I really believe the unmistakable message Jesus communicated to us through his washing our feet before that meal proved to be the final factor in the poisoning of Judas's heart against the Master. When Judas saw Jesus shuffling along the floor, calling each of us to an attitude of submissive servanthood, Judas gave up altogether. It was partly an excuse, of course. His greed was also a major factor. But Jesus' words and actions that evening made it clear to all of us that he had no intention of conquering our nation in the way we felt it needed to be conquered. This was not the Messiah Judas was hoping for, and it was certainly not the Messiah he was willing to accept.

In the years since Jesus' departure, the words he spoke to us at our final meal together prior to his crucifixion have become the foundation upon which the Holy Spirit has rebuilt my life. You may have read his words as they are preserved for us in the accounts circulating among us and wondered at how we could have been there and heard Jesus speaking and not understood at the time exactly what was about to happen and why. In clear, simple terms Jesus handed us his entire life, message, and purpose. He offered us a powerful visual illustration of his own approaching death through a small loaf of bread "broken for us" and a cup of wine poured out for us, the New Covenant in his blood. To accompany the New Covenant, he then offered us his New Commandment that we love one another just as he loved us.

He told us plainly he was about to die. He told us what we had already come to know in our hearts, that he and the Father are one. "He who has seen me has seen the Father." He promised us peace and told us that in the future we would share with him the same type of relationship that a branch shares with a vine. He himself would be our source of life and nourishment. All we had to do was abide in him. He called us his friends.

He warned us, too, of what was ahead. They hated him; they would hate us as well. But he was not going to leave us as orphans. He was going to send us the helper who would testify of him, convicting the world of the truth about himself. He told us we were about to enter intense grief but promised that our grief would be turned to joy. He was going to the Father. At the proper time we would join him. He then ended by telling us he shared these things with us so that in him we might have peace. He said that in the world we would have tribulation but that we were to take courage because he had overcome the world.

Then he prayed for us and for all those who would come to believe in him through us. It was a prayer unlike any other I had ever heard, a prayer that poured out from the very heart of God. He talked about the Father "glorifying" him through his approaching death. He affirmed his absolute authority over all men and his right to give eternal life to all those who came to him. He prayed for our unity in him and for our love for one another. He prayed that we would not be destroyed by evil and that the glory which he had known would now rest upon us.

When the Master finished praying, for a few minutes we all just sat in silence. No one spoke because there was nothing more to say. As I sat there with the Master, surrounded by my fellow disciples, I was filled with such intense, conflicting emotions. I felt honored as never before in my life, honored as only God himself can honor a man. But at the same time I felt a deep loneliness and apprehension. Though I did not yet understand the Master's words, it was impossible to hear them without anticipating the arrival of some great darkness over the earth. I did not know what was coming. I only knew I would do whatever I could, at whatever cost to myself, to guard and protect my Master. As he had loved me, so I would love him. This I could do. This I would do, no matter what.

❦

You, of course, now read the account of that evening knowing of the events that came upon us immediately following our final meal together. You know of the betrayal and of the hideous midnight mockery of a trial. You know of Jesus' crucifixion and death. You know, too, of his resurrection, his departure, and his gift of the Holy Spirit to each of his own. But can you imagine what it would have been like for me, without that knowledge, knowing nothing of God's great plan and purpose for his people, believing all I had and could ever hope for was Jesus with me in the flesh? Are you his child? If so, then it may help you to understand me at that point in my life by recalling yourself as you listened to the Master's words in the days of your flesh, before his Spirit opened your heart to his truth. Do you remember the way in which his words had no power to touch your soul, to change your life? At the time I simply could not hear what he was saying. Only in retrospect did it take on life and power. I certainly do not offer this as an excuse but only as an explanation. My supreme confidence that night still rested solely on my flesh. I knew nothing else. My love for the Master was unquestioned, but my ability to express that love was chained to the limited and wholly inadequate resources of my flesh—my personality, my strength of will, my fluctuating emotions of the moment. At the time I was certain it was an adequate basis for service. It was all I had ever known. How could I think otherwise?

Of course, there was that other matter—the Lord's prophetic announcement of my denials. "This very night, before a rooster crows, you will deny me three times." At the time, however, the Master's prophecy only caused my flesh to surge more intensely within me. I would remain true! I have made my choice! My resolve is absolute! Bring on the world! I will stand firm or perish in the process!

Jesus knew I would respond that way, of course. He knew my flesh perfectly. And he knew, too, that I knew my flesh not at all. That prophecy was his final gift to me prior to the crucifixion. It was the perfect mirror in which I would at last be able to see the reflection of myself.

One final touch was needed before our meeting ended. The flesh always needs an alternative to the reality of God. It needs a tool, a resource, a means by which it believes it can fulfill the work of God. My flesh was about to protect the Son of God from his approaching death. Very well, then my flesh would need a resource, a point of security. He knew

I had it—my sword, my alternative to the reality of God. I'd been carrying it secretly all week, just in case. Now he wanted me to bring it out in the open, to wave it about boldly so that everyone could see the true source of my security. Just prior to our departure, he forced my hand by saying, "Whoever has no sword is to sell his coat and buy one."

It was the moment my flesh had been waiting for. Immediately I reached under my cloak and drew out my weapon. Now at last they all could see the depth of my resolve. To my surprise, Simon the Zealot also produced a sword. As I stood there, brandishing the blade above my head, everyone within reach of my flailing arm jumped out of the way. It was obvious to all that my zeal vastly exceeded my skill with the thing. I looked at the Master; he looked at me and said simply, "It is enough."

We sang a hymn and then followed Jesus into the darkened streets, then out of the city to Gethsemane, a grove of olive trees at the base of the Mount of Olives just outside Jerusalem. The grove was quiet, secluded, and carefully manicured. We all knew it as one of Jesus' favorite places of retreat from the noise and chaos of the city.

2 3

The few lanterns we carried with us guided our way through the darkness. When we reached the garden, Jesus asked James, John, and me to walk with him a little farther into the grove. He wanted to pray, but he did not want to be alone. Even in the dim light it was impossible to miss the anguish in his eyes. He was not afraid, but he was clearly in the grips of some deep inner turmoil. He left the three of us with the lantern and walked a few more paces into the darkness, then dropped first to his knees, and then to his face as he prayed. We could hear him easily, praying sometimes with words, sometimes only with deep, agonizing groans. "My Father, if it is possible, let this cup pass from me; yet not as I will, but as you will."

For some fifteen or twenty minutes, the three of us stood in silence within our little bubble of light that valiantly held back the sea of darkness around us. It was so quiet, so black beyond the lantern's reach. At first I kept a firm grip on my sword. I had no apparent reason for fear, and yet I was afraid. The center of our world lay in deep distress a few feet from where we stood. Something was terribly wrong. I would stand guard. I would protect. I would be a strong tower . . . a mighty wall . . . a valiant warrior. But perhaps if I just sat down it would be okay. Ah yes! The others were following my lead. We could guard as easily from a sitting position. It seemed rather warm for this time of night. If only I hadn't eaten quite so much. The sword made sitting difficult. Maybe if I just stretched out a bit. Yes, that was better. The stars were so bright tonight. No moon at all. I couldn't see anything around us anyway; perhaps if I just closed my eyes, I could concentrate on listening more carefully for the arrival of any intruders . . .

"Simon, are you sleeping? Couldn't you keep watch for even one hour?"

The Master's voice jolted me awake. I sat bolt upright, groped for my sword, and mumbled something about having just closed my eyes so that I could listen more carefully.

He wasn't angry with me, nor was he disappointed. His perfect knowledge of me made disappointment impossible. He knew I was running in the flesh. He knew my flesh would fail. But there was a deep sorrow in his voice, a sorrow that grew out of his knowledge of what lay ahead. Our time to die was at last upon us both. This cup would not pass from him, nor would he lay it down of his own accord. The knowledge of what would soon come upon him could not help but create great sorrow within him. But there was more. I saw it in his eyes as I sat there fumbling for an explanation that did not exist. He felt sorrow for *me* as well. He took no joy in watching the foundations of my life disintegrate, yet he loved me far too much to deprive me of what lay ahead. My confidence in the flesh would have to die, and it would be an agonizing, pain-filled death. But even now he shared that pain with me.

He then offered my flesh a second chance. "Keep watching and praying that you may not come into temptation; the spirit is willing, but the flesh is weak."

Perhaps you know already what happened next. He retreated into the darkness. I determined to remain faithful. And then, once again, I slept. The second time I felt his hand upon my shoulder was even worse than the first. Neither of us spoke. What was there to say? I reached over and woke James and John. We didn't dare look into his eyes. In silence he once again departed into the night.

When I awoke the third time, it was not only the voice of the Master that drew me back to the land of the living. This time there were other noises as well. And there were torches and clanking and confusion. I heard Jesus talking to me.

"Are you still sleeping? It is enough; the hour has come; the Son of Man is being betrayed into the hands of sinners. Get up, let's be going; the one who betrays me is here!"

I grabbed my sword, sprang to my feet, and frantically tried to understand the scene around me. Members of the temple guard were everywhere, swords drawn and clubs held high. The high priest was there too, surrounded by his slaves and other temple officials. And there, at the head of the mob, was Judas. He approached Jesus and kissed him on the cheek, calling him "Master."

Jesus turned to him, and for just an instant their eyes met. Then Jesus spoke. "Judas, are you betraying the Son of Man with a kiss?" Those were the final words ever to pass between the two of them. Judas dropped his eyes to the ground and stepped into the darkness. I never saw the man alive again.

For a few seconds following Judas's exit, no one spoke, no one moved. Two armies faced each other on this tiny battlefield, both sizing up their enemy, both obviously fighting fear. We, of course, saw the glint of the swords and spear tips in the torchlight and feared for our lives. These who came in darkness to capture the King had every reason to fear as well. They knew the Master's reputation. They knew the reports of his power. They knew, too, their actions this night were driven by the forces of evil within them. Their hatred drove them on, but their hatred could not completely mask their terror of what this man might do to them if he chose to use his powers in his own defense. And between the two groups stood the object of this great confrontation, the only one apparently unaffected by what was happening, Jesus.

After several agonizing moments Jesus himself broke the silence. "Whom do you seek?"

One of the officials responded, "Jesus of Nazareth."

What happened next will seem strange to any who were not there that night, watching this ultimate conflict between good and evil unfold. On one side, empowered with the spirit of Satan himself, armed with their weapons of warfare, driven by their hatred and fear, bolstered by their sheer numbers, protected by the darkness of the hour and their evil intent, were all those who came to destroy the one whom they despised above all others. On the other side was Jesus and, cowering behind him, a group of helpless, pathetic disciples. And yet, when Jesus answered the official by taking a step forward and saying simply, "I AM!" his response pierced his enemies with terror. In that single, brief statement Jesus confronted his attackers with everything they needed to know about the person standing before them. The authority with which he proclaimed his identity shook the very ground upon which they stood. In that instant I knew what Moses had known so many years ago when he stood before the burning bush and heard the voice of God proclaim, "I AM WHO I AM!" They had come in their arrogance seeking Jesus of Nazareth. They found, instead, the great I AM, the absolute and supreme authority of life.

You think perhaps I recall this inaccurately? You think perhaps I see it now through the eyes of one who loves his Lord more than life itself, and who therefore embellishes a bit? I will tell you only that Jesus' single affirmation, "I AM!" so terrorized the mob before him that the entire force surged backwards, tripping and stumbling over one another until they lay in a pathetic heap of humanity upon the ground. I remember at the time thinking they looked as if they were all cringing under the anticipation of some mighty blow from on high.

But the blow did not come.

Jesus then spoke again. "Whom do you seek?"

After a moment the high priest stood to his feet and spat out the words, "Jesus of Nazareth!"

The others rallied to their feet behind him. It was obvious now that no divine protector would be coming to Jesus' aid. Their worst fears could be put to rest.

Jesus responded once again by saying, "I told you that I am he; if therefore you seek me, let these go their way." He turned and pointed to those of us standing behind him.

The high priest motioned to two guards standing next to him. They stepped forward, carrying ropes with which to bind the Master. If I was ever to act, I knew it had to be now. All the energy of my flesh suddenly surged within me. This at last was my ultimate test. The others could do what they wanted. Let them cower here in the darkness behind the Master. I at least would show myself strong. If I could reach the high priest and cleave his skull in two, perhaps it would cause enough confusion to enable Jesus and the others to slip away into the darkness. With a mighty bellow I heaved my sword above my head and charged out from behind Jesus straight into the enemy forces. Unfortunately, my speed and dexterity were not nearly as great as my resolve. The high priest saw and heard me blundering across the clearing in plenty of time to anticipate my actions. Long before I reached my target, he stepped behind one of his slaves, and when I finally brought my blade crashing down, rather than skillfully eliminating the head of the enemy forces, my sword twisted in my grip, cracked the poor slave a mighty rap on the skull, and then slid down the side of his head, slicing off his ear in the process.

The slave let out an agonizing wail and clapped his hand over the side of his head. I stood before him, still clutching my weapon, staring at the results of my mighty offensive— one little ear lying upon the ground at my feet. Half a dozen temple guards dropped their spears level with my chest and waited for the command to run me through.

The command that came, however, did not come from the enemy; it came from Jesus. And it was not directed at the soldiers; it was directed at me. "Stop! No more of this."

Jesus stooped down, cradled the severed ear in his hand, then stood and touched the trembling slave's wound. When he drew back his hand, the wound was healed.

I just stood there beside him, watching as Jesus used his final act of healing on this earth to undo the results of the best my flesh could produce. Then, after restoring the servant's ear, he turned once again to me and said, "Put your sword back into its sheath; for all who take the sword will die by the sword. Or do you think that I can't now call to my Father, and he will send more than twelve legions of angels? But then how would the Scripture be fulfilled, that it must be so? Shall I not drink the cup which the Father has given me?"

It was awful. In one mighty blast of energy, I gave my Master the best I had to offer and discovered that not only was my best not good enough, it wasn't even wanted. I dropped my sword to the ground, hung my head in shame, and slipped back into the shadows.

I could hear Jesus exchanging a few more words with his captors as the guards circled around him. Seized with terror, my fellow disciples now fled for their lives. From my hiding place in the shadows behind a nearby olive tree, I watched as they grabbed his wrists and lashed them together. I could still see him in the glow of the torchlight, standing there so utterly alone, silent, bound like a common thief.

⋈

The next few hours of my life are forever imbedded in my memory in vivid, agonizing detail. From my hiding place I watched as the hideous procession moved away into the night, leaving me in my silence and darkness and pain. For several minutes I didn't dare move. Then, just when I felt it might be safe to step out from behind the tree, I heard something moving in the darkness to my left. The sound sent a new jolt of terror through me, freezing me once again in place.

"Simon! Simon, are you there?" Even though it was a forced whisper I knew that voice.

"John! Is that you? I'm over here. Are you alone?"

"Yeah, everyone else took off running."

Together we made our way out of the garden and onto the main road. We could see the bobbing torches and hear the clank of the armor some distance ahead of us, moving away. We crept along in the darkness behind Jesus' captors, being careful not to be seen.

The procession wound through the darkened streets of the city until it reached a large, well-lighted courtyard outside the home of Annas, the father-in-law of Caiaphas, the high priest. There were servants posted at the entrance of the courtyard to keep unwanted visitors out. From deep within the shadows across the street, I could see inside the courtyard. A large gathering of priests, scribes, and other prominent leaders were bunched together in little groups, apparently waiting for some major event to take place. This was no spontaneous late-night festival gathering. Servants were coming and going, catering to the needs of those present, in the midst of what appeared to be an excited, almost festive atmosphere.

As soon as the procession surrounding Jesus entered the courtyard, the Jewish officials quickly grouped themselves together into what appeared to be a makeshift courtroom setting. John and I quietly crossed the street and hovered closer to the entrance to the courtyard so that we could see and hear the proceedings a little better. As we approached the gate, John suddenly whispered, "Hey! I think I can get us inside. I have some friends inside there, and I think that servant girl at the gate knows me and will let me pass. Wait here."

And with that he walked casually up to the entrance, smiled and nodded to the servant, who nodded in return, and then walked on in. A few minutes later I saw him once again at the gate, talking with the servant girl and pointing in my direction. She nodded, and he motioned for me to come.

My heart was pounding so loud, I felt sure the whole neighborhood could hear it, but there was such a crowd inside, I hoped I could keep to the shadows and not be noticed. I could see John a few paces ahead of me, walking into the courtyard. As I approached the gate, I attempted a casual nod to the servant girl, who nodded in return as I passed. Then, just as I passed by her, she raised her head in apparent recognition and said, "You too were with Jesus the Galilean! You are not also one of this man's disciples, are you?"

"I don't know what you are talking about, woman. I don't know him!"

The words were out of my mouth in an instant. I tried hard to look incensed at her accusation, but I could feel the little beads of sweat forming on my forehead. A puzzled expression crept across her face, but she said no more. I kept my eyes fixed on her until she dropped her gaze to the ground, and I slipped past her and into the courtyard.

"I don't know him . . . I don't know him . . . I don't know him." Had I really just spoken those words? I told myself it was simply a necessary deception so that I could keep close to the Master and watch for another opportunity to free him. That's the way of the flesh, of course. The flesh always has a reason, an explanation for its failure. But no explanation could free me from the anguish I felt in the pit of my stomach.

From a distance I could see the high priest and the other officials gathered around Jesus, asking him questions and discussing among themselves. John had positioned himself so that he could hear what was being said. The night was growing cold, and a number of the guards and household slaves were standing around a fire kindled in the center of the courtyard. My clothes were soaked with sweat, and I stood shivering alone in the shadows for a few minutes. Then I moved up closer to the fire, hoping for some warmth. One of the maids brushed by me, bringing another load of wood for the fire. She looked up to excuse herself, then suddenly went silent when she saw my face. She dropped her wood on the fire, then turned and spoke to one of the guards. He in turn looked at me and spoke first to those gathered around the fire and then to me. "This man was with Jesus of Nazareth! You are one of them too!"

"Man, I am not!" This time it was obvious my denial did not convince my accusers. But since they had apparently received no specific orders concerning Jesus' disciples, they said no more. As soon as they turned their attention once again to the fire in front of them, I slipped back into the shadows and edged my way cautiously closer to those gathered around Jesus.

I located John in the crowd and stood at his side. We could hear everything being said, and my height gave me a clear view of Jesus and his accusers. For some considerable time we stood there, watching, listening, discussing quietly between ourselves, as witness after witness brought lies against the Master. It was obvious what they wanted. Somehow, somewhere they would find "legal" grounds for executing their prisoner.

After more than an hour, as we stood there in helpless agony, I suddenly felt a tap on my shoulder and turned to face a man who appeared to be wrestling with some intense emotion.

"Did I not see you in the garden with him?" His accusation caused all those in our immediate area to turn and look at me.

At first I tried to make my denial sound casual and disarming. "No, of course not. Don't be ridiculous!"

"No, you're lying! That was my brother's ear you cut off. Your Galilean speech gives you away." Then he turned to those around us and said, "Certainly this man was with him, for he too is a Galilean."

The explosion that erupted from within me burst forth with such violence that it caused even the high priest himself to stop midsentence and look in my direction. "Listen, you little fool! I don't know that man, and I never have!" As I spoke, I stretched out my arm in Jesus' direction and punctuated my words with a jabbing index finger. "I have nothing to do with him, do you understand? I don't know him. I don't want to know him. I couldn't care less what happens to him. He's no friend of mine, and I assure you that I'm no friend of his!" And then, just so there could be no misunderstanding, I finished my tirade with a string of profanity intended to make it clear to all that I shared nothing in common with this Galilean rabbi on trial for his life a few feet from where we stood.

I did not realize I had been screaming until I heard the silence in the courtyard that followed. No one spoke. No one moved. I became aware of my arm, still suspended in midair, aimed at Jesus. The sound that finally shattered the oppressive stillness in which I stood was the sound that also marked the end of my life as I had known it. Somewhere in the distance a lone rooster crowed his declaration of an approaching dawn and at the same time announced my entrance into the darkest night of my life.

"This very night, before a rooster crows, you will deny me three times." Jesus' words surged into my consciousness.

I turned toward Jesus. Our eyes met, and in that meeting at last I saw myself. There was no hiding place left for me. So this was the great Simon Peter. This was the great leader of men. This was the great defender and guardian of the king.

Tears flooded up from deep within me. Agonizing sobs broke through my lips. Through blurred vision I shoved my way past those who blocked my exit and fled into the darkened street. I ran until at last I found some ancient, deserted alleyway, a place reserved for the filth and refuse of the city. Several curious rats squeaked their concern at my intrusion. It seemed a fitting place in which to live out the remainder of my existence—just another piece of worthless garbage in among the rest.

I sobbed my anguish until I could sob no more. Then at last I slept and in that sleep entered the only world in which I knew I could ever again find some measure of peace.

24

I don't know what woke me. Perhaps it was the growing stench of the surrounding filth as it warmed in the morning sun. Perhaps it was the increasing noise from the street at the end of the alley. I do know, however, that the world to which I returned was unlike any I had ever known before. It wasn't the filth. It wasn't the odor. It wasn't the noise. It was something else altogether, something deep within me, at the very core of my being.

Simon was dead. My heart continued to beat. My lungs continued their endless expansion and contraction. My senses continued to relay information to my brain. But whereas once there had been hope and life and aspirations and desires and a purpose for being, now there was only pain and shame and emptiness and death.

It was far more than simply regret for my failures or anxiety over the fate of my Master. Regret I understood. Failure I understood. Anxiety I understood. This was none of these. There was simply no longer any life within me.

Each of us constructs our lives on beliefs we accept as unshakable. These beliefs form the great support pillars of our existence, pillars on which everything else is built. We rarely or perhaps never acknowledge their existence in our conscious minds. Yet every choice we make, every word we utter, every goal we hold for the future, assumes their certainty.

For me, the greatest of those pillars, the one upon which all the others depended, the one rooted in the deepest core of my being, was the understanding that Simon Barjona would always ultimately prevail. If I tried hard enough, if I worked long enough, if I learned from my mistakes, if I regrouped following my failures, I could and I would succeed. This was not simply something I hoped for; it was the foundation of my life.

When this man, this Jesus, entered my world almost four years earlier, he brought massive changes with him. When I finally submitted to his lordship, he became my reason for being. His goals became my goals. His successes became my successes. His techniques became my techniques. His affirmations became my greatest joys, and his reprimands pierced me deeply. In a word, he became the center of my world.

But even though I had forsaken all and followed him, the central pillar of my life was still undisturbed. My goals were different. My techniques were different. My hopes were different. My reason for living was changed. But the means by which I pursued all of these remained unaltered. Whereas once my determination, my strength, my wit, my charisma, indeed, all my fleshly attributes had been focused on becoming Simon the great fisherman, through Jesus all those fleshly attributes had been refocused on becoming Simon the great disciple. The goals were radically different, but the means were identical—*me*.

Then, in one terrifying instant, at the very moment when he knew all my weight rested upon it, Jesus reached his almighty arms around that pillar and wrenched it out from under me, and everything that rested upon it came crashing down. Now there was only the shattered ruins of my existence surrounding a cold, black, gaping chasm where once my pillar had been.

If you have ever been there, you will understand. It wasn't just that I had failed. Failure I understood. Failure was simply a call to try harder and reach higher. This was not failure; this was death. The foundation of my life had collapsed, and now my spirit wandered aimlessly through the piles of rubble, through the broken bricks and crumpled mortar, listening to the wind whistling through the ruins of my life.

The increasing turmoil from the street at the end of the alley finally broke through my pain. I stood and then wandered toward the commotion. There seemed to be some sort of a parade in progress. Both sides of the street were lined with people yelling and pointing at something passing by in front of them.

At first all I could see were the mounted Roman soldiers, swords drawn, pushing their way through the multitude, making a path for those following behind. Then I turned and saw the reason for this procession. Three men stumbled along behind, flanked on either side by armed guards. Each one carried a large wooden cross on his shoulders. It was another one of those hideous Roman executions in progress.

The first two men were keeping pace with the demands of the soldiers, but the third man was having trouble. Even from this distance I could see what appeared to be streams of blood running down his face and neck and onto his naked shoulders and chest. He was wearing something on his head. He was bent nearly double, so I could not see his face. Then, just as he approached the entrance to the alley, he collapsed under the weight of the cross and fell face first into the dirt. The cross fell to the ground at his side, and for the first time I saw his back, or what was left of it. The flesh hung in shredded strips of what had once been skin and muscle. The brutal beating must have taken place several hours ago, for much of the blood was now dried and caked, though numerous red streams still oozed from the deeper wounds. I could now see that the thing on his head was actually a kind of mock crown, woven from the branches of some sort of wicked thornbush. The long spikes pierced deep into his head, causing the blood to run freely down his forehead.

Never had I seen a man so brutalized prior to his execution. I could not imagine what his offense must have been to justify such treatment. For several seconds he did not move. Then he groaned and rolled onto his side, and I looked into the bruised and swollen face of my King.

The soldier nearest him walked over and gave him a sharp kick in the side, demanding that he pick up his cross and continue on. Jesus brought himself to his hands and knees and then tried to hoist the wooden cross beam back onto his shoulders, but the loss of blood and the damage inflicted on his back and shoulder muscles made it impossible for him to support the weight. He dropped once again to his knees, allowing the rough wooden surface to scrape across the raw flesh of his back as the cross fell to the ground.

The frustrated guard looked at the spectators along the side of the street opposite me, then laid his hand on a man nearly my size, pointed at the cross, and told him to pick it up. The man stepped into the street, hoisted the cross beam onto his shoulders, then reached down and helped Jesus back onto his feet. With the weight of the wood off his back,

Jesus was able to continue on, and the gruesome procession once again moved forward.

When the last guard passed by me, I stepped out into the street and fell in line. I suppose I should have feared recognition, but I was far beyond fear. The depth of unrelenting, inescapable anguish within me eclipsed every other emotion throughout the remainder of that day. It no longer mattered whether or not I was recognized. It no longer mattered whether or not I too was executed. Nothing mattered anymore. The source of all life would soon be dead. How could it possibly matter whether or not my body continued to live?

I saw a number of familiar faces around me as we moved through the streets. Jesus' mother followed as close as the guards would permit. John walked beside her, his left arm around her, holding her close. Lazarus, Martha, and Mary were there together. A short distance away I saw my brother, Andrew. Our eyes met, but neither of us spoke. What was there to say? His eyes too were dark, swirling pools of pain.

When the procession finally reached Golgotha, the designated place of execution, the crowd fanned out at the base of the hill, watching the final steps in the execution process. The holes in which the crosses would be dropped had already been dug. The three crosses were laid on the ground, the three prisoners were laid on the crosses, and large metal spikes were driven through each hand and each foot. The soldiers then lifted each cross in turn and dropped them into the holes. Jesus' cross was in the center.

Of all the images I retain from that day, it is the memory of the Master's hands I recall most of all. I knew the touch of those hands as well as I knew the sound of his voice. I remembered the first time he placed his hand on my shoulder. I remembered the strength and the acceptance and the comradeship it communicated. I remembered the relief of feeling his hand gripping my arm as I sank below the waves that night I attempted to walk on the water. I recalled the countless times I was privileged to stand beside him, watching as he reached out and touched blind eyes, deaf ears, broken and deformed bodies, bringing sight, and sound, and wholeness with each touch. I remembered fixing my eyes on those fingers the day he took that little boy's lunch and kept breaking and breaking and breaking the bread and fish. I kept trying to see how he was performing the wonder taking place before me. In my mind I saw him once again as he stretched out those hands from the bow of our boat the night I knew we were all going to perish on the sea. I remembered the instant calm that followed, the peace, the rest.

And now I stood at a distance and looked up at those hands, crushed and bruised, blood flowing freely down his palms from the jagged wounds surrounding the spikes driven through them. And these drunken fools gambling below him had no idea what they were destroying.

For nearly three hours I stood in silence and watched. No one spoke to me; I spoke to no one. There were many in the crowd who were mocking him. The priests and other religious leaders obviously considered this a cause for great celebration. Others, like myself, clothed themselves in their private shrouds of grief. At one point I saw Mary and John approach the cross together. Words passed between them and Jesus, but I could not hear what was said.

Then, when the sun was at its highest point, beating down directly above our heads, a sudden eerie darkness crept across the land. Those who came to celebrate his execution were disturbed. They tried hard to pretend it was just a coincidence, but it made them all uneasy. Boisterous laughter and ugly jests were replaced by subdued conversations. Those who viewed this as their victory seemed more reticent to look directly at the dying figure before them. If there was any possibility this man's death was bringing darkness on the earth, was it possible he might bring even worse on those who were responsible?

For the next three hours, the darkness remained. Then, just as the darkness began to lessen a bit, I heard him speak his final words.

"My God! My God! Why have you forsaken me?"

His cry pierced the silence that now surrounded the cross. And then, "I thirst!"

And then, finally, "It is finished!" followed by one great sigh and then nothing more.

He was gone.

His body now hung unmoving on the cross, and the only world in which I wanted to live instantly ceased to exist. My future was gone. My great hopes and plans were no more. But in the end it was not the loss of my future, it was not the death of my hopes and my plans that brought me this endless pain. It was knowing that tomorrow morning I would wake to a world in which he no longer existed. I missed him more than I had known it was possible to miss anything or anyone. How strange! As long as he still breathed upon that cross, I continued to draw some comfort from his presence in our world. But now a great sea of loneliness flooded into my soul and mingled with my pain, bringing new poignancy, new dimension to my agony.

As I stood there in that strange half darkness, I suddenly felt the ground beneath my feet rumble and churn. It was as if the earth itself shuddered uncontrollably in its grief. There was nothing more for me here. There was nothing more for me anywhere. I turned and walked away into a night that would never end.

25

The love of God is poured out within us in so many different ways. At the time, walking the streets of Jerusalem that evening, unseeing and now almost unfeeling because of the numbing narcotic of ceaseless pain, the concept of the love of God was to my mind the ultimate absurdity. If ever I thought I had needed the miraculous intervention of a loving God in my own life, it was in that garden as I fought for the release of my King. If ever I knew with absolute and unquestioned certainty that our world desperately, urgently needed the miraculous intervention of a loving God, it was as I stood below that cross, watching Jesus die. And yet, there I was, having just witnessed what I would later come to recognize as the two greatest expressions of the love of God I would ever know yet possessing at the time not a glimmer of that love.

For several hours I wandered the city streets, speaking to no one, recognizing no one, having no longer any place I wanted to go and nothing I wanted to do. I considered returning immediately to Galilee and to my beloved Ruth. But what would I say? Could I share with her my shame? Could I tell her of my repeated denials of my Lord? Could I explain to her how our great march to victory culminated not in Jesus' coronation but rather in his brutal, bloody execution? No, it would be best for me to stay on here for a few more days.

As the piercing agony of the crucifixion gradually dulled into a silent, throbbing fog of pain, I became aware of my fear. How far would the high priest and his cohorts go in their efforts to cleanse their kingdom of the one they hated above all others? Would the Master's blood satisfy their lusts? Or would a dozen bloody crosses serve their purposes better? I must find Andrew and James and John and the others. We needed to discuss what steps should be taken to insure our safety.

I checked out several of our favorite gathering places in the city but found no one. In the end my wanderings took me back to Golgotha. If the others were gathered anywhere, it would be there. I would be safe enough now. The sun would soon be setting, bringing with it the onset of the Passover Sabbath, and even the Jewish leaders' seething hatred would not drive them to risk tarnishing their public image through violation of this sacred day of rest. I wondered too what the Romans would do with Jesus' body.

I arrived back at the hill just in time to see the outlines of two men carefully lifting Jesus' cross from the hole in which it had been placed for the crucifixion. The dead form of the Master still hung from the spikes. I watched as they gently laid it upon the ground and then began the tedious task of removing the spikes from Jesus' hands and feet. At first I thought they must simply be members of the execution guard completing their duties. But the obvious care with which they went about their work soon caused me to change my mind. There was a respect, a gentleness in their manner and actions. They laid the cross on a spotless sheet of white linen. They removed each spike, taking great care not to cause any further mutilation to the Master's body in the process. Then, when the body was finally freed from the wood, they lifted it up and placed it not on the ground but rather on a second clean linen sheet spread out next to the now empty cross. It was obvious these men were not Roman soldiers sent to carry out a duty. These men were disciples of Jesus, engaged in a work of reverent compassion.

I drew close enough to see their faces. One of the men I knew. It was Nicodemus, the man who became a follower and staunch supporter of Jesus after a late-night conversation with him. Nicodemus was a member of the Sanhedrin, the governing religious body of our people, and was among the wealthiest men in the city. The other man was Joseph, originally from Arimathea, a town about twenty-five miles northwest of Jerusalem, in the hill country of Judea. I did not know him at the time, but his clothes identified him as a person of great wealth as well. Nicodemus saw me hovering in the shadows. He did not speak, but his respectful nod in my direction told me he knew who I was and assured me I had nothing to fear. Joseph and Nicodemus wrapped the body of Jesus in the linen cloth and then placed it on a cart standing nearby.

As the two men moved the cart away from the base of the hill and into the streets of the city, I became aware for the first time that I was not the only one watching these proceedings with more than casual interest. As I fell in step behind the body of my Lord, I found myself a member of a procession of at least twenty-five or thirty men and women. Nearly all of the faces were familiar to me, most of them

228

well known. There was Jesus' mother, with John still at her side. There was James and Simon the Zealot. Andrew was in the group, as was Lazarus and his sisters, Mary and Martha. The funeral procession trailed along behind the cart until the two men stopped outside a luxurious home in the best part of the city. They carried the body into a spacious, well-lighted front room and laid it upon a table prepared for the task ahead. Several large rolls of white linen cloth stood beside the table along with what must have been at least a hundred pounds of a paste mixture of myrrh and aloes. The sweet, pungent fragrance of the mixture filled the room as we all filed in to watch the proceedings.

Little conversation passed between those present throughout the next hour as Joseph and Nicodemus prepared Jesus' body for burial. It helped, though, being there with these others who understood. We watched as the body was carefully washed and dried. Then the wrapping process began. At first a single wrapping of the white linen was placed around the entire body from the feet up to the neck. Then a thin layer of the myrrh and aloes mixture was spread over the linen, followed by a second layer of cloth, followed by another layer of the mixture, and then another layer of cloth, and so on until all the myrrh and aloes mixture was used and a thick, firm paste and linen cocoon encased the body. The head was then wrapped tightly in a separate long, unbroken length of linen.

It was getting late when the process was finally complete. The body of Jesus was now considerably heavier, and Joseph and Nicodemus solicited the help of several more hands to move it back out to the cart.

The procession then moved out again, following the cart to a tomb that only the wealthiest could have afforded. It was to have been Joseph's tomb, a vault chiseled out of a solid rock wall with a stone bench inside providing what we assumed would now be the final resting place for our Master. The door of the sepulcher was formed by a massive, round slab of stone, expertly crafted to seal off the entrance once it was rolled into place. It took eight men straining on the slab to finally move it into place.

And so, at last, the world came to an end.

✶

My recollection of the next several days is little more than a dark blur of mingled pain and fear. I stayed close to my fellow disciples. The report of my public denials and desertion was now well known to all of them. To their credit, though, their attitudes toward me seemed to reflect compassion and sorrow rather than condemnation. Perhaps their own sense of defeat and shame at doing nothing themselves to prevent the Master's death kept them from passing too harsh a judgment on me. We all saw the wisdom of staying out of sight as much as possible. Though no further arrests were being made, the possibility was enough to keep us all cowering in the shadows.

The day following the crucifixion, filled with remorse and faced with the consequences of his greed, Judas found a desolate piece of ground outside the city, secured a rope to the branch of an old tree overhanging a thirty-foot embankment, slipped a noose around his neck, and jumped to his death. The rope snapped his neck, the weight of his body then broke the branch on which his rope was tied, and his body, branch, and rope crashed onto the jagged rocks below. His chest and stomach were ripped open in the fall, and those who found his remains gave testimony to the hideous end of the one whose name has now become synonymous with betrayal among the people of God.

✶

The sun was not yet fully risen the first day of the week when I felt John's firm grip on my shoulder, shaking me into consciousness. Morning has never been a good time of day for me, but since the Master's death it was abhorrent beyond measure, bringing with it the obligation to face another sixteen hours of emptiness, fear, shame, and regret. The urgency with which he spoke brought me to a sitting position.

"Simon? Simon! Wake up! Mary's here. She just came back from the tomb, and the stone is rolled away from the door. The guards are gone, and she's afraid somebody has taken his body."

I got dressed as quickly as I could, and the two of us set off at a brisk pace, heading toward the sepulcher. The first rays of the morning sun were just touching the tallest buildings in the city, promising a glorious day ahead. I will not say I yet had hope. Perhaps it would be more accurate to say I felt within me the hope of a hope. For the first time since the crucifixion, the Spirit of God brought back to my mind the Master's promised resurrection on the third day. We walked on in silence for several minutes, my mind now recalling more and more of Jesus' prophetic words: "The Son of Man is going to be delivered into the hands of men; and they will kill him, and he will be raised on the third day." "Behold, we are going up to Jerusalem; and the Son of Man will be delivered to the chief priests and scribes, and they will condemn him to death, and will hand him over to the Gentiles to mock and scourge and crucify him, and on the third day he will be raised up." "For just as Jonah was three days and three nights in the belly of the sea monster, so will the Son of Man be three days and three nights in the heart of the earth."

The more I thought, the faster I walked. John's mind must have been moving in the same direction, for after several minutes of silence, I glanced over at him and saw a tiny smile creeping across his lips. He saw me looking at him, and for a few seconds we both stopped and stared at each other in silence. Then John's face broke into a broad grin, and he spoke the two words that signaled the start of the best footrace of my life.

"Three days!"

That was all he said. It was all he needed to say. We both took off at a dead run, heading for the tomb. It wasn't a fair race, of course, with me being built more for strength than for speed. John arrived at the door to the open grave a full minute ahead of me. When I finally came puffing and blowing up to his side, though, I could see the pain once again filling his eyes. A single glance into the dimly lit cavern told me why. From where he stood, looking through the door, the linen cocoon in the shape of the Master's feet could be clearly seen still resting on the cold stone bench.

I left John standing at the door and entered the cave. Having come this far, I wanted to make certain Jesus' body was still undisturbed. What I found when I entered that tomb altered the course of my life and the history of the human race forever.

The first thing I noticed was the absence of Jesus' head. The linen cocoon surrounding his body was still stretched out on the stone, but the cloth binding for his head was now folded neatly, sitting by itself at the end of the bench. And where his head should have been there was nothing . . . nothing at all. Then I looked more closely at the cocoon. There was something wrong with it as well. The chest and stomach were sunken in several inches as if some heavy weight had been pressed down, crushing the chest cavity. When the truth of what I was seeing finally surged into my conscious mind, I let out a sort of gasping bellow that drew John to my side. There was no body inside the wrappings! It wasn't just that the head was missing. The entire body was missing, having passed through the layers of binding, leaving the linen wrappings untouched, undisturbed in the form of a hollow shell. With the body removed, the still-moist linen and paste cocoon had sunken in slightly under its own weight.

What we were seeing could of course not be true. And yet it was. I knelt down and slipped my arm through the neck hole, feeling the emptiness within, to confirm what I now already knew—Jesus was alive! I had no idea where he was. But I knew he was alive.

I sprang to my feet, grabbed John around the chest, and then bounced him around the tomb in a mighty bear hug, screaming, "He's alive! He's alive! He's alive!"

Following my exuberant outburst, we both headed back to the city to report our discovery to the others. We walked together, talking over the deluge of still unanswered questions that now flooded our minds. The question that troubled me most deeply, though, and the one that now mattered more than all the rest combined, was a question I dared not put into words, a question for which I knew John could never give me an answer. If, indeed, the Master was alive, and if we were ever to see him again, how would he relate to me, the one who failed him utterly, the one who publicly, repeatedly denied him, the one who deserted him in his greatest hour of need?

26

Less than four hours later I had the answer to the question I feared most of all.

John and I literally exploded into the silent, dimly lit room in which our fellow disciples still lay sleeping. We were both blasting forth our accounts of the empty tomb and the linen wrappings before the door closed behind us. Our entrance caused several of our comrades to sit suddenly bolt upright out of a deep sleep, terror in their eyes, assuming the early morning chaos meant their own arrest and execution was now upon them. By the time everyone was awake and alert enough to hear what we were saying, they were all so irritated with us that no one was taking us seriously. Someone flung back a less than flattering proverb about the offensiveness of loud greetings early in the morning, and several others mumbled comments about the dangers of drowning our pain in too much wine. Within a matter of minutes the only thing we had successfully accomplished was to reduce the room to a collection of grumpy, muttering, half-awake men tossing insults back and forth at one another.

John and I continued our urgent efforts to convince the others, but trying to tell them about the resurrection of Christ introduced us to a principle we would see reconfirmed countless times throughout the rest of our lives. Facts alone can never successfully communicate the truth about the resurrection of our Lord. Only when those facts are combined with the work of the Spirit of God can the hearer ever make the transition from facts to truth.

In the end John and I decided it would be best for us to keep any additional comments to ourselves until our fellow disciples were better equipped to relate to our discoveries in a logical, rational manner. Having successfully roused the entire room with our entrance, we then fell silent and joined the others in the morning routines of life.

We were just finishing our morning meal together when the women arrived. Mary, Jesus' mother, was there, as was the mother of James the Less, along with several other loyal followers of the Master. The group was lead by Joanna, the wife of King Herod's steward. Throughout most of the past four years her social prominence in the Jerusalem community had not prevented her from boldly proclaiming her support of Jesus. The first words out of Joanna's mouth sent a jolt throughout every man in that room.

"We just saw Jesus! He's alive! He's whole! And he's coming to see you!"

A few seconds of stunned silence were followed by everyone in the room bursting into speech at once. All the women launched into vivid accounts of their encounter with the Master, and all the men pelted them with questions. The room quickly broke into four or five little clusters of shrieking men and women, all trying to hear and be heard above the noise. Gradually the account took shape.

The women had gathered at sunrise, planning to go to the Lord's grave as a group to mourn his death and, if they could find someone to help them move the stone at the entrance of the cave, to anoint his body with spices. When they arrived at the tomb, however, they found the stone already removed. They entered, expecting to find Jesus' body, but found instead two young men sitting at either end of the empty linen wrappings. The men were dressed in glistening white clothing, giving off a radiance that immediately convinced the women they were in the presence of supernatural beings. The two men stood as the women entered, and one of them spoke. "Don't be afraid; for I know that you are looking for Jesus who has been crucified. Why do you seek the living one among the dead? He is not here, for he has risen, just as he said. Come, see the place where he was lying."

At this point he encouraged the women to gather around the empty linen cocoon, and, to my immense satisfaction, the women gave a description of the empty shell identical to the one John and I had been trying to present to the others a half hour earlier.

Then the angel spoke again. "And go quickly and tell his disciples that he has risen from the dead; and behold, he is going before you into Galilee, there you will see him; behold, I have told you."

But the best was yet to come. The women took off out of the sepulcher, heading back to town as fast as they could go. But before they'd gone a hundred paces down the trail, suddenly there he was! He wasn't a ghost. He wasn't a product of their imaginations. He was real and he was alive! They dropped to the ground in his presence, but he opened his arms wide and embraced them in what was certainly the most wonderful group hug of their lives. Everything about him proclaimed victory. The first word he spoke to them was the single word "Rejoice!"—not that they needed any encouragement. Jesus did not stay with them long, but he did not depart from them before he personally confirmed the same message given to them by the angels a few minutes earlier.

"Don't be afraid; go and take word to my brothers to leave for Galilee, and they will see me there."

I will not say the others believed the women's report. Grief and loss can do strange things to people. It can cause some to see and hear what they want to see and hear. It can cause others to fear the reentrance of hope, believing it will lead in the end only to greater pain. I will say, however, that I have never seen a group of men pack more quickly for the journey home than we did that morning.

For me, however, there was one more tiny piece of information given to me by Jesus' mother, information that overshadowed all the rest. The room was still buzzing with a dozen different conversations when she approached me. No words had passed between us since before the crucifixion. When I saw her coming my way, I found myself unable to make eye contact with her. My sense of shame and failure was still so raw, so intense. What defense could I offer for my actions? What explanation could justify my failure? If I could have met her gaze as she approached, however, I would have known she was seeking me out not to bring me condemnation but rather to bring me hope.

"Simon, there is something else I think you need to know. Joanna did not quote the angel's words exactly as they were spoken. The exact words spoken by the angel were these: 'But go, tell his disciples and Peter, "He is going before you into Galilee; there you will see him, just as he said to you."' He mentioned your name specifically, Simon. He wants you there."

"'And Peter'? You're sure he said, 'and Peter'? He really said my name?"

"Yes, Simon, I'm sure. I heard him speak. The message the angels gave us mentioned you by name. And Simon, if you could have seen him, if you could have seen the way he is, you would know . . . everything is all right. In fact, it's not just all right, it's wonderful as it has never been wonderful before. Go to him, Simon. He wants to see you, and you very much need to see him."

And so I went, not because Mary told me to go, but because I knew I had no choice. Until I saw him, until I knew where we stood, he and I, nothing else mattered. The deafening babble of the dozen bellowing voices around me continued, but I no longer heard them. I walked in silence out the door and into the early morning Jerusalem street. I didn't know where to go, of course, but I also knew it didn't matter. I didn't have to find him; he would find me. I would return to the tomb and wait.

As I walked along the quiet lanes winding through the city, the angel's words kept running through my mind. "But go, tell his disciples and Peter . . . and Peter . . . and Peter . . . and Peter." Could it really be? I would have expected the angel to say, "But go, tell his disciples, except Peter," but that was not what Mary said. And why did the angel use that name—Peter? Why didn't he call me Simon? Surely that other name, that other wonderful name given to me by the Lord so long ago, the name that meant "The Rock," surely I lost any right to that name forever when I proclaimed to all the world, "I do not know him!"

My mind was so full of lies back then. It still is in many ways, of course. But at that point in my pilgrimage, even the basics of the faith eluded me. After four years with the Master, I still believed the serpent's lie that my past determined my future, my sins defined my true identity, and the limitations of my flesh designated the boundaries of the life of Christ through me. I was yet to discover that his declaration of me as "The Rock" was not and never had been based on anything I could do for him. It was, rather, his prophetic affirmation of what he would one day accomplish in and through me.

If I was permitted to retain just one memory of the risen Lord, it would be the memory of that first encounter. The garden surrounding the entrance to the tomb was deserted when I arrived. I had some vague notion of waiting for his arrival on the bench inside the cave, but I never made it that far. As I approached the doorway, without warning he was there, standing just a few feet in front of me. Until that instant I had not known how much pain, how much shame, how much fear and unresolved agony still remained within me. At the sight of him, I dropped to my knees and then to my face at his feet. Through uncontrolled sobs I spoke the words I most wanted him to hear. "Oh, my Lord, forgive me . . . forgive me . . . forgive me."

There was no question about it being him or about his being real. The thought never crossed my mind. I could feel his feet in my hands. Even through my blurred vision, I could see where the nails had been driven through his flesh.

Then, as I lay there on the grass at his feet, he knelt down, and I once again felt his strong grip on my shoulders, and I heard his voice speak my new name. "Peter!"

When I finally looked up into his face, I saw what until that instant I believed I would never see again. I saw him smile. And I saw in his eyes not just forgiveness, though certainly that was there in abundance, but something else as well. I saw victory—both his victory and mine.

He did not remain with me long, but it was long enough. Everything I needed to know he communicated with absolute clarity. He was alive. I was forgiven. He still loved me. He still wanted me by his side. And I did not have to be afraid anymore.

And so the longest night of my life at last came to an end as the risen rays of his love once again flooded my soul.

27

Those weeks between the resurrection and the day of Pentecost were exciting days for me, but they were difficult ones as well. Relating to the truth of the resurrection without the indwelling presence of the Holy Spirit drove me to all sorts of strange behaviors. I was flooded with truth about my Lord, but I did not understand what to do with it. That Jesus was alive was obvious. He threaded himself through our lives, appearing to one person here, to two or three there, to a small group in Jerusalem, and then to another gathering in Galilee. He touched us, ate with us, talked with us, and responded to our questions, making certain every individual within his tiny band of faithful followers knew beyond any doubt that he was alive.

That he lived was now the central truth of my existence. But I didn't know how this truth was to impact my life. My heart was healed, but my mind was still immersed in blindness, ignorance, and confusion. It was a strange time in my life, a brief time between two worlds, a time when I possessed huge quantities of truth about the Master yet continued to relate to that truth through the mind of the flesh.

We spent most of those days back in Galilee. I kept waiting for Jesus to reorganize his people for a second assault on Jerusalem. At the time it seemed to me to be the only logical plan. In my mind I could see it all so clearly—the excitement among the masses at Jesus' miraculous reappearance, the terror in the eyes of the high priest and his cohorts as he stood before them in his resurrected majesty, the immediate submission or panic-driven desertion of all those who once opposed him.

But the reorganization did not take place, and no matter how skillfully I tried to move my brief conversations with the Master in that direction, he never mentioned a renewed assault on Jerusalem. Our supreme victory, now so obviously within our grasp, seemed to be an issue about which the Master had no concern whatsoever.

And so once again my Lord set me up. It was the waiting that drove me to it, the not knowing, the not doing something . . . *anything*. He knew it would, of course. A portion of the truth is sometimes a dangerous thing, and I still had such a very small portion.

We were back in Galilee at the time. It was where he wanted us throughout most of those days—with our families, with our friends, out of the sight and the reach of those forces in Jerusalem who were already hearing and fearing the reports and rumors of his reappearance.

It was perhaps three weeks after our return home. Several days had passed since our last meeting with the Master. We didn't know what to do. It was all so unsettling. We knew he was alive, but we had no idea where he was, or where we should be, or what we should be doing. I have never been good at waiting. The truth is, it makes me crazy.

I remember that day so well. I rose early and once again began my caged animal routine. After several days with me pacing around the house, peeking out the windows, running out to talk with the others, then returning again to pace some more, Ruth was nearly to the end of her remarkable patience. She tried reopening the same conversation we'd been having for the past several days. This time she tried using questions in her efforts to move me toward the truth. Could we trust the Master? Did I believe he knew what he was doing? Could we rest in his ability to show us what we needed to do and when we needed to do it? Her logic, of course, was flawless, but it was also powerless to calm my undirected energy. The more skillfully her reasoning pushed me toward the truth, the more frustrated I became.

Our conversation continued until I found myself feeling trapped in the grip of the obvious truth of her words. I fumbled for some sort of rational rebuttal for several minutes, realized in the end there was none, and finally sprang to my feet and bellowed, "I'm going to go talk with the others! Maybe they'll understand!"

I found them grouped in Jesus' old house. Mary was still living there, along with James the Less and Thaddaeus. The house remained our central gathering place, and I arrived to find Thomas and Nathanael already there. James and John arrived a few minutes later.

We spent the rest of the day talking through the same unanswered questions we'd been talking through since the resurrection. My conversations with the others went no better than my conversation with Ruth had gone. It wasn't long before a grumpy, irritable silence fell across the group.

I hated silence. I hated inactivity. I hated not knowing what came next. I hated this feeling of having no control over my future. For some time we all sat in silence, watching the shadows grow longer in the room—another day nearly gone, another day of doing nothing. When I could stand it no longer, I finally sprang to my feet and blurted out, "I'm going fishing!"

For several seconds everyone in the room sat frozen, their mouths hanging open, their eyes bulging in my direction. They knew my proclamation carried with it far more than a simple announcement of an evening's leisure activity. Three years earlier Andrew, James, and John had stood with me on the shore of the Sea of Galilee as my Lord called me away from my boat, my nets, and my petty aspirations for life, and into his love. These men knew I was now making a conscious decision to return to that world in an effort to reclaim some measure of control over my own life. At the time, my decision seemed to be born out of my frustration with the inactivity and lack of direction. Looking back, however, I know it was really my frustration with Jesus. Once again he wasn't doing things the way I thought they should be done.

Our greatest strengths and greatest weaknesses will always grow from the same characteristics in our lives. Throughout my adult years I have known I could motivate people to follow me. At those times when I have been moving in the direction of truth and wisdom, this ability has been a great strength. At those times when I have been pursuing foolishness and lies, it has been a great weakness. That morning, as I stood among my comrades, boldly proclaiming my intention to return to Egypt, I led myself and six other men away from faith and back into the ways of the flesh.

The brief silence following my announcement was soon broken by a chorus of six voices saying, "Yeah, me too!" "That sounds good to me!" and "Hey! Wait for me!"

The sun was low on the horizon when we reached the boat and checked our long-neglected gear. When everything was finally in order, we pushed off and headed down the coast to a familiar location not far offshore.

It was a perfect night for fishing—just enough moon for light, a warm, gentle breeze blowing in from the lake. It was perfect, that is, except for one thing—there were no fish.

I tend to become intensely focused at those times when I am operating in the flesh and know it. It's a wonderful hiding place. It keeps me from having to think. If you would have observed me from the shore that night, you would have assumed we were bobbing in the center of the greatest school of fish in the history of the Sea of Galilee. I cast my net, pulled it in, cast it again, pulled it in, then cast it yet again as quickly and skillfully as I could. The fact that each pull brought up yet another empty net in no way deterred me. For nearly ten hours I hid behind a fruitless fishing frenzy that eventually caused my comrades to drop their nets and plop down on the deck in amazed disbelief at my utter refusal to accept the truth. Funny how we so often attempt to compensate for going the wrong direction by increasing our speed.

As the first rays of the morning sun burst over the horizon, I too finally acknowledged the truth and dropped down in an exhausted heap. I was soaked with sweat. My tunic, long since cast aside, lay beside me as the early morning sun bathed my upper body.

I think John saw him first—a man standing on the shore, waving in our direction. His voice carried easily to us over the water.

244

"Children, you do not have any fish, do you?"

We assumed the man must be a hungry early morning customer, hoping for fresh fish to buy. I do remember thinking it a little odd for him to address us as "children." The silhouette of his physique against the rising sun did not convey an impression of great age, but it was impossible to see his features from this distance with the light behind him.

John stood up and called back, "No!" assuming his response would end the brief conversation.

To our surprise, however, the man then called back, "Cast the net on the right-hand side of the boat, and you will find a catch."

None of us spoke a word in response to the stranger's instructions, but the sudden light in John's eyes and the hint of a smile crossing his lips told me we were both thinking the same thing.

I wonder if you know what it is like. I knew I was standing where I should not be standing, doing what I should not be doing. I was just a little boy, angry with my daddy, hiding from him behind the house, hoping with everything within me that he loved me enough to come find me and bring me back inside again. Running away is such hard work. Just one night of it and my spirit was already weary, and lonely, and longing for some way back. One other time in my life, following a fruitless night of fishing, a man told me to cast my net on the other side. When this stranger on the beach spoke those words, the most glorious hope suddenly flooded into me. I wanted so much for it to be him.

I sprang to my feet, lunged at my net, then gave it a mighty cast over the right-hand side of the boat. What then followed four of us had all seen before. There they were once again—hundreds and hundreds of fish forcing themselves into the net, each wriggling little creature fighting for the high honor of doing the bidding of his Creator.

So many emotions flew through me in those few seconds. I remember the strange sensation of realizing I didn't care about the fish. I didn't care how many there were. I didn't care what price they would bring. I didn't care if the net broke apart and the entire catch was lost. I remember, too, marveling at the realization I didn't really want to be here, in this boat, hauling in this net—not today, not ever again. For the past three years there had been in the back of my mind the belief that I had given up a great career in exchange for the Master. This perceived "loss" was a sturdy beachhead for my flesh. But as I strained at those ropes that morning, seeing below me the greatest success a fisherman could ever achieve, I saw, too, the utter foolishness of my fleshly mind. When my Lord called me to himself, he took nothing from me but emptiness and in return gave me purpose, and fulfillment, and life. I'd come out that night thinking I wanted fish. Now I knew—I didn't want fish; all I wanted was him.

As the others continued to fight with the massive catch, John and I let go of the net at the same time, stood, and faced the shore. Then John turned to me and said what we both already knew. "It's the Lord!"

We were only a few hundred feet from shore. I grabbed my cloak, tied it around me, and plunged into the water. A few floundering strokes brought me close enough so that my feet could touch, allowing me then to churn my way onto the beach. The others followed in the boat, dragging the bloated net behind them.

For a few minutes I just stood there alone with Jesus on the shore, huffing and puffing and dripping. At first he didn't say anything, and neither did I. I felt like such a fool, but he did nothing to intensify my sense of foolishness. He could so easily have lashed out at me, asking me if I really wanted to return to my fishing, asking if I had some complaint with the way he was handling my life. But, of course, that was not his way. He never condemned. He never asked questions for which I already knew the answers. He never spoke either more or less than needed to be said. And at this moment his presence with me here on this beach, following this night, communicated everything I needed to hear. His eyes twinkled, and a smile crossed his lips. Daddy cared enough to come find me behind the house.

I shivered a little in my early morning wetness, and Jesus nodded toward the warmth of a fire kindled on the shore. The aroma of several sizzling fish cooking on the coals mingled with the wood smoke to fill the air with the most wonderful scent. I crouched by the fire with Jesus sitting across from me, and we waited until the others arrived. James and Andrew tied the net onto the side of the boat, and then everyone came ashore. As soon as the boat was beached, Jesus suggested I grab a few more fish from the net so we could all have breakfast together.

The breakfast the seven of us shared on the beach that day was perhaps as close to perfection as I will ever know on this earth. We talked and laughed about the ridiculous fishing venture of the previous night, with lots of comments about whose idea it had been. Then Andrew got going with a vivid reenactment of my frantic net-flinging marathon, capturing my antics and utter stupidity in a way that got us all howling until I thought I was going to be sick. We ate until we were stuffed, and when the food and conversation finally ran out, we stretched out in the warmth of the mid-morning sun.

Of course, it wasn't the food or the warmth or the laughter that made it so intensely, painfully good. It was just being there with him. He stayed with us longer that morning than at any other time between his resurrection and his final departure. He wanted us to know that though many things were now radically different than they were prior to his resurrection, one thing remained the same. His being with us was still his greatest joy and highest priority.

I want so much for you to understand what it was like. He wasn't just stopping by to check up on us. He wasn't policing the troops to make sure we were ready for battle.

He wasn't there primarily to communicate some profound new truth. He wasn't laying out battle strategies for conquering the world. He was simply doing the one thing he wanted to do most of all. He was being with us. Every one of us there that morning felt it. His sharing in our silly little jokes and joining in our laughter and conversation, poking at fish still too hot to eat and stretching out next to us in the morning sun, was as important to him as anything else we would ever share together. In a thousand quiet ways, he told us again and again that it wasn't what we were doing that brought him joy; it was just us.

I must have dozed off for a few minutes as I let my soggy clothing bake in the sun, because I remember suddenly opening my eyes and looking up at the Master sitting next to me on the beach. I sat up, and for a few seconds we looked out across the Sea of Galilee. Then he turned to me and spoke.

"Simon, son of John, do you love me more than these?" As he spoke, he motioned toward my boat and the net still bulging with fish.

Hearing him ask the question flooded me with a tremendous sense of relief. He knew the answer to his question already, but he also knew I needed to say it.

"Yes, Lord; you know that I love you."

Then he said, "Tend my lambs."

He stood, and I stood with him. Together we walked along the shore in silence. Then he said a second time, "Simon, son of John, do you love me?"

It surprised me a little to hear him ask the question again, but I responded immediately, "Yes, Lord; you know that I love you."

And he said, "Shepherd my sheep."

Only a few seconds passed before he questioned me a third time. "Simon, son of John, do you love me?"

At first his words brought me pain. Why, three times, would he ask me this same question? Could it be he didn't believe my words? I felt an agonized tear tumble down my cheek. Then I remembered that awful night and my three vehement denials of my Lord. He was offering me this opportunity to replace each of those lies with the truth.

"Lord, you know all things; you know that I love you."

And Jesus said, "Tend my sheep."

Then the Master continued to speak. "When you were younger, you used to dress yourself, and walk wherever you wished; but when you grow old, you will stretch out your hands, and someone else will dress you, and bring you where you don't wish to go."

I knew what he was saying. The time would come when my allegiance to him would bring about my own execution. But if you think the prophecy he offered that morning created fear within me, you are wrong. On the contrary, it filled me with hope and with assurance that I would never again deny my Lord, even to the point of death. The great fear of my life was put to rest. Both my calling and my faithfulness in that calling were assured. He knew I understood. He smiled and spoke once again the two words I'd heard him speak to me three years earlier, by this same boat and these same nets. "Follow me!"

I heard the sound of someone approaching from behind and turned to see John coming our way. Because Jesus was offering glimpses into the future, I couldn't resist the urge to ask, "Lord, and what about this man?"

The Master's gentle rebuke brought with it two truths that have served me well ever since. "If I want him to remain until I come, what is that to you? You follow me!"

First of all, Jesus wanted me to know that no man ever has either the right or the ability to understand God's dealings with anyone but himself. No man is ever told another man's story. No man can ever have the faith to live another man's calling. The implications of Jesus' words were obvious. He would lead John in the path that fit him perfectly, just as he would me. But the only path I am qualified to live, and the only one I can relate to with trust and understanding, is my own.

In the years since I heard the Master speak those words, I have seen countless men and women living and dying in circumstances that would have shaken my faith to the core. Yet I have seen them face their callings with boldness and confident assurance in the love and living reality of their Lord. And each time, when I have found myself tempted to question the Lord's dealings with others, I have heard his words once again in my mind: "What is that to you? You follow me!" He provides each of us with the faith we need for just one calling in life—the calling he has given to us alone.

And there was a second treasure for me in the words he spoke, one that now forms the deepest foundation of my life. It came in his repetition of those words, "You follow me." You see, he wanted me to know that the fundamentals of my discipleship were never going to change. Three years earlier my life with the King began by my response to those same words, "Follow me!" At the time it was an obvious, logical request that I physically walk with him, eat with him, listen to him, learn from him, and be with him on a daily basis. But here is the amazing thing, the thing I never could have anticipated had he not revealed it to me. Even though he now lives in his resurrected glory, even though his physical presence would soon be removed from this world, even though I would no longer be able to see him with my eyes or touch him with my hands, the basics of my life with him were never going to change. Through the gift of his Spirit, I would continue to live in the reality of his constant presence with me. My calling now is identical to the calling he first offered me on that beach so many years ago—"Follow me!" And now, each day I continue to live in his presence and hear his voice and follow his leadership one day, one step at a time.

I will tell you something now that I don't think you will believe unless you have known it yourself. You would, perhaps, think that once the Master was physically removed from this world, it would leave a huge, aching void in my life. The truth is, life has been so much better now that he is gone. Before I experienced this, I could not have believed it either. Before he left, he told us himself, "I tell you the truth, it is to your advantage that I go away; for if I do not go away, the helper shall not come to you; but if I go, I will send him to you." I know now what he meant. When he was still with us in the flesh, he was limited to the physical body in which he dwelt. He could talk with only one person at a time. He could focus on only one individual need at a time. If he was talking with John, or with Andrew, or with James, then he could not be talking with me.

But now, through his Holy Spirit, I live in the living reality of his presence every second of every hour of every day of my life. Do I value the days I spent with him in the flesh? More than life itself. Would I trade what I have now for what I had then? Never! There are no deep secrets to my walk with the King. The walk began with his words, "Follow me!" The walk now continues on exactly the same basis.

I began this account by reminding you of my words to you in my second open letter to the churches: you have received a faith of the same kind as ours. I hope now you can understand why I made that statement. Each true child of God lives in the reality of the presence of Christ in exactly the same way as I do. And each of us shares his same simple calling to "Follow me!" He will not lead you where he has led me, but he will lead you just the same, in the path that fits perfectly with his life within you and his purposes for you.

Though I saw the Master one more time, on the day of his departure, that day on the beach was my final personal audience with the King. It was an audience carefully designed by him to provide me with everything I needed to know most about the road that lay ahead.

Epilogue

I did not expect them to come for me so quickly. Even now I can hear the sound of their boots outside my cell. There is so much more I wanted to tell you about him and about my life in his love since his departure. But it is clear my King knows I have said enough. What you need to understand of the weeks and months following my encounter with the Master on that beach you can easily learn from Dr. Luke's excellent account now circulating among the churches.

It is best this way. I doubt I could find the words to explain it to you. If you already know him, then you too know what it is to live each day, each moment in his presence. If you have not yet met him, then I think you would not believe me anyway.

There have been those within the church who have sought to elevate me to some high and lofty status. I suppose there will always be some who will seek to do so. When I have seen this in the attitudes of those around me, I have known they simply do not understand. I am in no way unique. I am just a man, like any other man. I brought noth-